DELL'S RAGE

DELL'S RAGE

A NOVEL BY
ML BIDDISON

Dell's Rage/ML Biddison – First Edition
ISBN -978 1719329422

Prologue

The girl in the mirror didn't look like a killer—she looked Irish. Light green eyes flashed above peach-pale cheeks and a flush of freckles skipped across the bridge of her long straight nose. A bush of curly hair, a dusty red like the surface of Mars, framed her face. No piercings, earrings or tattoos modified her appearance and she wore no lipstick. She'd never had time for that stuff, which anyway would've made her stand out in ways she never wanted. She didn't want to be noticed...especially by men.

Lingering over her image in the gas-station restroom, Dell wondered about her heritage. She'd heard the Irish had a quick temper and tended to rise tall, attributes that fit her—but she had no other clues about her origins. Abandoned as a toddler, she was shuffled through a series of group homes, existing and thriving even, until adolescence intruded at age twelve. Somehow she had learned to read and write along the way and had refined her skills in the practical arts of stealing...and fighting.

Inured to the pains of battle over the years, Dell wore the marks of those encounters with some pride. As her talent and speed grew, she was able to keep others from getting what they always wanted from her, mainly parts of her self that she was unwilling to give. All too frequently she had to deal with nasty older boys in those places that Child Protective Services naively termed 'safe environments'.

Often she would escape into fantasy with the aid of the public library, where she'd be lofted into environs she had never been, exposed to experience otherwise beyond her reach. The library was not close-by, but she never wasted time getting there. She'd spend hours devouring every word and picture that sparked her imagination. Eventually, darkness or hunger would intervene, and the reality of her life on the streets was always waiting with a new lesson to grapple with.

Then, there was Savior. He had approached her one afternoon as she lingered at a local grocery near the cold sodas, hoping for the clerk's inattention. Savior had struck her fancy as no one had before, with his dark hair, smooth face and dimpled smile. He had a big black car, and a quiet way of talking. He was her shining knight, come to take her cares away, and shortly thereafter they were off.

Yet another stupid mistake in a series of dumb moves she had learned to live with over the years.

But that was then, and this is now. A dead man lay slumped in the big truck outside, and someone would come looking for her soon enough. She finished splashing her face, reached down for the brown Sierra Club ruck-sack, and pushed out the door.

Chapter 1

Martin Planck reeled with thoughts of his sisters, aunts and uncles, who threatened to disrupt his uncluttered plans of doing nothing this summer. They were planning a twenty-fifth annual family reunion, right here in Dakota Country. In his back yard! Well, maybe not literally, but close enough. Sioux Falls was charming, said Sara. An ideal spot, according to Sandy. We would love to come west for a get together, shouted Sally! Relatives on both coasts waxed enthusiasm. They would plan to converge on the city in just six weeks, at the end of May, right when the semester was ending. Right when he had planned to get lost for a month in the hills to hunt for signs of solitude.

He had dreamed of a two-wheeled journey through the badlands, joining with the locals, finding out what sort of folk put themselves out there permanently. Now he was taking only a week, during the regular Easter break, and he would leave the two-wheeled venture for later, probably toward the end of summer. Primary, as always, were the wishes of his scattered family. He would serve as tour-guide, and solicitor. He would referee the rumbles, play host to the fantasies, and placate the offended. He had a lot of loose ends to tie up before then, though most likely any plans he made would be ultimately vetoed.

Coming off this reverie, he looked at the gas gauge, noticing the needle was nudging below the last mark. In the distance there was a large Conoco sign. *Any port in a storm*, he sighed.

He noticed flashing blue and red lights under the gas station marquee as he pulled next to the pumps. There were three Stanley County Sheriff's SUVs ahead of him, next to a metallic green Peterbilt semi under the truck canopy.

Sheriff Vern Warner conferred with a deputy outside the minimart doorway. He looked up as Planck eased his Ford two-door next to the pump.

Plank slid out of the seat, stood and pocketed his keys, then strolled toward the Sheriff, greeting him. "Hey Vern. What's going on?"

Warner flicked his tan Stetson above his eyebrows as Martin approached. He gave him a half smile. "Hey, Marty...you're a long way from home. What ill wind brings you out here?"

Martin looked to the semi, then out over the grassland. "Just needed some gas. You got the whole place lit up, Vern—what's the occasion?"

Warner and Planck were used to seeing one another at county meetings and the odd drug-raid or traffic incident. Planck taught Journalism at University Center in Sioux Falls, and frequently fell into Warner's path. He ranked up there as one of the top journalists in the state and often worked freelance for several local news outlets.

Warner was a hands-on sheriff who always cut a good image in his sheepskin leather coat, Stetson, and six-shot Smith & Wesson holstered high on his hip. He didn't mind crossing boundaries on occasion, either. There was usually precious little to keep him busy in Stanley County, so he put his nose in where he could. He was competent, and Planck liked him. Despite the constant tension between news gatherers and law enforcement, Warner viewed him in a similar manner.

"We have an incident here, Marty. Not sure whether it's newsworthy, yet. Why don't you just fill up, and call the office in a couple hours?"

"That's okay Vern, I'm not in the middle of anything." He moved shoulders forward and back, trying to get the driver's kink out of his neck. "I think I'll just hang out here a bit, if you don't mind—maybe get a sandwich..."

"Suit yourself." Warner turned to one of the deputies. "Hey Charlie, don't go pulling on that until Madeline can look at it!"

Planck went into the minimart, nodded to the young attendant, whose black hair had been slicked back into a ponytail, and headed to the sandwich bin. He selected a ham and cheese—it was either that or a lettuce and bologna—chose a bottle of water, and was back at the register. "Some excitement here today?"

The teen looked up from the graphic novel he held. The cover, a slash of red and purple, featured a girl in a Roman centurion skirt wielding a curved sword with lots of splashing blood. "Damn straight—about made my week!"

Planck slipped easily into interview mode. "Did you see what happened?"

"Naw, nothing. Except there was this truck out there parked forever, so I went to look, and this guy was just there not movin'! Dead, I think. Called the sheriff, for sure."

"You say 'forever'. Would that be longer than a couple of hours?"

"Since early this morning—didn't even know he was still there."

"He didn't get gas?"

"No, the truck pulled in around sunrise...then this girl walked in and said she needed to use the restroom. Then nothin'. After a while, I got to noticin' the truck still there, so I went to look. Saw him lying there with his mouth open—gross."

"So, there was a girl? You think she was with the truck?"

"Yeah...what else?"

"What'd this girl look like?"

"Oh, she would have stood out in a crowd. Tall skinny kid, kinda pretty, lots of red hair. Wasn't dressed up—wore dark pants...a baggy coat, and...oh yeah, a back-pack."

Marty realized this girl had to be connected with the dead trucker, and he found himself becoming more interested as the tale unfolded. "Sooo...you say she was a kid...about how old?"

"I'd say 'bout sixteen or eighteen. Couldn't have been much older."

It appeared there was a mystery here that might add up to a good feature. "Have you told the sheriff any of this?"

Sheriff Warner watched as the Deputy Coroner's grey Toyota swerved into the Conoco station driveway. It came to a precise stop behind the first SUV. The DC eased herself from the vehicle, and slowly surveyed the scene before closing the car door. She moved straight to Warner. Madeline Highwater was small, and looked even smaller in her dark three-piece suit and plain black slippers. Her confident, precise movement lent her a large presence, however.

She dusted crumbs from a hasty breakfast off her jacket, and looked up at the Sheriff. "What do we have here, Vern?"

"Not sure, Maddie." He glanced over to where Deputy Bradford was crawling over the semi, snapping photos. "There's the body of a man in the truck, probably the driver. Appears to be in his sixties. No signs of injury. Haven't ID'd him yet—was waiting for you, Maddie."

"Right." A slight smile twitched across her lips. "Well, let's get to work..."

Highwater slipped gloves and a camera out of her bag as she turned toward the truck cab, where the body of a graying, bearded man slumped against the steering wheel.

As she was climbing up into the truck's cab, Deputy Greg Daniels finished his work combing through the grassy area between the truck and the store. He excitedly approached the sheriff. "Look at this, Vern...I think I found his wallet!"

Warner examined the displayed worn black billfold. "Umm...we'll see if he's missing one. There an ID in there?"

"Yeah, an Illinois license and a couple credit cards. No cash, though."

Warner looked around. From where he stood, nothing of interest broke the horizon. The gas station, a couple of out buildings, and a water tower were the only structures. The grass undulated everywhere, the highway cutting through it. The nearest town was eight miles south of here. Hell, the whole county had less people in it than most small towns. This guy might have been headed to Midland, or Eagle Butte, or maybe he was just lost, but nobody travels out this way hoping they'll find an ATM.

"Over there, and no cash...interesting," he mused. "Hey Maddie, is that guy carrying anything in his pockets?"

A muffled, "Nothing there, Vern," Her head poked out the cab door, "but he does have a broken finger." She held up her right index finger, then turned back to her work.

The Sheriff rubbed his neck and directed his attention to Daniels. "Greg, get on the radio and follow up on the ID. Let's see where this guy has come from."

"Show me what you got, Maddie." He pressed a rag to his nose and climbed up next to the woman. She held up the corpse's right hand for him to see.

"There doesn't appear to be any other injuries. Off hand, I'd say this guy suffered a heart attack or stroke. I'll know more tomorrow after we do some lab work."

The door from the minimart swung open and Planck walked out into the sunlight. Shading his eyes from the glare, he walked toward where the sheriff was just climbing off the semi. Warner looked over at him. "Marty. I thought you'd left already."

Planck ignored the remark. "Vern, did you talk to the clerk, yet?"

"We talked to him briefly. We'll get to him again, soon. Why, you get an exclusive—one day in the life sort of thing?"

"This might be of interest. There was a girl here—young woman. She showed up about when the truck rolled in."

Highwater interrupted, emerging again from the truck's cab. "Something else here, Vern. Look here." She pointed to the dead man's pants. "Dark spots here, not blood, and unless I'm not my mother's daughter, I'd say they were semen stains."

Chapter 2

Walking was tiresome, and sweat trickled down her neck and chest. The river had to be nearby. Seagulls always meant water. *Damn birds didn't know they were supposed to be on the ocean.* But this country was about as far away from any ocean that you could get. So they stayed on the river.

She was down to her last two power bars and was getting kinda tired of the same old yuck. She wished she had a plan. It would be nice to get to the actual ocean. That would be a plan—no, that was a goal, not a plan. She needed a plan. The last few days it was to get as far away from Chicago as she could, but now she needed to get someplace, not away from somewhere. The river was close. She would make that her plan, then figure it out from there, depending on what was happening.

Something unforeseen could always change her plan. Maybe she would find a boat and float down the river to New Orleans. That's a plan. But she probably would stick out even more there. Whatever—she could handle it. Spring was a time for optimism. Good thing she didn't have to do this in winter. That would suck.

The dusty roadbed she followed cut straight through an endless field of tall grass and purple colored flowers. Kinda pretty and the air smelled fresh and sweet. The road rolled on to the horizon. A warm spring breeze buoyed her back, and she never felt as powerful as she did right now. The large semi-automatic pistol tucked into a side pocket of her pack was a welcome weight. She felt she could face anything. Hell, she didn't even need the pistol, but it might give her an advantage at some point.

A rumbling noise behind alerted her and she turned to face it. A roiling dust cloud grew larger as a vehicle of some sort came in view. Dell stopped and waited for it to get closer—a pick-up. A pretty old one.

The truck slowed down as it neared, came to a stop where she stood, and a window cranked down.

"You lost, honey?" The woman appeared to be in her late thirties. She had a kind, weathered face, and lively grey eyes that danced up and down as they looked her over. "Where you headed?"

"Oh..." She glanced down at her dirt covered boots, "I was kinda headed to the river. You going that way?"

The woman did not hesitate. "You bet, honey, hop in!"

Dell nodded, tossed her ruck-sack in the truck-bed, opened the door, and clambered up onto the bench.

The pick-up moved off leaving a billow of dust behind. "My name's Francie, what's yours, sweetie?"

Dell remained silent for a moment, looking out at the waving grass. She knew this was just the first of many questions, but she didn't mind. She was perfectly fine with not answering anything she didn't want to. "It's Dell...short for Adele, I guess."

"Oh...like the singer. Well, Dell...what brings you out here into the middle of nowhere?"

"Don't know any singer." She paused, and glanced sideways at the woman. "Must be somewhere...you're here, aren't you? Francie? And I guess you been here a while?"

Francie was used to dealing with teen angst, in its many forms. "Ok, wrong question. Here's a better one—are you hungry?" She darted a look to Dell, then back to the road. "I've been out all morning. Was just coming back for lunch, and I'd be happy to feed you."

Dell said nothing. Appeared to be considering while her stomach growled in betrayal.

"Actually, my place is right on the river, just south of the reservation. It'd be wonderful to have some company for a while. What do you say?"

The girl wrinkled her nose and scratched it. She hadn't had anything but power bars for two days, and the offer was sounding really good right now. "Yah, okay," she murmured, examining her hands, "but I can't stay long. Got people waiting for me in...Montana."

"Montana, huh. That's where you're from? "

"Not exactly, no. Actually...I'm from Baltimore. I've hiked the Appalachian Trail, and now I'm headed west. Trying to break in these new boots!" She pointed to her Timberland lace-ups, looked at Francie with a slight smile that said, you know I'm bullshitting, right?

Francie was just grateful for the conversation. Did she really care what was going on with this disheveled young woman? Who just got into her truck? Who was obviously not from around here, and had no visible way of maintaining herself? She was intrigued with the whole idea of someone, who was entirely on their own, living by their wits from day to day. How does she do it? She must be in really big trouble.

The pick-up rumbled over the road for several miles, as the occupants kept to themselves. Dell tried not to think about her situation. The dead truck driver didn't bother her...too much, she kept telling herself. *He damn well got what he deserved.* She was somewhat apprehensive about Savior. She knew he wasn't happy about her sudden departure, after she had broken that other creep's nose and locked him in the closet. She didn't know if he was going to do anything about her leaving, but she didn't really care. That was kinda the last straw. She was used to the pawing and the grunting, but when that old guy came at her with pliers, no way. She decided there was more to life than being someone's freaky toy. She was not going to let any guy make her do stuff anymore. Not ever!

The truck hit a rough patch. She looked over to find Francie watching her.

"You in trouble, sweetie?"

"Why...what do you mean?"

"You just...you are just emitting those dark vibes right now. I've been there, I know what they look like."

Dell tried to smile. "Yeah, trouble is my middle name. So, how about you, Francie? What do you do?"

"Ummm, trying to change the subject, I guess? Fair enough." She swerved around a medium-sized pot hole. "I'm the mother of two boys. One's about to graduate from high school. The other is not far behind. The boy's father died several years back...been on our own ever since, on a ranch. Breeding horses. It's not easy, but I wouldn't trade it for anything..." Looking at Dell again, "Now your turn."

Dell tried to keep from grimacing. She looked straight ahead at the road, and took a breath. "Well, I'm on my own, too. And I like it, I guess...do a lot of traveling, which is a good thing, and meet a lot of people. Most of them are nice, like you, but some...well, that's why I keep traveling."

She smiled and looked at her hands again, and her ragged nails. "I keep thinking I need to get a plan and get someplace to call home...never really had one. But I could really use a bath— that's why I'm headed to the river."

Francie laughed. "You're welcome to use the bath at our place. We have hot water!"

Chapter 3

Francine Parker had lost her husband, James, when their youngest was just seven years old. The tractor had rolled over on him as he was pushing manure over the bluff. He was in all sorts of pain for three days before he passed. Donnie took it real hard. He idolized his father. Jimmy, three years older than his brother, coped a little better. Ten year olds can do that. Nearly eight years had passed, and Francie did okay with the ranch. She sold stud service all over the country, and had several award winning stallions in demand. Customers would either bring their mares around, or more frequently, she would ship harvested semen in special containers to breeders from as far away as Denmark. She also served as a part time counselor at the Stanley County Schools, a job that forced some discipline into her otherwise chaotic life.

"This is our turn." She slowed the pick-up to a crawl, and turned the wheel sharply to the right, entering a rutted tire worn lane between two pastures. "It's just up here about a mile."

Dell noticed the landscape gradually change. More trees now scattered themselves about. Some Dogwood and Pine, but mostly Cottonwood. She recognized them from books she'd looked at on her visits to the library. Not many around where she grew up, and those that were there were all the same type, planted because they weren't much bother. A large expanse of silver came into view through the trees, and she guessed it was the Missouri River. It appeared to be a vast lake, and she could barely make out the other side. "Wow, that's the river? It's a lot bigger than I thought."

"Yep, that's it...they dammed it up in Pierre, southeast of here, way back in the mid-fifties. What you're looking at is actually Lake Oahe."

A left turn brought them to the house, situated in amongst

the trees, on a bluff overlooking the lake in the distance. It was a large buff-yellow prairie style home, with two stories, a shake roof, and a long front porch. Yellow roses planted in a row all along the porch were just starting to bloom. A hundred yards down a slight incline away from the house stood a barn and stalls. They matched the house in color, but corrugated tin covered the roof. Dell could see several horses snorting and whinnying their greetings from pipe corrals that were attached to the stalls.

"Grab your gear, and let's see what we can scare up for lunch."

Sheriff Warner had finished talking to the store clerk, and watched as Maddie's Toyota followed the ambulance out of the parking lot, heading to the lab in Pierre. They would get a driver up here to move the truck out to where it belonged. The cargo consisted of rolled paper, which proved uniformly uninteresting. But the CSI team from the capital would have to go over everything, and already the cab had been taped, as had the women's rest-room. Deputy Daniels had confirmed the deceased driver was from Chicago, and Warner was now treating the incident as a crime.

A warm breeze kicked up, and dust motes created halos of sparkling light over the scene. "We have theft, probable assault, and possibly murder linked to this," the Sheriff told Daniels, "and we have a suspect. Contact Chicago PD and see if they have any reported runaways fitting the description. Also notify the Pierre FBI office—tell them we'll send prints as soon as we get them."

Planck stood within hearing distance, hands in pockets. Although he was not part of the conversation, he was ready to put his previous plans on hold and do what he could to help find out what happened here. Besides, it might turn out to be a great story. He moved closer to the sheriff. "Vern, if I'm right, and you're looking for this girl, there are two things you should be doing."

Warner gave him his attention. "Go on, Marty."

"Well the way I look at it, she's either on foot, or caught a ride on her way out of here. It's been about four hours, so that means she is still within fifteen miles or two hundred fifty miles from here. So start looking fifteen miles or so down the road, and..."

"Yeah, I've thought of that," The sheriff interrupted, "Charlie, get State on the box, and see if they have any reports of hitchhiking girls from any of their units. It's been too damn long to set up roadblocks. She'd be long gone by now. After you do that, Charlie, why don't you mosey up the road, and see what you can find? She is probably running that way—she'd be crazy to go back the way she came."

"How do you figure, Sheriff?" Bradford asked.

"Well, Charlie, the truck is obviously out of Chicago, right? And that way is away from Chicago, right? Who would be crazy enough to run back the way they came?"

"Right, Sheriff." Charlie climbed into his SUV, cranked it to a start, and roared out of the station.

Warner turned back to Marty. "I think we have to know more about this girl to figure out what she might do. Fingerprints will help, if we're lucky. Once we have her identified we might find she has family in the area or maybe get a clue about what she's doing out here."

Planck added, "One scenario is that she is running hard from something, and will not allow anyone to get in her way. That truck driver may have tried to stop her, and she was having none of it. The heart attack was her opportunity."

The sheriff continued, "That would be a reason for not reporting it to anyone, but there was a struggle of some kind, as evidenced by the broken finger, and if she was being assaulted, she might've been able to break his finger to get away. Not reporting an assault tells me she was probably doing the assaulting, though."

"Or she just didn't want anyone to know where she

was...bringing us back to the question, who or what's she running from?"

"Then there's the sex thing," Warner said, looking back at the truck cab. "We have to figure out whether this girl was forced to perform a sex act, or whether it's just something she does. You don't get ejaculate without sex...at least that's been my experience."

Planck was intrigued by the girl. She had been described as younger than most of his students, yet she was out here on her own, taking what she needed and dealing with it. Then he mentally kicked himself, trying not to make a romantic figure out of her. *Come on, Marty, get real. This girl is desperate, and probably illiterate, and slovenly, and a sociopath, and hungry to boot. She doesn't give a damn about anything, and will not let anyone get in her way. So, why is she running? Why does anybody run? Because the pain gets unbearable. Okay, pain from what? She was said to be healthy, so it's mental pain, then. Alright. Someone is making her feel awful. What does one feel awful from? Too much school? Too little freedom? Doing unpleasant things? Come on, every school kid has to deal with that. Okay. How about doing...horrible things? Unspeakable things? That feels right. She was a slave, forced to do unspeakable things. So she took off. From where? A foster home, probably—few people are going to treat their own kid like that. There I go, jumping to conclusions again. But, more than likely, she's in the system, somewhere.*

"Sheriff." Marty became animated. "You've got to contact Chicago CPS...she's in the system!"

"How do you figure?"

"She's not running away from home. She is not acting like a normal kid. This girl has been abused for a long time, and she's running because there's nothing else she can do. I just know it!"

Chapter 4

Francie introduced the boys when they trudged up the path from the school-bus. A black-and-white Border-Collie mix accompanied them, running ahead, then circling back around, making sure they were still coming.

"Dell, this is Jimmy and Donnie. Donnie and Jimmy, this is our guest, Dell. I think she'll be staying for a day or two. Oh, and that's Panda," indicating the dog.

Dell had watched the pair approach, with growing apprehension. *Calm down,* she told herself. *They're just Francie's boys, not like some wild coyotes coming to sniff me out.*

"Hi." "Hi." The boys greeted her tentatively.

Dell waggled fingers in return.

Francie continued, "The boys spend over an hour on the bus getting to and from school in Fort Pierre every day. I usually take them down to the road in the morning—have to be out and about anyway." She turned to her sons. Both had brown unruly hair, the older one's a bit lighter in shade. Dell thought one was somewhat younger than she was, and the other a bit older. She immediately noticed a sparkle of humor in his eyes.

"This here is Jimmy. He loves math and science, when he's not riding and wrestling with horses. And Donnie, he's a freshman this year—first year on the football team. She pumped a fist in the air, "Go Bufs!"

Donnie gave Dell a puzzled look, "You go to school?"

"Oh...I did." Dell's eye's opened wide in momentary panic. "Actually school's out already where I'm from, so I'm on an adventure."

"Yeah," Donnie persisted, "What grade you in?"

Francie didn't let him continue. "Come on boys, let's get inside and get things arranged before dinner."

And that was that. Dell was welcomed into Francie's home

with no further vetting. She was introduced to Irma, the house-keeper. A simple dinner of beef stew, bread and tapioca pudding was consumed. Afterward, she went with Jimmy to feed flakes to the horses, while Donnie gathered the eggs for breakfast. She couldn't believe her good fortune. She was given a room! "Dell, this is where you'll stay tonight. You can put your things in the drawer there. Bathroom's down the hall on your right. We get up at five thirty...you need anything, just give a holler."

The night was black and cold. Every so often there was a snort from one of the horses, awakened by a possum sneaking by, or maybe a raccoon. Then it was the owl—Hoot...hoo. Hoot...hoo. Dell couldn't sleep. How could she sleep when everything was so quiet? Could she really be missing the horns blaring, the sirens every ten or twenty minutes, the car alarms and the occasional gunshot? And she couldn't forget the nightly arguments between disappointed women and their tormentors down the halls and in the streets. And screaming. The diesel trains rushing by with the hyper air-horns and the crossing guards ding, ding, dinging. With these impressions drifting through her mind she was soon fast asleep.

She awoke with a start! It was still dark. Dell held her breath and listened hard. She had a lingering vision of Savior climbing in through the window.

There was a faraway clank, then a scraping sound. She eased out of the bed, threw on her oversized coat, opened the bedroom door a crack, and peered up and down the hall. There were lights on downstairs, and buttery smells coming from the kitchen. It was morning already, even though it was dark as the other side of the moon.

Dell dressed and walked down to the kitchen, where Francie and the boys were preparing breakfast.

"Hi there," Francie called. "We've got toast, potatoes and eggs this morning!"

Donnie lifted his eyes from his task at the stove, "Actually, we have this every morning except Sunday."

"Go ahead, take a seat," Francie instructed. "I'll get you a plate.

"Thanks...smells really good. Dell eased herself into a chair facing the dark window. "So, what happens on Sunday?"

Jimmy looked up from where he was devouring the last of the egg with a piece of jellied toast. "On Sunday we starve!"

"Yeah," said Donnie, "That's when we have to go to church."

"We don't starve. We just do church first, then we eat in town after. Irma gets the day off," Francie explained, "and we shop for necessities and sometimes visit with friends."

"What day..." Dell hesitated, "is it today?"

Francie started, "I'm sorry? What's today?"

Jimmy looked at her like she had just stepped off a train from Patagonia.

"Really, I never know what day it is anymore..."

Jimmy gave her a puzzled smile. "One day pretty much like the other around here—except Sunday."

Donnie shouted, "It's Thursday! Tomorrow's TGIF!"

Francie intervened, "Time to finish up guys. The bus will be here in 45 minutes and animals are waiting. Dell, you can go with Jimmy to feed the horses. Tomorrow, Donnie will teach you about chickens. In a half hour, we'll head down to the road."

Dell rode fence with Francie all morning. They bounced along in the truck, stopping at points where the wire fencing was sagging or broken. Afterwards, they repaired broken water basins, mended hot wire, replaced broken siding in the covered stalls. Francie mentioned that the plastic irrigation piping was broken somewhere, "but we'll save that for another day." Then Dell was taught how to drive a Ford 601 Diesel five-speed loader-dozer. The noisy vehicle was used to move manure into one pile, where it was covered, and allowed to compost.

Dell was dirty and sweat was running into her eyes when Francie stopped her with an upheld hand. "Hey Kiddo, let's take a break. I'd like to show you something."

They took the pick-up and rode down the hill over a rutted

dirt trail, then around a curve where a wide expanse of dark blue water sprang into view. They were near the west bank of the Missouri River, known here as Lake Oahe. The truck continued on down to a floating pier at the bank, where a twenty-five-foot cabin cruiser was moored. Dell thought it retro-fabulous, with a white hull, and dark hardwood trim everywhere along the deck, outlining the teak planks and around the port-holes forward, then onto the top and aft decks. The fittings were all polished brass. A two-piece windshield projected amid-ship, sweeping up over an eighteen-inch steering-wheel. The wheel area was covered over with a canvas canopy, but was otherwise open to the weather. Two large outboards jutted out of the stern.

"What do you think? You want to take it out in a couple days? Think you'll still be hangin' around then?"

Dell was overwhelmed. A speed boat! This was so far from what she had been thinking or even expecting to pop up, she didn't know what to say. She looked at Francie. "What is going on? Why are you doing this for me?"

Francie gave her a quizzical look. "What—you don't like boats?"

"It's just that...I was, you know, lost. And now you are giving me all this stuff." She started to giggle, but caught herself. "Okay, yes, I like boats, especially fast ones. Does this thing go fast?"

"Oh, it's fast...what do you think?"

"I think it'll be a good break from all this work you're laying on me. Sure. And I guess I don't have other plans for the next couple of days...and I think I can't wait until Saturday."

The next afternoon, after Dell had chased the chickens with Donnie, she caught up with Jimmy on the pad next to the stalls, who was brushing down a tall, black, fidgety horse, which kept snorting and stamping his feet, producing mini-puffs of dust with each hoof. Panda danced around the horse, looking for an excuse to correct him.

Dell was dressed much the same today, long black pants and lace-up boots, except for a long sleeve plaid shirt that she had borrowed from Francie. She appraised the horse. "What's wrong with that one?"

"Oh he's just like that...too close to the mares. It makes him sort of hyper."

"What's his name?"

"We call him Jonny, although he doesn't always answer to that. Sometimes we have to give him a little whack." Jim looked at her intently. She was very distracting, even though she didn't appear to work at it. He realized that from the time he first saw her yesterday, he had found it hard to keep his eyes off her. "I guess guys are like that sometimes."

"Like what?" she asked.

"You have to whack them, before they pay attention."

Dell's eyes, wide with awe, were glued to the horse. The stallion stood about 16 hands, according to Jimmy. *They had to be awfully big hands!* His coat was shiny and brilliant, like polished obsidian. Dell had never been this close to such an animal before.

"Can I brush him?"

"Sure," Jimmie handed her the brush. "Just put your hand in the loop. Let him smell you first, so he knows you're a friend—don't let him bite you, though."

Dell placed her left hand near the big horse's nose, and he nuzzled her arm as she began to stroke his mane. "Do you ride him?

"Oh, yeah!" Jimmy replied, "He likes to run."

"When can I ride him?"

"How long have you been riding?" He asked, "Can't let you on him unless you're a good rider."

"Well, I've never ridden before, but I'm sure I'll be able to stay on him. I think he likes me."

Jimmy looked from Dell to the horse and back. "I hate to bust your bubble, but if you are going to ride, you need to start a little slower. Over there..." He indicated a small pinto two stalls away, hanging its head over the gate, intently watching the show.

Dell had always dreamed of having a horse and riding one,

just like most girls she had been acquainted with in the past. She daydreamed so intensely about every detail of grooming and riding her animal in those early years that she was convinced she would be able to get on and hold on with no problems whatsoever. "So that's a better horse for me? What you're saying is I should ride that horse first?" She nodded toward little paint. She shrugged. "Okay, Jimmy, if that's what you want me to do—saddle up the pinto."

"Not so fast, girl. We have to finish what we're doing here first, then maybe think about going for a ride."

"Oh, come on!" Dell begged. "You said I needed to ride that one, what's her name?"

Dell quickly mastered the art of picking hooves, cinching down the saddle and adjusting the stirrups. She became acquainted with the small pinto, named Lady, who was greedily gobbling down a carrot as Jimmy saddled up the stallion. When he was ready, he turned to Dell and her horse. "Ok, let me help you up. First thing is to always mount from the left side."

Dell was way ahead of him. She grabbed the reins, placed a toe in the stirrup, and swung easily over onto the animal.

"Which way?"

She kicked the eager pinto into a steady canter toward the horizon. Jimmy mounted hurriedly, and took off after her.

Donnie came running out of the barn shouting after them, "Hey, where you guys going?"

The only answer was a thick cloud of dust.

Dell slowed down when she saw the river. She reined in her horse and dismounted near a green muddy beach, where dozens of startled cranes took flight. A big pale moon was swelling above the water.

Jimmy and the stallion pounded in behind her, Jimmy jumping from the mount as he came to an abrupt halt.

He moved up to her as she crouched, contemplating the wide blue expanse. "So, all that about not knowing how to ride, you were just making it up?"

A puzzled look, then she gazed back at the drifting birds. "I've been rehearsing for years, but never with a real horse. It's just like I imagined it." She threw him a generous smile. "Thanks for the lesson."

"Sure," he looked down at his boots, "Glad I could help."

They lingered for a while, skimming rocks into the water, occasionally glancing at one another as the bounce count reached six or more.

Jimmy had so many questions for Dell, but only was able to give voice to one or two. He couldn't help but notice her hair wafting in the breeze, the heat shimmering off her exposed arms, as she moved. "Why," he asked, "are you here? I mean, are you going to stay? It would be good...if you stayed."

Dell looked him in the eyes. "It's real hard to say where I'm going to end up. I really like it here, but I really can't say right now."

Jimmy suddenly moved close, touched her arm and brushed his lips over hers. She stepped back. "Jimmy, I can't! I mean, I like you, but I really can't! It's just, well, I'm way too old for you...I..."

"Sorry," he said, lowering his head, "Just an impulse...I was thinking...I don't know what I was thinking."

He looked around, then at the sky, as if judging the distance between here and the moon. "I guess we'd better be heading back for supper—getting a little late."

"So, you're going to let me ride Jonny, then?' She smiled up at him.

He looked like he was gathering his arguments together, when she implored, "You saw how I can ride—come onnn!"

Dell felt Jonny's nervousness, as he bustled beneath her. She calmed him with her whispers, and assured him with the firm grip of her thighs as they bolted across the grassland toward the house. It was exhilarating! She could go on riding this horse all night. But reality loomed as they approached the stalls. Jonny slowed to a halt, and Dell jumped off. She gave him a hug around the neck, and was leading him to the grooming pad when Jimmy caught up.

He brought Lady into the pad opposite the stallion. They quickly removed the horses' saddles in silence and prepared them for the evening, giving each a bucket of oats.

"When you're ready to tell me how you learned to ride, I'll be listening," he said. "And, you know, I don't see how you could be older than me. If anything, you're younger."

"Oh, I'm older. Much older, believe me."

Chapter 5

As Francie and Irma prepared the evening pot-roast the phone rang. Irma answered, and after a brief minute passed it to Francie. "Is the Sheriff's Department. He's asking for you."

Francie wiped her hands on a towel and accepted the receiver. "Hello, this is Francine."

"Hello, Mrs. Parker. This is Deputy Daniels at the Sheriff's Department. We're calling folks in the area to see if we can find a young lady who has gone missing."

"A missing girl—who is it?"

"Well, she's not from around here, Mrs. Parker, but we need to find her and wanted to know if you or your family might have come in contact with this young lady. She has been described as young, probably mid-teens, fairly tall, with red curly hair, wearing dark clothing. Have you seen anyone around fitting that description?"

Francie gripped the phone with both hands and glanced at Irma, who was pretending not to listen. "I...don't see a lot of people up here. Is she in some kind of trouble?"

"I can't discuss that Ma'am. We just need to find her—she was last seen Wednesday, near Langdon's Conoco out on the highway, and she may have been headed in your direction."

"Okay. Tall, with red hair. I'll ask the boys if they have come across anyone like that."

"Curly hair, Ma'am. They would've noticed. This girl may be dangerous, Ma'am, so if you see her, please contact us immediately."

"I'll call you if we get any information, Deputy. Please give my regards to Sheriff Warner."

She hung up the phone and turned to Irma. "Oh, shit!" she said.

At that moment Donnie came bursting through the back

door. "Finished with the animals, what's for dinner? Jimmy and Dell went riding."

Francie looked momentarily alarmed. "Where are they now?"

"They're here!"

At the door Jimmy ushered Dell into the kitchen. "Old ladies first." Jimmy said, directing her through with his hat.

"Yeah, you're just afraid I'll kick you if I get behind you…"

They both wore broad smiles as Francie directed them to clean up because dinner was about to be served.

When they had finished, the boys rinsed their plates. Irma rose to clean up, chatting with Donnie while he helped put the food away. Francie took Dell aside, "Dell, when the boys go up to do their homework, I would like to talk to you in the den before you get too far, okay?"

Dell tensed up, sensing something unpleasant. "Sure—got nowhere to go."

Chapter 6

"Dell, I just received a disturbing call from the Sheriff's Department." They were seated in matching armchairs facing each other. Francie was on the edge of her chair, Dell was curled up, with bare feet tucked under her. "They said they were looking for a missing girl about your age, with red hair. They wouldn't tell me why they were looking, but they said she was dangerous...is that you?"

Dell looked out the window, not quite knowing how to answer. Finally she said, "Don't worry, I'm not dangerous."

"Well, why are they after you, Dell?"

Again the silence...then, "I guess they think I'm a criminal. But I'm not."

"You want to tell me about it?"

"I probably should pack up and be moving on..."

"Dell, you can't just keep running—they'll catch up to you in the end! Why don't we just sort it out now, and get through it? I'll do everything I can for you, but I need to know what I'm...what we're dealing with here."

"I can't! It's not something I can just talk about. It's me, it's the way I live." A tear trailed down her cheek.

"You know, Dell, I think that whatever you can tell me about your circumstances is not going to be as bad as you think it is. I'm a good judge of character, and I like having you around. The boys like you too, so let me in. What's going on?"

Dell hesitated, then it all rushed out. "I've been having sex with boys since I was nine years old. There! Is that somebody you want hanging around your kids?"

Francie blinked several times. The truth is, she suspected the girl had been abused as a young child, but it was a shock to hear such details revealed. "Dell, I am sorry. When that happens to a nine year old, it's not her fault. I..."

Dell didn't let her finish, "I have sex with men, too. For money! And I'm sick of it!"

Francie hesitated. It was difficult to get her head around what Dell was telling her.

"That's why I'm out here. I'm running from that. I had to get out of Chicago as fast as I could."

"Did something happen to make you...decide to leave?"

Dell wiped away more tears. "I might as well tell you as anybody. I'm a whore! I've been a whore since Savior took me, and set me up. He took the money, and I did what was asked. I didn't feel anything. Then some pervert tried to hurt me, but I hurt him instead, and I got out."

"So, that's when you came here?"

"Yah, I hitched a ride with a trucker going the long haul. But it was the same old scam. We went for hours, and I was finally relaxing, when he pulled a gun on me! You don't want to hear the rest."

Francie was with her at this point. "So, he demanded sex, and you, what? Told him to bugger off?"

"OK, we parked over there, the gas station. He had this gun, and so I, well...sucked him off. You know."

Francie nodded, "And..."

"Yah, well, he was real distracted, and I grabbed the gun at just the right time. I think I heard his finger snap. I sat up and pointed it at him, but he was shaking out of control. That's when I searched for his wallet and took his money. I figured he owed me."

Francie was silent for a moment, trying to digest what Dell was telling her. "So what happened then, Dell? Why is the Sheriff interested? Is it because you took his money?"

"Maybe, or maybe it's because he was dead. And they think I killed him. But I didn't...he killed himself. By messing with me! That's what I think."

Francie tried to calm the thoughts ricocheting in her mind. She had to get this right. "Dell, I think the best thing for you to do at this point, is to..."

Dell interrupted her. "I'm not going to turn myself in. Don't you see? They will just put me back into the system again. No matter how this goes. I cannot let Savior find me!"

"Okay, okay, let's just look at this from all sides. The sheriff is a good man. He'll look at the facts and see that you had no fault in the death of that trucker. Then he'll just..."

"Send me back to Chicago, because I'm too young to make decisions for myself, right?"

"Well," Francie was stumped, "maybe we have to think about this some more and come up with a better solution. Why don't we put this on hold until tomorrow? We have some time, right? The Sheriff doesn't know you're here."

Later, Dell lay on the bed in her room. Moonlight spilled over the covers through the open window. She was getting used to hearing the owls calling, and the occasional restless Mockingbird. But she didn't sleep. She had all her gear together—waiting for the right moment to slip away, when everyone would surely be deep in slumber. She would miss them. Francie cared like no other woman she had known, and the boys were so accepting of her. Jimmy had even tried it with her. Although she had put him in his place, she didn't mind. She liked Irma, and Panda, and she had better stop with this maudlin thinking or she would never be able to do what she had to do.

Dell awoke to a soft red light from the window. Outside a mist hugged the ground, glowing red from the rising sun. It was morning already! Immediately paralyzed with indecision, she tried to move. These people got up very early. Maybe she had missed her chance! Then she realized it was Saturday, and might still have a few minutes. Quickly slipping into her boots, she grabbed the rucksack, and clambered out the window, making way too much noise.

She found it difficult to see where she was going because of the mist, but managed to keep from crashing into anything on her way to the driveway. She knew they would miss her soon and would mount a search on the road, so she turned toward the river, instead. She would make her way upstream to the north and west, until finding a way to cross. Then she would disappear into the Cheyenne River Reservation. She risked a chance of standing out there like a cuckoo in a robin's nest. But it could be easier to lose herself because of communications difficulties between the rez and the rest of the world. She had learned from studying maps that there were reservations all over this state. They were a lot like foreign countries, with few people and lots of space. Reason enough for her to have chosen to run there, with the added bonus that it was plenty far from where she had come. She also had money enough to pay for help, if need be.

The mist continued to thicken as she approached the river, the color gradually changing from red to yellow. Dell couldn't see how close she was to the shoreline, but she could hear the lapping of the wavelets. And she heard something else. There was a scraping, as if something was being dragged through the sand and gravel. Then some banging and clanking.

Dell froze. She moved slowly sideways, off the road into a ditch, where she crouched down in the grass. The shuffling sound moved closer, and shadowy figures quickly moved past her, on up the road. Toward the house.

Chapter 7

Francie didn't sleep well. She awoke early, with the red mist of dawn floating through the sheer-curtained windows of her bedroom. She knew something wasn't right with Dell. She slipped off her bed, threw on a robe, and made her way down the darkened hallway to the girl's room. She knocked softly, and went in, to discover an empty bed and an open window. She peered out the window in a vain hope that she was not too late. Nothing there but the quiet swirling mist, insulating against the small disturbances of the night. She had no choice now. Back in her room, Francie grabbed the phone receiver, and punched the button for the Sheriff's Department.

A woman answered on the second ring. "Sheriff's dispatch. Is this an emergency?"

"Hi, this is Francine out at Parker Ranch, near Mission Ridge—when will Sheriff Warner be in?"

"We don't expect the Sheriff for another three hours, Ma'am. Is there something I can do for you?"

"Well, uh, we received a call from your office yesterday inquiring about a young girl who was missing? And I believe we have seen her, but she's gone."

"And what can I do for you, Ma'am?"

"You can let the sheriff know that she was here, and maybe you can find where she went from here. Is there anyone you can send out?"

"Do you remember who you talked to yesterday, Ma'am?"

Francie thought back on the call. "Umm, I think...Daniels. Yes, it was Deputy Daniels. I told him to say 'hello' to the sheriff for me."

"Right, Ma'am. I'll put in a call to Deputy Daniels. He should be in shortly. You say this is regarding a missing girl?"

"Yes! Daniels said she was dangerous! He seemed to think it

was important."

"Okay, Ma'am. Thanks for the call Ma'am." The dispatcher disconnected.

Francie was frustrated. She would have called the Sheriff at home, but did not have his number. She had to get moving if she was going to catch up with Dell and try to persuade her to stay. Good thing it was Saturday. No worry about getting the boys off on time. They would get themselves up and the animals would be looked after. She would try and track Dell down before she got too far. She dressed, slipped into her boots, grabbed a strobe light and headed out the front door.

On her way down the front drive she hesitated. Dell would make sure she couldn't be followed, so she would do the unexpected. Don't head down the road. It's the first place anyone would begin. Where then? Only one other way—toward the river. Francie turned right, and started down the rutted drive. She switched on the strobe, and swung it back and forth over the road, from brown fence to green-yellow grass. She curved steeply down to the left, then straightened again, noting how stark everything appeared in the morning mist. She moved quickly, thinking about her first meeting with Dell. The girl was like no one she had ever encountered. Obviously a feral child, she lived entirely on her own, by her wits. She had been doing that, above and apart from the system fate had placed her into, for countless years. She was like a wolf-child, a female Mowgli, living within the system, and only recently trapped within a different system of slavery, which she had finally escaped from. What were her values? Who did she care about? Francie decided those were moot questions, to be answered only when they became relevant to her ultimate fate. Right now she only knew for sure that the girl had found a place in her heart, and she cared very much what might happen to her.

The mist was still dense, but the light had turned a pale yellow. As Francie proceeded, step by step, she became aware she was not alone on the road.

Her light played back and forth, showing nothing but shadows, when one of them moved.

A figure with a rifle rushed toward her and growled. "Down on the ground!"

She stood, dumbfounded, when a hand reached out, swatted away her light, and pushed her. "Down!" said the figure.

Chapter 8

Marty lay half-awake when his phone rang. He sprang out of bed and punched it on. "This is Marty."

"Hey, Marty. Sheriff Warner. I could use your help on this. Just got a call from the Parker Ranch, a Francine Parker. She may have seen our girl and I know you got a bead on her."

"Yeah? Where's she at, Vern?"

"Up near the river a ways. Daniels and me will be up at Mission Ridge in about an hour, if you wanna meet us there."

"Got it. See you in an hour."

Marty was ensconced in a cheap motel in Hayes. He had a feeling that something was going to break in this dead trucker incident, and he thought it might turn out to be interesting. He quickly brushed his teeth, packed his overnight bag, and banged out the door into the courtyard. He keyed the entry to his six-year-old Ford and slammed it into gear. His stomach told him it was past feeding time, but he tried to ignore the signals. Food would come later.

It was an hour and a quarter at top speed before he reached the Mission Ridge Station. The Stanley County Sheriff SUV was waiting by the stop sign, and he pulled alongside. Windows were rolled down.

"I was beginning to think you weren't coming," the sheriff admonished.

Planck noted that Deputy Daniels was slumped over in the passenger seat, deep in sleep. He answered the sheriff. "Your hours go by faster than mine, Vern. Where to, now?"

"The Parker Ranch is about fifteen miles northeast of here, up Bennet Road. The turns are not well marked, so you best follow us, Marty."

They caravanned over several dirt roads at slow to moderate

speeds, depending on the visibility over the next few miles. Finally, there was a sign at a nondescript intersection marked 'Parker Ranch'. When the dust settled, they turned and slowly rolled up the road between fields of waving prairie grass.

Planck pulled alongside the Sheriff's vehicle. Windows were downed. "What's the plan, Vern?"

"We'll just go on up to the house. Francine had called about the girl, but said she was gone, so we'll just go up there and scope it out."

They led Francine back toward the house. Several men accompanied her. She couldn't see how many. All had military type rifles, and they sounded very serious. She wondered if they could be connected with Dell in any way but couldn't imagine how the girl might be associated with these strange men. She did not fear for herself, but did worry about the boys. Irma wouldn't be in until later, so she was okay for now. These men were here for a reason, and if she could figure it out, then maybe this could end quickly without anyone getting hurt.

"How many people in the house?" Apparently the leader, as he was the only one who spoke. Of medium height, maybe five-eleven, he wore his black hair long with a sparse mustache over his lip. He dressed himself in dark blue coveralls, like a plumber. They all were dressed that way, Francie noticed, and they all carried backpacks.

He shoved her shoulder. "How many?" he demanded.

"Uh, there's just me and the boys," she responded. "Two boys. They are young, you won't need to worry about them." Although Francie was worried, greatly. She continued to ask herself, *what are these militants doing here?*

"The boys," the leader asked, "where are they?"

"Still in bed. I'll go get them up."

"Not you!" He gestured to one of the minions, "Ali, check upstairs."

"What do you want?" Her shrill voice betrayed her loss of

control. Nothing in her experience had prepared her for this. "Why are you doing this?"

The leader studied her, then slowly looked around the house. "Don't worry about it. All will be over soon." He proceeded through the living room into the kitchen, moving items, lifting lids, and opening drawers.

They urged Jimmy and Donnie downstairs, both dressed in loose flannel pajamas, prodded by the military style weapons.

"Hey, Mom!" Donnie shouted. "Mom, what's happening?" Echoed Jimmy.

"Shut up!" ordered the thug with the rifle. He kicked Jimmy halfway down stairs, but the boy caught himself on the railing. He turned and yelled at his attacker, "Stop that, you piece of shit!" This earned him a slam in the ribs with a rifle butt, and he stumbled onto the landing. Donnie grabbed him, and they supported one another the rest of the way down.

The leader herded the family onto the peach patterned couches in the living room, where he addressed them. "Is this everyone?"

Francie was shaking. "Jimmy, are you okay? Where's Panda?"

Jimmy's lip bled down his chin. "I'm okay. They locked Panda in the bedroom."

"Ok, enough!" The gunman shouted. "My name is Djibouti. I will be your host for the next several hours. Just behave yourselves, and we will get along fine. We are using your house as a base of operations, and if you don't get into our business, then you will be fine."

One of his company approached and conferred with Djibouti for a few seconds, gesturing here and there with his weapon.

Francie spoke up again. "What is your business? You know we have people coming soon."

"What? Out here you don't even have a paperboy." He appeared slightly amused.

"You will pay dearly if you harm any of these boys!"

"Madam, we expect to pay dearly for what we are doing, so

just don't get in our way, and you won't be harmed."

Satisfied with everyone's acquiescence, he continued, "Madam, what is your name?"

Francie replied.

"Okay, Francie. I will need the keys to your vehicles. All of them, including the launch down at the dock."

"I don't see what you can possibly hope to gain from this. I suggest you leave now!"

Djibouti calmly turned to Francie and slapped her loudly across the face. "One last time, Francie—where are the keys?"

The slap stung, but it seemed distant and did not elicit her cooperation. Francie did not believe the intruders would not harm them. She felt she had to delay them as long as possible, because she knew they would have no use for her when they got what they wanted. So she simply stood and stared at the man.

"Which boy should I shoot first, do you think?"

Jimmy rose from where he was made to sit, and lunged at the man. He was easily stopped by one of the men, who stepped in front of him, and roughly shoved him back into his seat. Francie lost her resolve then. "Please, you don't have to hurt anyone— the keys are over there on the desk." She indicated the roll top desk in the entrance way, by the front door. "In the dish. Everything you need is there. Will you go now?"

Djibouti directed one of the men to the desk. "I think I will be honest, and tell you that we are not leaving anytime soon. We have some complicated business to attend to."

As the keys were found and retrieved from the dish on the desk, another one of the men stepped in off the porch. He stood bigger than the others, exhibiting a completely bald head, dotted with sweat. "Djibouti, there is a vehicle coming up the road!"

Djibouti jerked Francie by the arm. "Who is coming?"

"I told you we have people coming. I called the sheriff— you'd better get out while you can."

A look of concern flashed across the intruder's face. But only briefly. Djibouti directed two of his men outside. "Ali, you and Muncie hide yourself out in front with Roark, and wait for whoever it is!" He looked again at Francie, "I don't think we have to be too concerned at this time. Whoever is coming, you cannot possibly have told them we are here."

Francie was immediately worried about the sheriff. These people had assault rifles, and there were six of them that she had counted, maybe more. She tried desperately to think of how she could distract them enough to gain an advantage. Maybe when the sheriff arrived, she would have a chance to get the shotgun from the pantry.

Djibouti seemed to read her mind. He spun her around and shoved her toward the couch. "Go sit with your boys, and stay put!"

Outside, the men lingered near the porch, listening for sounds. There was the definite slow rumble of a vehicle, which seemed to be making its way carefully up the road in the distance. Ali directed one of the men across the drive, toward the lake. "Muncie, take cover over there. Roark," he waved to the other man, "you hide up there, near the porch. When they get here, we'll wait 'til they stop and get out before we take them."

Both men complied without a sound. Muncie, a dark pudgy man with an unkempt mustache, found a large Cottonwood nearby, close to the drive that led to the river. He shuffled over to the tree, unslung his AR-15. He found a comfortable spot within the roots of the tree, and sat back facing the house where he could peer around to the road. He placed the rifle across his lap and waited. A slight noise behind him caused him to look around. He barely had time to register the sight of something dark rushing at his head before the heavy blow snatched consciousness in a flash of red.

Roark was in a rosebush, cursing the thorns in his arm, when he was suddenly hit in the side of the head. He staggered back, dazed, when a figure in black appeared with a rifle and smashed him again. He went down with a sharp moan.

Ali was alerted by the noise. "Roark!" The sound of the vehicle was growing louder. He looked across the road to where Muncie had disappeared. "Muncie," he shouted, "go check on Roark." There was no response. Ali looked down the road to where the vehicle would soon appear, then rushed over to where he last had seen his compatriot, rifle held at the ready. There was no sign of Roark. He called again. "Roark! Muncie!"

Chapter 9

Dell quickly familiarized herself with the AR-15s. She pulled the magazines out and threw the bolts to empty the weapons. She pulled each trigger several times, and flicked the safeties on and off, then on again to get a feel for them. Then she reloaded and decided to place one next to the pump shed behind the house. The weapon would be good there until needed, if it came to that. The other she would stash somewhere in front. If seen, she didn't want to appear as a threat. There was still the concealed semi-automatic in her pack she could rely on if needed.

Dell didn't know if the men would survive the thrashing she gave them, but if they did they wouldn't be much trouble for a while. She had dragged them off into the grass, and tied their arms and necks together with belts and boot laces.

She had known Francie and the boys for only a short while, but felt they had formed a bond like none she had ever known. They demanded nothing from her, and had no interest in directing her life or any part of it. She felt they only wanted good to come her way, and only expected goodness in return. Well, she was ready to give. She realized that Francie was right. Running off was a mistake, and now bad things had begun to happen. She didn't know if she was to blame, but found herself ready to defend these folks in every way she knew how. There had been six attackers, and now there were four. The others had to be on their guard now, and were not going to be so easy. If she had any inkling of what they were after, she might have been able to use that to her advantage, but she didn't have a clue.

Djibouti and two of his men had made a quick search of the perimeter before headlights appeared at the end of the drive. The invader directed his men inside, where they made ready. He ordered Ali to put the family in the den, and placed one man at the door.

Planck arrived at the Parker Ranch house shortly before seven AM just behind the sheriff's vehicle. The sun was glaring over the roof of the house, placing it in silhouette, making visibility poor.

The two vehicles eased to a stop in front near the covered porch. Planck got out of his sedan and crossed to Warner's SUV, but the sheriff held him back. "Wait a sec, Marty. Let's sit here awhile. That girl is supposed to have been here. She may still be around."

Marty looked over to where the drive angled to the left of the house and down to the river. "I'm going down there Vern, see if I can find anything." He again checked his surroundings, then followed the road down to the river.

Warner looked at Daniels, now just waking up. The house was dark and no one had appeared to greet them. He didn't like it, and said as much to the Deputy. "If that girl was here, no telling what she might have been up to. He pulled his sidearm before heading up to the porch. "Daniels, you head around back." Warner slowly climbed the steps, went up to the door, and tried the knob. When he found it unlocked, he opened it and walked in.

"Good morning Sheriff—you will please drop your gun." Djibouti and three of his men were situated around the entranceway, so that there could be no question of doing what was advised.

Warner slowly lowered his Smith & Wesson. "Excuse me—who are you?"

Francie spoke up. "I'm sorry, Vern. These men showed up early this morning, and sort of took over."

"Took over?"

"Don't concern yourself, Sheriff. We won't be here longer than necessary. But I'm thinking that you will have to give me the gun, and join the family."

Djibouti gestured to Ali. "Check outside for his friends, but be careful!" He then gingerly took the revolver from the sheriff's still hand, as Ali edged his way through the entrance.

A moment later gunshots sounded outside. Djibouti rushed back to the doorway. Ali immediately appeared, pushing Deputy Daniels through ahead of him. Daniels was limping and bleeding from his right leg. Djibouti raised an eyebrow, and pointed to the other of the two couches. "So who is this? A not so smart policeman?"

Ali blurted, "There's two cars out there, Djibouti! This one was trying to sneak around the house."

The leader turned to the Sheriff. "How many others, Sheriff? Tell me!"

Warner remained mute. Djibouti appeared frustrated, his brows wrinkling. "Here's what I think, Sheriff. You blundered in here by chance—but no. Another car was following. That means someone else has accompanied you and your deputy! Am I right?"

Warner looked at him blankly. "You're entitled to think what you want to."

"No, wait." Djibouti was changing his mind. "Two of my men are missing before you arrived. That means someone else has intervened." Djibouti scratched his head.

"We'll have to force their hand." He looked to his henchmen. "Ali, you and Carlos—grab the youngest kid...and Francie here. Bind their hands. All of them!" He indicated Warner and Jimmy as well.

Zip ties were produced, and wrists were tightly bound. Djibouti grabbed Francie's arm and steered her toward the door. He barked over his shoulder, "Carlos, grab the kid and come with me."

Outside the morning sun peeked over the roof of the house, glaring harshly off the windshields of the two vehicles in front.

Chapter 10

Marty hadn't gotten too far down the heavily rutted drive when a girl appeared in front of him.

"Whoa!" He jumped. Then apologized. "I'm sorry, you startled me." She was young, yet seemed totally in control, and she had come from nowhere.

Dell appraised him, and decided he wasn't one of the invaders. "Keep your voice down," she hissed. "Who are you, and what are you doing here?"

"Well," he whispered back, glancing around cautiously, "I'm out here with the sheriff, and we are looking for this...ah..." He suddenly realized that he might have found what they were looking for. She was tall and slender, with a mass of curly, reddish hair. She wore dark jeans, a red plaid shirt rolled just above her elbows, and was carrying a backpack in her left hand. The shirt couldn't quite hide well defined muscles in her arms. "My name is Martin, and I'm a journalist out of Sioux Falls. Do you live here?"

"If you're not one of them, then you'd better keep out of the way. There's trouble here and you'll stay out of it, if you're smart."

Martin had no time to reply. A voice shouting from around the front of the house immediately caught their attention. "Whoever's out there, we've got your friends. If you want them to stay healthy, show yourselves!" Then, "You've got one minute!"

Dell frowned and her eyes got hard. She whispered to Martin, "I have to help them—you get lost."

She brushed past him, beginning to focus on what needed to be done, and trotted up the drive.

Djibouti, holding Francie in front of him, was about to shout another order, when a young woman jogged easily from around the house and halted a good twenty feet from where he stood. He noted her unkempt curly hair, and the fact that she was as tall as he was. She carried a pack over one shoulder.

"Who's this now?" Djibouti smiled. "And what have you done with my soldiers?"

Francie was shocked to see her, and blurted her name, as did her son. "Dell!" "Dell?"

Dell allowed a small smile, and looked at the intruder. "I don't know about any 'soldiers', but I see lots of lowlife scumbags here. Let these people go, whoever you are."

"You—I take it they call you Dell—you are in no position to make demands." He pointed his rifle at her with his left hand, while continuing to hold Francie's wrists with the other.

"Dell, honey, don't anger him. Maybe we can find out what he wants…"

Dell looked at Francie, and her whole body began to thrum with rage, but since early childhood she had been a master at hiding her feelings. She flicked her chin up. "Alright, big man. Let's go inside and listen to your demands."

"I don't have any demands, darling. Now who is out here with you? Who drove that second car, there?" He gestured with the rifle to Marty's Ford, parked next to the Sheriff Department SUV.

Dell glanced over to the vehicles. "That's my car. I drove in right after the sheriff. Is he inside?" She hadn't met the sheriff, but wasn't surprised that he had walked right into this one. In her experience, law enforcement types were mostly bluster, and not very smart.

Francie twisted around to look at her captor. "So if you have no demands, then why don't you move on, and leave us in peace?"

"We will leave soon enough, but we will be here at least until tonight." He took one last look around, and gestured at Dell with his weapon. "Go ahead of us, into the house."

Dell moved quickly up the steps, and disappeared through the front door.

"Carlos, take the kid, and get in there with the girl, and tie her up!" Djibouti was suddenly struck by a feeling he was losing control of the situation, and unease about his missing men gnawed at his thoughts.

As Dell sailed through the door, her senses turned hyper and telegraphed an immediate assessment of the situation. One thug with a rifle was in the kitchen, looking out the back window. The other was in the chair next to the couch, where Jimmy sat alongside a uniformed man, who she assumed was the sheriff. A prone deputy occupied the matching couch. The man in the chair, surprised by her appearance, began to rise. Jimmy spotted her at the same time and shouted, "Dell!"

The man smiled at her and was about to say something, as she continued straight toward him, her intention not apparent on her expressionless face. Internally, her rage outlined everything she saw in a red halo, and the world around her shifted into slow-motion.

She stopped inches from the man, but her head continued forward, snapping into his nose with a loud crack. Before he realized what happened, she grabbed his shoulders and kneed him swiftly in the groin. As he gasped in surprise and pain, she rescued his rifle before it fell, raised the weapon and popped off two shots at Ali, who had been slow to move from the kitchen window. He dropped from sight.

As Carlos pushed Donnie through the front door, he jumped at the noise and tripped backward, nearly dropping his weapon. Donnie broke free.

Dell had turned, racing towards the pair, the forgotten rifle clattering to the floor. She leaped, twisting her body around, her leg arcing in a lightning fast kick, boot connecting hard with Carlos' chest.

The blow crashed him into the door frame. Dell snagged his weapon on the fly and whirled, dropping down to one knee, then coming up fast, she pivoted the rifle around to point at Djibouti, silhouetted in the doorway. The man froze, his mouth gaping, while still holding Francie's bound wrists.

Dell screamed at him, "Freeze, asshole!"

He instantly let go of Francie, and almost dropped his weapon. Then gripped it hard and turned to run stumbling down the porch stairs.

At that moment, the back door slammed. Apparently, Ali had only been winged by Dell's hurried fusillade, and had made a quick exit as well.

Dell, breathing deep, with sweat and blood running down her face, tended to Francie. "Are you okay?" She dug into her jeans, produced a large folding knife, and cut the zip ties. Francie gave Dell a measured look, and turned to Donnie. Dell handed her the knife, and she quickly undid his hands.

Donnie embraced his mother, and held her tight for a long moment. Francie said, "We're okay, Donnie. Now let me get to the others."

"Over here," the sheriff said. He was looking dazed. Francie cut his bonds, and he quickly got to his feet to check on Daniels as Francie cut the ties around Jimmy's wrists.

Jimmy looked at Dell, who was a different person than she had been a moment ago. She stood with her eyes shut, and shoulders slumped.

"Dell," said Jimmy, "good to see you."

"Hi, Jimmy," she panted. "I'm sorry I left. I don't know what I was thinking. I won't do it again."

"All right," Sheriff Warner was quickly recovering from the ordeal. "I'm not sure I believe what I've just seen. " He squinted at Dell. "Are you...I don't know how to put this. We have been looking for a young woman, fitting your description. I...can't believe what I've just seen." He sat back down, and shook his head. "Okay, let's get these guys secured." He looked toward his captor, who now lay moaning with a broken nose in front of him. His gaze shifted to Carlos, who was writhing in pain as he lay by the door. "I'll call County Medics. We need to get these guys to a hospital. You too, Daniels." The deputy began moving and struggled to sit up. Warner took another look around the room, then walked to the desk and picked up the phone.

Chapter 11

Planck watched the girl disappear around the house, and he suddenly felt inadequate. Her presence puzzled him as did the ultimatum from the unseen intruders. She had told him to get lost, but surely, there might be something he could do. He didn't know these people, but they were obviously under siege. He looked around for something that might give him an edge, and spied an object leaning against a nearby cottonwood that didn't quite fit in. Moving closer, he discovered it was an assault rifle, an AR-15.

He thought about it—definitely not a normal ranch tool—then picked it up. It was loaded, and fully functional. While carrying the weapon back toward the house he tripped over what he first dismissed as a fallen tree branch. A second look revealed the leg of a man clad in a dark jumper. The individual lay hogtied and appeared unconscious. Marty decided that this one must be the victim of his own folly, and assumed he was put out of commission for a good reason. He continued toward the house.

While closing in on the rear of the home, he heard two gunshots from within. A moment later, the back door crashed open and a dark man, clad similarly to the other he had just left, limped quickly outside and stumbled down the steps. He had long stringy hair, with a splotch of blood oozing across his shoulder, and appeared to be desperately trying to leave the vicinity. He spotted Marty just as the AR-15 Marty held was leveled at his chest.

"Stop right there, Mister! Where are you headed, you think?"

The man stopped and glared his frustration at Marty.

"Turn around," Marty gestured with the rifle. "Let's get up to the front of the house, and sort this out."

As they rounded the corner, they nearly collided with a

wide-eyed Djibouti, who veered off at an angle and continued running like he was on fire. Distracted, Marty was surprised by his prisoner, who turned on him, knocking the rifle to the ground. Before He could recover, the prisoner had leapt away through the tall grass, following the trail left by his comrade.

Martin retrieved the fallen weapon, hefted it and looked after the fleeing figures. They had made themselves invisible by this time, and he didn't think it would be wise to pursue them. Assuming he should find out what was going on in the house instead, he approached the front and jogged up the steps to the door. He tried the handle, and cautiously cracked it open. Before him was a scene difficult to interpret.

The sheriff talked on his phone near the kitchen. Two injured men lay on either side of the floor. A wounded deputy propped himself on a couch. A woman stood with arms about two boys and the girl he had met earlier on the trail below. A medium-sized dog jumped and spun around the woman, who focused only on the people she hugged.

Martin said, "Hello, is everything alright here? What's going on Vern?" This directed toward the sheriff, who looked up and gave him an index finger signal.

The sheriff put down the phone. "Marty, did you see anyone out there?"

"Oh yeah, Vern. I ran into two guys, but they left in a real hurry despite my best efforts. What happened here?"

Warner looked over the scene. "I don't think I can describe it adequately without help, Marty. We're going to have to all sit down and discuss this amongst ourselves." He gestured around the room. "That means Missus Parker here, and the young folk, too. Maybe together we can figure out what just happened."

Francine turned to the sheriff. "Vern, I was forced to give that guy all my keys, including the key to the launch down at the river."

Planck looked back out the door. "That might be where those two are headed. If they reach that boat, Sheriff, we may have trouble catching up to them."

The sheriff addressed Francine. "Will you be able to handle things here, Francie? I got help coming, so it shouldn't be too long."

"We'll be fine, Sheriff. The boys will help, and Dell is here if anything else comes up." She gave a questioning look to Dell, who was now sitting quietly with the boys, checking Jimmy's ribs for bruises. "You will be here awhile, won't you Dell?"

The girl looked up, a smile touching her lips. She nodded slightly and turned her attention back to the boys.

Planck and Warner left the house and headed around to the road leading to the lake. Along the way, Planck remembered the man he had almost tripped over, and stopped. "Sheriff, that girl was coming through here before she met up with you and the others, and I think she left an injured man or two in her wake, over there in the grass somewhere."

"Show me."

Martin led the sheriff over to where he thought he had tripped over a body. They saw plenty of trampled grass, but no men, injured or otherwise. They were about to give it up, when Warner bent down and picked up a knotted shoelace that had been cut. "I think, Marty, that we may be looking for more than two men down at the boat."

"We'd better get moving."

They began a steady jog down the trail, weapons held ready. As they came within sight of the launch they observed three men carrying bundles toward it from a beached skiff. One of the men they hadn't seen before. Near giant in stature, his head bald and glistening in the sunlight. Intent on their job, the men yelled and cursed when Warner ordered them to drop what they were doing. "All of you. Get on the ground!"

Two complied. The third kicked up sand as he ran toward the water and dived in, swimming like he had a place to go. Only there was nothing. The river here spanned miles across, and even Michael Phelps would have trouble making it.

Marty watched him splash, and kept his AR-15 leveled at the

others. Warner stepped among them to bind their hands with zip ties. The universal handcuffs. A sudden movement from the power launch caught Marty's eye. He swung the rifle around as a fourth man lifted himself above the railing and aimed his rifle at the sheriff.

Marty yelled. "Stop!" But the man did not have a chance to comply, as Planck let off a volley of three shots. The man was thrown back in a confusion of splintered wood, smoke and blood.

Chapter 12

For a while it was quite a circus at the Parker Ranch. Ambulances parked in the drive next to the house, as were three large black SUVs with government plates. Inside, EMTs prepared to transport Deputy Daniels to the hospital for treatment of minor wounds. Two other men, suspected of home invasion, were in pretty serious shape. One suffered a broken nose, and injuries to his groin. The other had sustained broken ribs, and a dislocated hip.

Three FBI agents questioned the witnesses.

Agent Joiner addressed Francie. "So, Ma'am, you say there were four men here, holding your family hostage?"

"There were actually six men initially, Agent Joiner. And the sheriff and Deputy Daniels there were being held as well."

"Six, then." Joiner had introduced himself as Special Agent in Charge. He looked to be in his mid-fifties, and Francie thought that job stress had probably taken out most of his hair. What remained was salt and pepper grey, cut very short. His suit matched his hair.

"That's right. Two of them went outside when they heard the sheriff."

Agent Spanner, a thirty-something man with dark hair, spoke up. "So what happened to them?"

Francie looked at Dell. "I don't know. There were just four here when the sheriff came in. They made him drop his gun, and we were all made to sit tight. Then two of them decided to take us outside to draw out the others—me and Donnie."

"So there were more deputies with the sheriff?"

"You'll have to ask the sheriff that."

"Okay," Joiner continued. "How did you escape? I mean, you did escape—what happened?"

The third agent, a female in a dark blue striped suit, was

checking out Dell. She observed the girl didn't seem to fit in with the rest of the family and decided she was either a girlfriend of one of the boys, or maybe a neighbor.

"Well," Francie continued. "That's when Dell came in. When they brought us back inside, Dell was sort of...kicking one of them. I saw one man had hurt his nose, and the other two ran away."

The female agent addressed Dell. "I'm Agent Maddis. Where are you from, Dell?"

Dell looked down at the floor. She was not going to answer any questions she didn't want to. She made up her mind, and looked up at the agent. "I was outside."

"No, I mean originally. Where do you come from?"

Dell just looked at her. They looked at each other for a long minute. Jimmy broke the silence. "Dell has been with us as long as I can remember. She's like, uh, my older sister."

Agent Maddis stared at Jimmy, then back at Dell. "Okay, so Dell, did you put these guys' lights out?"

Dell smiled at Jimmy. "They were threatening my family, so I acted."

Sheriff Warner sat in the coarse sand next to the classic motor launch, explaining to four FBI agents out of Pierre why he had called them. "I believe that you'll find a large amount of explosives on that boat, gents. This is not no hit and run!"

One of the agents, Billings, had a satellite phone he was talking on, gesturing with his free hand. "Yeah, we have one dead suspect, and two have been subdued. We'll need a crawler out here to look for the third—he went swimming. Couldn't have gone far, but this is a big area. How long? Okay, will keep you posted."

He clipped the phone back in his belt and shaded his eyes from the glare as he perused the river. He then turned to Sheriff Warner. "What was it that tipped you into this operation, Sheriff?"

Warner rubbed the back of his neck, and pulled his hat down tighter against the breeze coming off the water. "Well, Agent Billings, it was more like 'tripped' not 'tipped'. We were out here on an unrelated matter, when these folk got in our faces."

"There were you and your deputy, and..."

"Yeah, we had a journalist, who had been in on this other case we were investigating. He was tagging along." He indicated Planck with a nod to Marty, who had been relieved of his 'found' rifle. "And a good thing he was along on this one—saved my butt. Also, good thing I deputized him before we came out here, otherwise there might have been some complications." He gave the agent a blank look.

The agent ignored him. "Tell me about the injured deputy, Sheriff. He get injured at the outset, when you first arrived at the ranch?"

"That guy over there." Warner indicated Ali, who was on the ground with the big man, awaiting their fate. "He caught Daniels in a firefight. Daniels was still outside the ranch house, and that man was sent out to look for him."

Billings took in the man the sheriff had indicated, noting the blood on his shirt. "Looks like Daniels gave as good as he got."

"You can't credit Daniels for that one. It was the girl did that."

"Girl? He was shot by a girl?"

Warner looked back up towards the house. "That's right, Agent Billings—saw it myself. She's part of that other matter I was telling you about."

"I'd like to hear more about this girl. She up at the house now?"

"As far as I know, unless you folks chased her off. She was still there when we took off after these bozos. Anyway, hadn't been for her, you might not have known about these explosives here until they were put to whatever use they had in mind for them."

Billings' phone jangled just then, and he pulled it out and pressed a button. "Billings."

Planck walked over to where the sheriff was conferring with the agent. "Well, Vern—I don't suppose you have any theories as to what the hell is going on here?"

"Oh, I have some ideas, Marty. Not sure they're correct ideas. These clowns were intent on blowing something up, and there is not much around here except for that humungous dam and power plant downstream. Just speculating, of course."

Agent Billings finished his call and turned back to the sheriff. "We don't have any sightings on the man who dove into the water, but they're out looking, and if he survives, we'll get him. There's a good chance that he didn't survive, however. If that's the case, we'll find his body. Count on that." He looked out over the river. "Oh, and to set your mind at rest, we've been getting intel on this operation for months, just no details. It's a good bet that your speculation about sabotage is right on."

The agent then turned his attention to the other investigators, who were waiting for a clean-up crew to handle the explosives. "I'll head back up to the house with the sheriff. You guys wrap up with these boys and head on up when you're done. I'll point the cleanup boys in the right direction when they find their way out here."

Agent Billings, Planck and Warner began their trudge back up the rutted pathway to the ranch house.

"So what about this girl, Sheriff? She shot one of the perps? Was she armed, or what?"

The sheriff thought awhile, as Planck looked on, wondering how he was going to handle this. "I'm not sure how I can explain about the girl, Agent Billings. Let's just say she was instrumental in subduing these terrorists. I think, basically, she took all six of them down, by herself." He looked directly at the agent. "She clobbered two of them outside before we arrived, as near as I can figure. Then she came into the house like a tornado, and biff-bam, three more were down, and the fourth was running fast."

Agent Billings smirked, shook his head, and pursed his lips

in thought, glancing again at Warner and Planck. "This girl, you think she is military?"

Planck eyed Warner, who replied. "You maybe should talk to her—I just saw her for a few minutes, and didn't get a chance to really question her at length."

Chapter 13

Dell was going over in her mind what she might tell the FBI when they finally began digging into what she was doing here and how she had managed to defeat these invaders. She didn't really know, herself, except that she knew she had to react and the best way to do that was to do it without thinking. She'd had years of practice subduing bullies in the alleys and fire escapes of the South Side where she grew up. It was always easier not to think about what she was going to do or how she was going to do it because, if she started to think about it, then the fear would creep in. And the fear would cripple her. That happened once, when she was nine, and she barely survived. She had never let it happen again.

Francie tried to protect Dell as best she could. The FBI and the sheriff were all over her, not letting her relax for an instant. Billings, Maddis and Joiner were incessant in their questioning. "Do you belong to any militant groups, Miss?" "How long have you been using firearms?" "Did you know any of the terrorists, Miss?" "What type of military training have you had?" "Did you know what the terrorists were planning?" When did you first come to live with the Parkers?" "What sort of drugs are you using?" "Are you a U.S. citizen?" "How old are you?" "Can we see your ID?" "What is your last name?"

All were answered with terse single-word answers—no, never, no, none, no, no, none. The last three or four questions she didn't answer at all—just sat and stared blankly at her interrogators.

"Answer the questions, Miss."

Francie intervened. "Stop browbeating her! You'd think she was the criminal, not the one who stopped these bastards! I think this incident has exhausted all of us, and you need to stop with these irrelevant questions! Dell has no connection with these criminals. Isn't it obvious?"

"I'm sorry, Missus Parker, but we need to know who we're dealing with, and the girl here is being less than cooperative." Agent Maddis turned again to Dell. "What can you tell us about yourself, Dell?"

To Dell, the female agent appeared to be playing good cop, with her softer demeanor, but she didn't mind. She figured she had to placate them somehow, so she began making stuff up. Stuff she hoped they would have difficulty verifying. "I was born in Chicago, so I guess I'm a U.S. citizen. I've never thought about it. I've never had a family, so I don't have a last name—never had need for one. Don't have an ID either. I know who I am, and nobody else really cares, so what would be the point?" She looked up from staring at her shoes. "When I was really young, I was singing 'Farmer in the Dell' all the time, so they named me Dell. Better than 'Farmer', I guess." She smiled, and looked at Jimmy to see if he was buying any of this. "Maybe someday I'll have a last name. I guess I'll need one if I ever get a bank account. Oh, and I've never used any drugs, just toughed it out."

Maddis rolled her eyes and looked at agent Billings, who continued with the questions. "The sheriff has filled us in on what you did here today to stop these guys. And we applaud that. However, you seem to be something of a loose cannon, Miss, and we just need to assess whether you might present a further danger, at this point, to anyone else."

Francie butted in again. "We know Dell wouldn't hurt anyone who wasn't a threat. She has become a part of our family, and we can vouch for her." She looked over at the boys, and both nodded their agreement. Panda, who was lying on the floor between Donnie and Jimmy, thumped his tail. "I'm sure if Irma, our housekeeper, were here, she would make it unanimous."

Sheriff Warner was looking hard at Dell, trying to come to some decision. He had some questions for the girl, but didn't want to make a federal case out of it unless he had to. "Agent Joiner, it looks like we've about wrapped up things here, as far as you're concerned. We got the bad guys, and you're doing your bit to tie up the loose ends. I may have some questions for the girl here on another matter, but that doesn't concern you folks at this point. If it should involve terrorism, or interstate commerce, I'll be sure and let you know."

They left off trying to get more information from Dell at the sheriff's urging. In two more hours, the Federal investigators finally left for the day.

Irma arrived as the Feds were leaving. She looked furtively about and cast her eyes down when she came close to an agent. She whispered to Francie, "You have some big trouble here?"

"We had a problem with some gunmen, Irma, but it's done with. You arrived at just the right time." She suspected Irma might be nervous with federal agents around, but Francie had never once asked her for documents, so all she could do was speculate.

She and Francie prepared a lunch of 'build them yourself' sandwiches, with chips, fresh bread, mayo and aioli spread, three different cheeses, turkey and ham, and home-made pickles. All four of the guys tore into the meal, and Dell was no slouch. She kept up with them, until the third one, half of which was left for Panda.

"So, Missus Parker," Planck began.

She smiled up at him. "Call me Francie."

"Okay, Francie. How long have you been out here, doing the ranch thing?"

"The ranch thing?" She was amused at his turn of phrase, and decided to play along. "Well, we started ranching, my husband James and I, about twenty years ago when we both graduated from college. We didn't think we could survive in the City, what with all those 'stop signs', so we decided to get married and head for the hills. And here we are! James didn't quite make it this far, but he's still with us in spirit, all of us. The boys and I." She started to tear up and looked around the room. "Dell, too. If she wants."

All the heads in the room turned to the girl, who was bending over with something for Panda. She looked up at the silence and sensed that she should speak. "I guess we're sort of in this together, now? I mean, I would love to stay here, but I don't know what that means, exactly. Yet..."

Apparently, that was the right answer. The boys grinned, made faces and punched each other. Francie just smiled.

Warner exchanged glances with Planck. "Well, Francie. Looks like you've got a new boarder...but Dell, I'm sorry to say that we have a few things to clear up first. I would appreciate it if you could come talk to me out on the porch for a bit. What do you say?"

Francine interrupted. "Sheriff Warner, you can have your talk with Dell on the porch, if you like, but I am going to be there as well."

The sheriff scratched the back of his bare head and puffed his lips.

Francine continued. "Listen, Vern. This girl has every right to be represented when questioned. You cannot question her without counsel. Now, I know we don't have any attorney present, but as a counselor, I believe I'm the next best thing, and I won't let you talk to her alone."

Warner knew it would be a smart move. He sure didn't want anything to come back on him, should he have to turn the girl over to the county prosecutor. "Okay, Francie, you and the girl, come with me. Shouldn't be more than a few minutes. Marty, you stay here. This has to be private."

Planck offered no argument. "No problem, Vern. I'll help Irma and the boys clean up."

Chapter 14

"So guys, what can you tell me about Dell? Is she going to be a good ranch hand?" Marty sat at the table while Jimmy and Donnie dried and put away the lunch dishes, as Irma stole glances at the journalist. "What have you found out about her already?"

Donnie turned his head to Marty. "Gosh, she can sure kick butt!

Jimmy smiled at his brother. "That was pretty awesome, but I think she can do a lot of things if she likes doing it. Like riding. She sure can ride a horse! And I don't think she's been around horses that much in the city where she came from."

"Did she tell you where she came from?"

Donnie answered. "She said she was from a big city back east. Don't know where exactly."

Jimmy corrected him. "Chicago, Donnie, and it's not that far away. But it is big. Bigger than any city we've ever been to."

"Yeah, biggest city we've been to is Pierre."

"Not exactly, Donnie," his brother corrected again. "We went to Sioux Falls once. That's totally bigger than Pierre."

"So, guys." Marty sought to get them back on track. "I guess you like her, then?"

The boys traded glances. "Yeah, she's fun, and pretty." "Tuff, too! Don't forget tuff!" "Kinda makes it more interesting around here." "You know, someone new."

"Yeah," echoed Jimmy, "It's good having someone around who says things you couldn't have predicted they were going to say...know what I mean? She's not like anyone I know at school. You know what they all think about things, either this or that. With Dell, you don't."

"How so?"

"Okay, the other day we were talking about age. I thought she was younger than me, and she said 'Oh no, I'm way older than you', and I thought she was just, you know, bee-essing me, but now I kinda wonder...maybe she's, you know, an old spirit?"

Sheriff Warner sat on the shaded front porch enjoying the early spring afternoon with Francine and Dell. He looked out over the waving grasses—Prairie Smoke, and cord grass, interspersed everywhere with small purple prairie crocus and black eyed Susan. The sky was spread with stratocumulus clouds, like an infinitely big pillow had burst across the heavens. It was pleasant, but his task was not.

"I suspect, Dell, that you are the person who left the scene of a fatality at the Conoco station on the highway about 25 miles from here Thursday morning. Are you that person?"

Dell looked at Francine, who answered with her own question. "Are you asking if she was present at the gas station at the time, or did she wrongfully leave the scene of a fatality?"

The Sheriff heaved a sigh. "You're right, that was two questions. Dell, were you present at the Conoco station Thursday morning, when a big green semi was parked there?"

Dell was expressionless for a moment, then she answered. "I was there, yes. Do you want me to tell you the whole story, Sheriff, so this questioning doesn't take forever?"

"That would be excellent, young lady, if it is the whole story."

"Ok, I'll try not to leave anything out." She looked down at her uneven fingernails. Francie suspected she was gathering up for another whopper, but thought maybe that would be better than anything she might help her come up with.

"The truth is, I was hitching a ride with that trucker in the green semi, and we arrived at the station very early in the morning. He stopped the truck and said he needed something out of the glove box, then he pulled this gun on me and said I had to have sex with him, or he would hurt me. So I did what he wanted, and when he was most distracted, I grabbed the gun out of his hand. His eyes got all big and he started shaking, so I grabbed his wallet that was laying on the dash, and took his cash so I could have money to get away from him. I got my pack and washed up in the restroom, then lit out, trying to get as far away from him as fast as I could."

Francie interjected. "That's when I came across her, Vern."

Warner pursed his lips in thought. "So, Dell. Did you know the man was dead?"

"I thought he might be sick, or having some sort of attack, but he wasn't dead when I left him. I didn't really care what happened to him, it was my chance to leave!"

"Where did you catch a ride with the man?"

"It was at a truck plaza, outside Chicago."

"Didn't he try anything with you earlier, before you got to the gas station where you left him?

"That was the first chance he had, 'cause it was the first time we stopped."

"Where's the gun you took, Dell?"

"I ditched it along the road back there somewhere."

"And I suppose you're going to tell me the money has all been spent!"

Dell started to respond, but Warner stopped her. "Never mind. I'm going to buy your story for now, even though I think you may have fudged on some of the details. You see, there is no way I could prove otherwise, that I can think of at present, and I think Francie here is a good judge of character, so we'll just leave it at that. One more question, though. Who are your folks in Chicago, and why did you decide to leave them and come all the way out here? Oh, and how old are you?"

"Well, that sounds like three questions, Sheriff," Dell responded, and Francie smiled at the girl. "But that's okay. As to my folks—I don't have folks. There are a lot of people living on the street in the City, and I was one of them, for as long as I can remember. It's really hard, and I thought I would try to go somewhere where people were nicer." Her eyes drifted to Francie's, and she smiled. "Oh, and I'm eighteen."

Warner thought that as good an explanation as any for why

they hadn't found anything to match the girl's prints. She apparently was off the grid, truly! She had no ID, no Social, no license, not even a library card. "Okay, Dell. I'm satisfied for now. If I get wind of anything that looks like you've been into, don't think I won't come back out here, though." He rose and started toward the door. "And if you should come across that pistol you took from the trucker, call me. We would like to check and see if it's been involved in any crimes."

"Any other crimes, you mean, Vern," Francie called after him.

Chapter 15

The next day, the Pierre Capitol Journal blared the headline, "Teen Wonder Girl Captures Terrorists." The story byline was Martin Planck. It read, 'Terrorists planned to blow up the Oahe Dam power plant on Saturday, but they were thwarted by a young woman using Super-Hero tactics. The teen, identified only as Dell, took on the six terrorists who staged an early morning raid at a ranch house near Mission Ridge. Dell, a resident of the home, surprised the gang, who were holding the Parker family, the Stanley County Sheriff, one deputy, and this reporter, hostage. The girl disabled two of the terrorists waiting outside, then stormed into the house, where she took on four others, disabling three of them. One shot was fired. Sheriff Vern Warner said "I can't believe what I've just seen," before securing the terrorists. A search is continuing for the sixth terrorist, who remains at large. Dell, who lives at the ranch with the Parker family, said she recently moved to the area from Chicago. She said she had no formal martial arts training, but she'd had a lot of practice taking on criminals in the City. The FBI was called in to investigate the incident. Agent Arch Billings of the FBI's Pierre office, said they had been getting intel on the terror operation against the dam for months. The facility provides much of the power to the northern and central parts of the United States.'

The story, accompanied by a small picture of Dell leaning against a porch railing, was picked up on the AP wire, and soon was news across the country.

Peter Savior rested in the Diamond-Back lounge following his afternoon workout at the gym. He was sipping a mojito when approached by Fred Tulley, his sometime business partner. Tulley sat on the empty stool next to Savior. "Pete, been workin' out? I can always tell—you're drinkin' the Mojito."

Savior just nodded.

"Hey, remember that slut you had working for you who broke Lonnie's nose?"

Savior looked at the man. "Don't remind me—haven't thought about her in days!"

"Well, now you should start thinkin'—look at what's in the paper." He tossed down a Tribune, folded open to an article on page five. "That look like your girl? She appears to be breakin' more noses, now."

Savior grabbed the paper and began to read. After a minute, he looked up at Tulley, and reminisced. "You know, I don't know what happened to her. Man, she was ready to do anything a guy wanted, in the mouth, up the ass, two or three guys at a time—anything. Boy, did she love to fuck! And she was good at it too—the best. We even did some videos. Then one day she kicks Lonnie in the balls, cracks him in the head, and runs off. With my money!" Savior stroked his goatee as he contemplated the news article. "I can see her taking Lonnie unawares, but all those guys? They must be real pussies." A smile slowly spread across his face. "You ready to take a couple days off?"

Tulley returned the smile. "You want I should talk to Lonnie, give him a chance to get some payback?"

"That's good, and maybe find an extra guy, too. I think we don't want any surprises—she may have suckered some hick friends who're willing to protect her."

"I got just the guy. His name is Roach, and I think he is ready to cool it in the country for a while."

Savior grinned and finished off his drink. "I'll get packed and have the car here tomorrow morning at ten. That good for you?"

Francie, and the boys, accompanied by Dell, drove into Pierre Sunday morning. The family would attend the local Presbyterian Church, while Dell elected to go shopping. She told them she had never been in a church, and was not going to start now. She felt that any connection with spiritual life would be one-on-one, and on her terms. They thought that would be fine, seeing as how Dell was in desperate need of a new wardrobe.

"There's a Penney's there, but the mall doesn't open until ten," Francie cautioned.

Dell smiled at her. "Don't worry, I'll wander around, get a snack, and wait 'til it opens. I'll be okay, honest!" Noting Francie's concerned look, she continued. "And I'll meet you outside the store at noon, like we said. It's not like I haven't been on my own before."

Francie silently chided herself for her mother-hen tendencies, but it was so close to yesterday's totally unexpected confrontations, that she was still on edge. She found also, that she was a little concerned over what Dell might choose to outfit herself with, given free rein. She told herself to stop thinking about it.

After they dropped Dell off near the Mall, Donnie leaned over to his brother. "I'll bet you she gets cowboy boots."

"I think she'll have a fancy skirt, a leather vest, and a Stetson," Jimmy answered. "A mini-skirt, maybe."

"You wish," his brother chided him, and punched him in the shoulder.

Dell wandered up and down the streets near the mall. She really didn't want to window shop in closed storefronts, but there was nothing nearby that sparked her interest, so she ventured across the parking spaces. The mall was an indoor type, with parking around the perimeter, and walk-ways leading to the various store entrances. A JC Penney and a Sears served as anchors on either extreme. The Sears had an auto service shop tied to the outside end. In between those two, small vendors catered to specialized wants, such as jewelry, teen clothing, sport shoes and the like. A food court occupied space mid-mall, where pre-cooked pseudo-ethnic foods could be sampled. A medium quality steak-house lurked nearby.

Dell had the jitters. She didn't want to be there, and sure didn't want to be found by anyone at the moment. Realizing she was free again, she toyed with the idea of disappearing. Why did she have to meet up with Francie and the boys as agreed? What connection did she have with them, other than they took her in, fed her, and gave her a place to feel at home? And, of course, protected her from the authorities.

Thus, fighting with her emotions she wandered around behind the buildings and let her feet take her down into a gully. A trail through the brush led her to an encampment of some sort. She burst into a clearing, defined by lines of hanging material and pockets of rubbish, and the smell of rotting oranges. She stopped abruptly. A man sat cross-legged in front of her. He languished near a baby stroller filled with plastic bags and appeared to be counting on his fingers.

"Oh, I'm sorry!" She held her breath.

The man looked in her direction, but not directly at her. Then he looked in the opposite direction. He seemed to dwarf his surroundings, displaying a bush of reddish-orange hair similar to hers, but more kinky than curly. He was definitely an African, with tight, bright skin, the color of wet mud. Gazing across her, he asked, "What did you bring me?"

The question was directed at her, she was sure, but it was too familiar, as if he was expecting her.

She swung a glance over her shoulder. "I'm sorry?" she reiterated, this time as a question.

He looked her up and down, then off to the horizon. "You are Irish. I'm Irish too, you know." His smile was all knowing. "Some just look at me and they say 'there's a cotton-pickin' Negro, but they don't know that I'm related to Saint Patrick. Looks can be deceivin', and that's why I'm not sure about you. You look like a sweet girl, but then you wouldn't be here, would you? I guess it's very dangerous being you. Being here. You never know what kind of creatures you'll meet up with." He looked directly at her, now. "It's a good thing it's only me, heh, heh." He laughed quietly, and turned his attention once again to his fingers.

"I was just looking around. I didn't mean to intrude." She wondered what he could possibly know about her nebulous origins. "How do you know me?"

"Know what? I'm sure I don't know you. Just blabbin' like a crazy fool, waiting for the summer, so I can get naked! I could use a new spring outfit, though."

"Do you live here all the time? Even in the winter? I'm from Chicago, and the winters are horrible there."

"No, child. I take advantage of the rails, and head to the Desert in the winter, where I idle in the sun. You should too. No use staying where you're not wanted!"

Dell furrowed her brows. "Why do you think I'm not wanted here?"

"Oh there's them that want you, and them that don't. Then there's them that's out to get you, I bet. So you should stay or go. Either way, it's going to be a fight, ain't it?"

Dell became uneasy, and looked around. "If you say so. But, is there anything you might need? I gotta go. Some money?"

"Money? You know, I was just saying, 'what I could use right now is some money!' You giving away money? That isn't very smart. Girl like you needs money as much as anybody. But you got it, I'll take it! Heh, heh. You're not from around here, I guess. What you doin' with money? Can't buy you friends. Do you need friends? No, I don't think so—you got friends. Good friends. Can't do better than that. Sure, I'd like some money. What'll you give for some good advice?"

She saw that he was dressed in black overalls, with a green canvas coat hanging over his shoulders, and no shirt. "How do you know I have friends, and what sort of advice would you have for me?"

"Oh girl, you're much too shiny not to have friends. People with no friends are dull and grey, and they are not too nice. You are nice?" He reached into his hair and ruffled it a bit. "You're here, and so young. Now let me tell you, things are not good for long, so get ready. You don't want to throw away what you have, but look out. There are things out there. Bad things. It's good to have friends—I know!" With that he began weaving his fingers in and out in what seemed like a mathematical progression.

"Wait, my name's Dell. I'd like to know yours."

He stopped whatever he was doing, and peered at her through thick eyebrows. "You are in great danger, Dell. Stick with your family—they're the only ones who can help. I'm Pan. I know."

"Pan? Only one name?" Dell wondered again how this man could know her.

"Peter Pan! Maybe you've heard of me?"

She moved closer and peered at him intently. "It sounds familiar. Why should I know you?"

"Everyone knows me, except you I guess. It's because I can fly! Maybe I'll teach you. What do you have for me?

She reached into her pocket and handed him one hundred dollars in twenties, about half of what she was carrying. "You might need this for a new coat, or something."

He looked at her hand, and snatched the money. "That's about right."

Dell kept her rendezvous, and the boys were delighted to see that she was sporting a new green baseball-type hat, with the Buffalos logo displayed on the front. Her copious curls of hair had been gathered into one large pony tail that sprang out through the hole over the back buckle. "Hey guys!"

They traded fist bumps.

"What else you get, Dell?" This from Donnie, who was betting she would return a Delta Queen.

She held up a small bag. "Just some clean undies, nothing special. I pretty much have everything I need. I did meet an interesting guy, though."

Chapter 16

Martin Planck treated himself to a beer after his article got picked up by the AP newswire and spread all over the country. This put a big feather in his cap, and he wondered if any of his students would have picked up on it when classes resumed again next week. It would be a good study lesson. The news is always unexpected and you have to be ready to record it whenever it happens. While it certainly wasn't Watergate, it was an interesting story. What could be better than a young unknown girl foiling terrorists? He probably would be smart to do a follow-up. He would see about an interview with that girl—do a thorough background piece, and try to get some words to live by. A noble goal—Words to Live By. It beat the bank-robbery and drunken car-chase stories by a mile. If it could be made interesting. That's what took a skilled hand. The stories with angst, something unusual that folks could relate to. This mysterious girl had it, he was sure. She had come from somewhere, and therein lies the story.

This woman now, Francine Parker—he had her number, and would give her a call tonight. He knew she would be close to home, and probably the girl, Dell, would be close by. Meanwhile, he would head to Pierre to learn as much as he could about that dam and power plant which may or may not hold the key to the safety of the Free World. If he was lucky, he could snag a motel room at a full service facility that came with an ice machine.

"Hi, Missus Parker...I'm Martin Planck. I hope you remember me from the other day?"

Francie didn't miss a beat. "Oh, yes. You're the reporter with Sheriff Warner. I remember, you asked me about the 'ranch thing'."

"Well, if it's not too much of an imposition, I was hoping to talk further with you and that girl Dell, who's staying with you. I was thinking that I could visit you folks, maybe first thing tomorrow?"

"What's this about, Mister Planck?"

"Actually, I am following up on a story I did on the incident at your ranch the other day. I would just like to get some background information for a kind of human interest story on the girl. I think that readers would love to hear about her."

"You know, Mister Planck, I don't think you would get much you can write about. Dell is a very reticent girl about her own life. She is not going to tell you much, I can guarantee. I'll see if she is willing to see you, however, and you can come by if you like. We'll either be at the house, or Irma can point you in the right direction."

Martin was satisfied with that. After he completed the call with Francine, he decided it would be a good idea to let someone know where he was going to be, just in case. He placed a call to the Sheriff's Office and asked for Sheriff Warner. When told the sheriff was not in, he left a message to the effect that he would be following up with the girl in the terrorist incident, and if he learned anything new, he would relay the info to the sheriff.

FBI Special Agent in Charge Joiner frowned with displeasure. As he argued on the phone with the sheriff his volume reflected his irritation. "Listen Warner, I recall you telling me you would keep us in the loop regarding this Dell person, and I haven't heard squat yet! How long does it take to get significant information out of a single girl?"

"There's nothing to report, Agent Joiner. You're right, I told you I would apprise you of anything significant, but we haven't been able to find anything out that you don't already know, so I'll be damned if I'm going to make stuff up just to satisfy your bosses!"

Joiner stroked his hand through his phantom hair, the remnants of which were showing more silvery white color than black. "Ok, listen Warner, I'm maybe a little under the gun here. This is a big deal, and we have to close the book on it if we can, so I'm maybe a little pushy on the details. I would appreciate it if you could help me out on this one. We feel this girl is too much of a loose end."

"Well, we haven't found the missing terrorist yet, and I'm sure that's getting on your nerves, but here's a plus...we, at least my journalist friend, is following up with the folks at the terrorist attack site, tomorrow. We hope to get something new to chew on then."

"Your journalist friend?"

"Yeah, Agent. We're operating on a shoestring here, and we use all the resources we can to get the job done."

Joiner rolled his eyes. "Look, Warner, I think you're making a big mistake working with a journalist. You can't trust these guys when the shit hits the fan. Just my opinion, of course."

"Noted. I've known Planck for a long time. He's not just a journalist, he's kind of a multi-faceted fellow. Stays out of the way when he needs to, and offers some good insight at times. He hopes to find out more about this girl, and if there is something significant, I'll hear about it."

Martin Planck negotiated his Ford sedan over the rutted excuses for a road that led to the Parker Ranch, slowly through the heavy mist before actual morning. The sun didn't seem to want to make its presence known today, at least not at six thirty Monday morning. He knew the Parkers were early risers, and if he was late, he probably would have a hard time catching up with them. The mist turned a brilliant red as the sun peeked over the river, then slowly turned a dull orange and yellow. Planck knew that sunrise was a critical time in the successful operation of a ranch, especially if one has school-age children that need to get to class more than an hour away. He figured he would be just in time for breakfast, unless the spring break has thrown their schedule way off.

When he finally pulled into the drive thirty minutes later, he was pleased to see that Francine's pick-up was still in front of the house.

Planck knocked at the door. After a minute, it was opened, and Irma peered out into the semi-darkness. "Oh, it's you, Mister Planck. You're so early."

"Thought I would need to be early, with this crowd."

"Ok, you are expected. Come in, if you please."

Planck entered the house, removed his wind-breaker, and hung it on the peg near the entrance. Irma led him to the kitchen, where the Parker clan was still enjoying breakfast.

"Hi, Martin, can I get you a coffee?" This from Francine, who was tending to the French Press when Planck entered.

"That would be great." Planck never could pass up a good cup of coffee in the morning. He moved into the kitchen, nodded at the boys, and took a seat at the end of the dining table. Dell was conspicuously absent.

"So, Martin. Or can I call you Marty?" Francie looked directly at her guest. "You get going awfully early. Anxious to see me, I guess."

Martin didn't miss a beat. "Good to see you, Francie. I know you are running a working ranch here, and I didn't want you to have to accommodate me in any unusual manner, so I decided to act accordingly. Am I on time?"

"Yeah, well, I'm sure we can work you in. Boys!" She turned her attention to her sons. "Finish up, then get your butts outside. I'll see you back here in twenty minutes."

She turned back to her guest. "Mondays. What exactly are you looking for, Marty?"

Planck could tell she was enjoying the day. "Actually, I was hoping to be able to talk to Dell, if that's possible."

Francine glanced at the clock. "She is usually up at this time and out with the boys...but I did tell her last night that you wanted to speak to her. That could have spooked her a bit. She is a complicated girl, and I still don't know how she'll react to different things. She may not be excited to see you, hard as that is to believe."

Planck took another sip of his coffee, smiled and raised the cup. "Good coffee!"

Francine smiled slightly, and just waited.

"You know, Francie, I am not going to put her on the spot. Just try to get to know her a little. What she did the other day was worth talking about, but I don't want to get into her head, or ask her stuff she doesn't want to talk about. I'm around young people all the time, and each one of them has a story to tell. I was just hoping Dell would tell me a little of hers."

Francie was okay with that, if it would help get Dell a little more used to interacting with people. "Let's see if I can rustle her up." Francie slid off the chair, walked through the great room, and disappeared up the stairs, taking them two at a time.

Martin took in the Parker kitchen. The stove was a large black Viking six-burner, looked to be gas operated, probably propane. Next to that was an equally massive refrigerator-freezer, also black. The walls were decorated with photos of horses. The table he was seated at appeared to be oak, with six legs and room for expansion. It was bare except for four place-mats. Above the table hung a wagon wheel sporting six hanging lamps, apparently on a dimmer-switch so as to create mood when needed. Martin wondered if Francine ever needed the dim lighting. He knew she was isolated out in the middle of no-where, with two, make that three, children who probably took up most of her free time. But she was a pleasant woman, and good looking to boot, and it was hard for Martin to imagine that she had no romantic life now. After all, her husband had been gone for quite some time.

Why was he thinking about her this way? Was it just because he was male, and any eligible female was fair game? *Come on, Planck, get a grip!* Martin couldn't help but think he had not had a serious relationship for two years, ever since the marriage broke up with Betty. Or she broke up with him, rather—opting for a connected businessman, who stormed into her life, mounted on a seventy-five-thousand-dollar RV. Six weeks later, they were off to California. Martin thought it was true love with Betty, and they had a wonderful time, until she was attracted by the blinding glitter of Bob, Dick, whatever his name was. He was so much younger then, and over the intervening two years, he felt he had begun to understand what had happened, and was adamant that it would never happen again.

Francine appeared at the head of the stairs and slowly made her way down to where Martin was waiting.

"Dell's not there."

"She's probably out with the boys, doing the chores."

"Yeah, you're right. She didn't want to see you, so she slipped out with the boys. It's what she does."

Francine did not look convinced. Martin tried to persuade her that nothing was amiss. "Let's wait a few minutes, and she'll be with the boys. Then I can ask her a few questions, and we'll be done."

They sat and sipped their coffees. Martin asked if running a ranch was as difficult as it sounded. Francine said sometimes there were unforeseen circumstances that made for crazy times, fences down, flooding, that sort of thing, but mostly it was routine. "I do part time counseling at County Schools in Fort Pierre three days a week, so there really is no down time."

At that point, some slams and crashes in the hall announced that Jimmy and Donnie were finished with the animals, and ready for their Easter week projects.

Francine was on her feet. "Hey Jimmy, Donnie—was Dell out there with you guys?"

Jimmy looked puzzled. "No, Mom. I didn't see her this morning."

Francine frowned and tightened her lips, looking as if she had just been slapped. "We'd better get you boys off to the fairgrounds now. She'll turn up soon—maybe when Martin here leaves." She looked pointedly at Planck.

"I didn't mean to scare her off." Planck finished his coffee. "Maybe we can do this later in more neutral surroundings, where she won't feel trapped by my presence."

"Maybe that can be arranged," Francine answered. "I think it depends on Dell. I'll broach the subject when she comes back to the house." *If she comes back,* Francine thought. She worried whether the girl really considered this her home yet, and knew that she was still very unsure of her place here. She might bolt at any time for the slightest of reasons, and Francine knew that she would miss her a great deal. More than she might have thought two days ago.

As Planck turned to leave, he smiled at Francine and tried to reassure her. "I'm sure she'll turn up as soon as I'm out of here. However it turns out, I'm glad we got to talk a little bit, and I hope it's not too long before we can see each other again, Francie, regardless of whether Dell is willing to come along."

"I would love to," she said, taking his hand in hers before he turned to go. "I will let you know soon what gives with the girl, and we'll take it from there."

Chapter 17

Dell became aware she couldn't see. Gradually she realized there was something covering her eyes, some sort of tape. She also could not move. Her feet were bound, and her hands had been fastened behind her, then tied to her feet, like being hog tied. This was a new one—she couldn't remember being hog-tied before. Sure, she had been bound, and hand-cuffed, and held with a rope around her neck, but never hog-tied. They couldn't get between her legs like this, and mostly that was the ultimate goal. Even though she had been a willing participant in her degradation for so many years, they still wanted what she was unable to give, and that was her innocence. That she had lost in the distant past, and it was no longer hers to give.

Her head throbbed with pain, and when she tried to cry out, she could only whimper, because her mouth was taped shut as well. She tried to think. *When did this happen?* The last thing she could remember was being out before sunrise watching the mist roll in over the river. Francie had asked when they got home yesterday if she would talk to Mister Planck soon. He wanted to do a feature story on her.

It was just a few days ago, when the shit-bags had taken everyone captive, and now she had a story to tell. Maybe Planck wanted to know who she was that made her so violent. She'd had a hard time getting to sleep after that day, which was no surprise. She worried that she had to keep herself inconspicuous if she wanted to live a normal life. That's why she ran out to the middle of nowhere in the first place. She couldn't let just anybody know who and where she was, as that knowledge would probably put her in danger. She knew about danger, and tried to avoid it when she could. But she didn't want to appear she had something to hide, either—that would just make people all the more curious. So she had decided she would talk with this guy, but make her story as dull and as vague as she could, so he would lose interest.

Somebody got to her this morning! She had been careless, and that's why her head was aching now—why she was so helpless, now. *Stay calm,* she told herself, *and think!* Before she could act on her own, she had to free her hands. But she couldn't see what she might use as a tool. *Stay calm.*

She gradually became aware of a definite up-and-down motion, and now began to detect a constant throbbing, like someone pulsing a mixer. She was in a boat. Being taken somewhere to be dealt with on arrival, she thought. *Get free now!* She tried scooting from where she was and could feel vinyl cushions giving beneath her. Abruptly, she plunged over an edge, landing with a soft thump. She lay with her back against a flimsy panel that moved when she pushed on it—a sliding door that covered an under-bench cubby. Her fingers found a rough edge. Twisting and scooting, she positioned her hand and foot bindings against the edge, then began sawing against it, pushing hard. After what seemed like forever, one of the zip ties snapped and she was no longer hog-tied. Legs thrust out in relief. As she worked on her wrist bindings she heard a hatch slide open.

She felt his presence a second before he spoke. "Hey, cunt. Looks like I come just in time. Well, good. Less work for me."

Dell let out a muffled snarl, as the tape across her eyes was painfully ripped off, taking with it a good portion of her eyebrows. She tightened her lips as he tugged at the tape there. Now she could see that she was at the prow of the ship, below two small bunks, and through the hatch a small dining area was visible. Directly above her hovered a fat man with a broad grin, wearing cut-off jeans and a black tee-shirt that read 'Corona'.

She looked away from his leering face. "What do you want?"

"I want to fuck you, of course." His grin got even bigger. "We drew straws—I get to go first." He began to unbuckle his belt.

Dell wanted to puke. She hated being helpless, and her fury

rose. Ways out of the situation were considered and rejected in rapid succession. Then, a decision, and she smiled coyly. "Well if you want to have a better time, you might untie me, and I'll make it good for you."

"Oh no, kid—I'm not crazy! They told me what you can do." The man dropped his shorts. He wore no underwear, and he was in an obvious state of excitement.

"Ooh, what a nice big cock you have," she purred. "Maybe you could just loosen my feet, and I can spread wide for you."

"You are such a slut. Okay, hang on." He bent and fumbled in his shorts pocket, coming up with a pocket knife, which he flicked open, and quickly cut through the zip tie holding her ankles. He tossed the knife onto a counter, then grabbed her waist and legs, and heaved her up on the bunk, where he yanked down her jeans and panties. "You are not a lightweight, kid. Come on, spread those legs for me."

"Okay, big guy. You sure you don't want to free my hands, too, so I can stroke that nice big cock of yours?"

"You're just fine, baby, now shut up!" He spread her legs apart and thrust his swollen member into her. "Ooh, you little slut, come to papa..." His eyes rolled up in ecstasy.

Dell hadn't had sex with a stranger for weeks, and she felt her body respond. Slight moans issued from her throat, turning quickly to cries of anguish. She would not let this happen! Focusing on the violation, her rage surged. She raised and bent her knees, clamped her ankles together, and squeezed as hard as she was able around the man's ribcage, just under his arms.

He yelled in surprise and pain, and tried to pummel her in the face. He was so close, though, and with the hold limiting the use of his arms, the blows were ineffectual. Dell continued to squeeze, and he screamed with the last gasp of breath, and began a fit of coughing. She rolled over, and flung him out of her and onto the floor.

Lifting her bent legs even higher, she coaxed her constrained arms beneath and around her body to the front. As the man began to rise, she was on top of him, bringing the zip-tied wrists across his throat.

He struggled hard for half a minute, then went limp. The zip-tie had cut into his windpipe, leaving an angry red slash. Not caring whether the man was alive or just unconscious, Dell flung him aside, and looked for the knife to cut the rest of her bind-ings. After freeing herself, she slipped her clothing back on and moved quickly into the galley.

There, the throbbing was louder. A faint smell of diesel per-meated the space. Behind a small folding dining table Dell saw two steps leading to a closed hatch. She moved up the steps and carefully inched open the double-doors. The light was almost blinding until her eyes became accustomed to it. A skinny man with a scraggly beard peered over the side while seated on a cushioned bench. Silvery water shimmered beyond to the hori-zon. She slowly closed the doors, sat back, held her aching head, and tried to think about her next move.

There must be others out of sight, piloting the boat, one...maybe two. Any more, and they would be with the gob out there so three more, max. Who are they? Find out later—ass-holes hurt me, and they're not going to do that again. The hatch was the only way out, so how to disable the lone troll in the way?

She had to squint while examining the cabin in the semi-darkness. As her eyes adjusted, she peered across the galley to the walls, up and down, and over to the wall next to where she sat. She spotted something there. It was a flare gun, anchored to the bulkhead with Velcro. *Let's see how this works*, she thought. Pulling it off the wall, she turned it over, playing with the mech-anism. It was an orange-colored plastic pistol, with several flares attached to the back. The barrel broke open easily with slight pressure on the hammer. She loaded a flare and closed the barrel. She figured there would be time to load one more flare before the others knew what had happened. Up the stairs again, she put an extra flare in her teeth, cocked the pistol and flung open the doors.

The man sat where she last saw him. He snapped his head around at the noise, just as the blast from the flare gun caught him and lifted him screaming against the flag stanchion. Fire and smoke erupted from his chest. The report sounded like a shotgun. Dell flipped out the burning plastic cartridge, slipped the new one in, and cocked the plastic weapon. As she stepped on the first rung of the ladder, a face loomed at her from the bridge above.

"Back, asshole!" she ordered, pointing the gun at his belly as she climbed further up into view. Another man, still at the wheel, turned to look at her. "Don't do it, shit bag!" she yelled as this one reached for a semi-auto pistol tucked into his belt. "Carefully drop it on the deck and kick it over here."

The man complied, as his mate backed up next to him. Dell was all the way up now. She squatted to retrieve the pistol and continued to watch him. He looked very familiar. The leader of Saturday's attackers. What was his name? She should know, they had talked about the leader...Djibouti! The slippery asswipe must have eluded the feebs.

"Djibouti, what gives? You didn't get your fill of me yet? What should I do with you this time?" She looked out to the shore, several miles distant. Djibouti said nothing.

"I guess the feds will want to close this case up. What do you think, should I take you to them, or would you rather take your chances in the water?"

The other man jerked his head and snaked his hand around to the back of his waist.

As a gun appeared, two explosions from Dell's pistol sent the man crashing over the rail.

"Goddam dumb bastard!" Dell screamed. She looked again at the lone survivor. "Look what you made me do, you ugly cocksucker! She stamped her foot, and Djibouti backed into the wheel, hands held high.

Chapter 18

"Hello, Martin? This is Francine. Listen, I'm sorry to bother you so soon, but I'm at a loss as to what to do, here." Francine had looked all over the house for signs of Dell, then had driven out to the road and back. She finally went down to the pier a half mile below the house and discovered the motor launch was missing from its mooring.

"I think Dell has taken the launch...to who knows where."

Pleased that Francine would call him for help, Planck wanted nothing better than to do so. "The boat? Does she know how to operate that?"

"Martin, that girl doesn't need much instruction on anything. She just looks at it, and does it. I don't know how, but the fact remains, the launch is missing."

Back at the motel room in Hayes, Planck had been about to pack up when Francie made the call. Now plans had to change. "Listen, Francine, I'll head back out there, but first I'm going to call the sheriff. Is it okay with you to get him involved?"

"You know, she might be just out on riding around, making sure you have left, and could be home at any time. So I didn't want to call Vern in on this, unless necessary."

"Okay, tell you what. I'll just tell him what's going on and that we may need him in an official capacity, but that I'll let him know when we find out more. Does that sound good?"

"Okay. Do you think you can be here soon?"

"I'm on my way, Francine."

Sheriff Warner was annoyed. "This girl again, Marty? Do you think I have nothing else on my plate in this office? Strike that—of course you do. So what is it now?"

"Well, you know Francine, Vern. And if she is worried about something, then there is probably something to it. So I'm headed back out there to check it out, and if we both think there is something that needs to be dealt with, then me or Francine will give you a heads up. Fair enough?"

"You sure that's the only reason you're going back out there, Marty?"

"Well, Vern, if you mean I smell a good story and don't want to be caught napping—you could be right. Or if you mean something else is going on—you could be right..."

Martin stopped by the motel office to pay for another night, and began the trek back to the Parker Ranch. This was his first official day of Easter break, and so far it was not going as planned.

Jimmy and Donnie tried to calm their mother. "You know, Mom, Dell told us she was sorry she left us and was never going to do it again," said Jimmy. Donnie echoed his brother. "Yeah, Mom, she promised, so she's gonna be back. You just wait!"

Francine hugged the boys close to her. "I know, boys. I'm just being crazy, I guess. Nothing will happen to her—we all know Dell. So she'll be home soon. Now let's just forget about this, and you get to work on your fair projects."

After the boys went off, she busied herself with some gutters that had blown down during last week's big wind storm. *Last gasp of winter,* she guessed. *It's never calm for long around here.*

Within the hour, Martin's Ford rumbled into the driveway. After emerging from the car he spotted Francine on a step ladder to the right of the porch. She climbed down and took off her gloves. "Thank you for coming back, Martin."

Dressed in blue jeans, and a yellow sweat shirt with 'Wheaties' blazoned across the front, she looked to Martin like a woman totally without guile whose aura grew brighter every time he looked at her. "I see I've caught you in between projects for a change. Do you have an ambulance standing by?"

"You caught me at my best, certainly. What say we go inside and get a drink, okay?" She led the way, and soon they were sipping lemonade in the kitchen.

After basking in her radiance for a few minutes, Martin got to the point. "So, no sign of Dell, but the boat is missing? Why don't we walk down to the pier and have a look around. Maybe we'll find something that'll tell us what's happened."

Francine was perched on the edge of a dining room chair, looking like she would bolt at any unexpected noise or idea. "That's right—the boat is missing. Maybe we can scan the area with our tricorders and see if we come up with something."

"Well, I don't have any of those, but we may spot footprints or something else to indicate what may have happened— whether she was alone, or what not. Won't hurt to take a look around."

"You know, Martin, when you put it like that, it sounds very reasonable. Let's do it."

They walked side by side down the drive to the boat launch and pier. As they neared the coarse sandy beach, Martin slowed to a stop and faced his companion. "We need to be really careful here and see what we're stepping on, all the way up to the dock."

Francine nodded, and Martin continued. "I think if we look closely, we can possibly spot fresh footprints, which in all like-lihood will be Dell's. Then we can see by the stress on the toes and heels, whether she was moving fast or slow, and maybe determine if she was alone by assessing whether any other marks were made at the same..."

Francine shook his elbow. "Martin! What's that?" She pointed to a craft silhouetted on the river's horizon.

Both peered to where she indicated. Definitely a boat, located maybe a half mile off shore, and headed their way.

Chapter 19

Dell had come back! Now mid-afternoon, the sun glared off the water like it had moved next door. The blinding light obscured their view, and until the craft slowed near the pier they could not be certain it was her.

At first the boat edged up to the dock, bumped and drifted off. Finally, it slowed enough so that after knocking against the dock posts, it just settled in.

Francie shouted up to the craft. "Throw down the bow line!"

When everything had been secured, two figures clambered down onto the dock. Dell appeared to be holding a pistol on a long-haired man who looked very familiar.

"Dell!" Francie had many questions. "Who's that with you?"

Martin interrupted. "I think that is the guy who had us captive last weekend."

Djibouti didn't look happy. Dell kept shoving him with her boot to keep him moving. "Hi, Francie. Glad you're here. You too, Mister Planck," she said, acknowledging the journalist with a wave of her pistol.

She wore a grim expression, but was clearly relieved to be on solid ground again. She wanted nothing more right now than to be sipping a soda with ice on the porch.

"This one didn't want me to throw him into the river, so I brought him back with me. Would you please get on the phone to the sheriff, or whoever, and get him out of here so I won't shoot him?"

Francine was alarmed at Dell's haggard appearance. She had a dark bruise on her left cheek, and what looked like dried blood matted the hair on top. "Oh, Dell!"

Martin studied the prisoner, while addressing Dell. "Why don't you give me the gun, Dell, and I'll watch this guy awhile so you can relax. Then you can tell us where you found him."

Dell kept her eyes on the prisoner as well, but glanced at Martin. "You're here to talk to me, right? I guess we're going to have to get that done with. You'll be ready to shoot this jerk if he gets funny, right?"

"Looks like you took all the fight out of him."

"He's tricky," she said. She handed Martin the Colt. "It's cocked, but the safety's on."

Dell moved toward Francie, and they embraced for a long moment. "We were getting worried about you, sweetie."

"I'm sorry," she said, close to tears. "Where's Jimmy and Donnie?"

"Oh, they're busy today...I thought you might have taken the launch, just to clear the air for a bit, but..."

"I didn't!" She pointed to Djibouti. "That...person took it, and me with him. I think he was planning to get back at me for the other day, and I just made it easy for him by walking right into a trap."

Francie tried to keep her calm. "It's going to be all right, Dell, we'll get this sorted out. Right now, why don't we..."

Dell interrupted, trying to keep her voice steady. "I had to shoot two of them. And there's another fat bastard down below. They're all dead."

Francine's mouth flew open at this. Shocked but not surprised, she was coming to know Dell's capabilities, and felt the emotional toll being exacted on the girl. "Did they hurt you, sweetie?"

"Just my head—it still aches from when they knocked me out, but I got a hard head."

Dell didn't bother to mention she had been raped as well. The rape left no marks she had to explain, and she didn't want people going on about it. Given what she'd been through in her short life, the incident had not been totally traumatic or unexpected. She felt sick about the dead men, though. She had never deliberately killed someone before.

Martin started to get antsy. "We need to contact the sheriff or someone who'll take this criminal into custody. So let's move on up to the house, folks. We'll talk details then."

They agreed and walked in silence the half mile back up to the house, Djibouti in front, prodded by Martin.

It seemed like hours before Sheriff Warner arrived. Everyone remained on edge during that time. However unlikely any escape attempt while being watched, they had no idea what might be going on in his mind. They all found it difficult to relax with a terrorist in the room.

When he demanded to relieve himself, Planck was not about to let him into the bathroom alone, so he accompanied him and stood by with the pistol while Djibouti used the facilities. He relaxed a bit when the criminal was safely back on the couch, a lamp-cord wrapped securely around his wrists.

The boys appeared when it was getting on to meal-time, and they exchanged hugs with Dell. No one was willing to turn their backs on their house-guest to prepare a meal, so chips and sodas were passed around, and the boys decided to take them up to their room while the adults waited for the authorities to arrive. Dell sipped on a soda, but ate nothing.

Chapter 20

The sheriff got there in an hour, followed closely by three black SUVs driven by the FBI. Dell saw them and rolled her eyes. She was not happy with what she knew was coming.

"Looks like you've been a busy girl, young lady." The sheriff tossed his hat on the rack after entering. Warner was not looking forward to the meeting with Dell either. It would take considerable effort cleaning up yet another mess surrounding this precocious young woman. She was like the eye of the hurricane. Dell nodded to Warner and continued looking out the window.

Agent Maddis approached Dell as the family sat waiting in the living area, while eight or so other investigators fluttered about. "We have two people deceased on the boat, Dell—one without his pants on. And he was strangled, it looks like." She looked at Dell expectantly. "You may remember me, Agent Rene Maddis?"

The girl looked back without expression. "He raped me." She said it matter-of-factly, like it was to be expected. "I just wanted to keep him from...continuing."

"So, you killed him?"

"I just got him off me. But don't worry, I'm okay. Just another day in the life."

Maddis furrowed her brow. "There was another man, shot with a rocket, looks like. Did you do that?"

"I don't know. Was he complaining?"

"He's dead, Dell."

"Sorry. I didn't plan on hurting anyone. I was just sitting down by the beach, and the next thing you know, they did this to themselves. Ask Djibouti. He was in charge of the whole thing. Why don't you ask him, and leave me the fuck alone!" She had lost her composure with the agent, and silently chided herself.

"Okay, Dell." Maddis raised her hands defensively. "We are questioning Djibouti—we're just trying to get a complete picture of what happened."

Dell glanced at Francie, who shook her hair and rubbed her neck, as she stared up at the ceiling.

The door creaked open again, admitting a small, prim woman dressed in black. Madeline Highwater, Stanley County Deputy Coroner and Chief Medical Examiner, stood in the doorway until spotting the sheriff. She didn't smile, but nodded to the others in the room, as she wound through them to Warner. "Vern, got a moment?"

"Yeah, Maddie, what's up?" He gave the DC his full attention.

"Causes of death are obvious on both bodies we examined. One suffered extensive injury and burns to his torso, when hit by an explosive flare. Bits of the device were still in the body. The other man's windpipe was severed with a garrote of some sort. Ostensibly a heavy zip-tie, which was found near his body, with blood on it. Both men died quickly."

"No chance of accidental death, then?"

"Oh, you know, Sheriff, the one guy, he...no." She looked up at Warner, who towered more than a foot over her. "No accident in either case. I understand the girl has admitted killing the victims?"

"Yes, she did, and FBI is working her over real hard." He looked across the room, where two agents were now questioning Dell.

"Dell, we are getting an entirely different story from Djibouti than you are giving us."

Dell looked at the agent who called himself Joiner. She shook her head slightly and curled her lip in disgust.

"That's right. He told us they were just taking the boat to get as far away as possible, and you had stowed away, then snuck up on them."

"So, Sheriff?" Highwater was trying to keep Warner's attention. "Unless you want it done differently, I think we can save the county some expense here and skip the autopsy."

Warner went over Hightower's assessment for a second, making sure he heard her correctly. "Yeah, yeah. You're right. I don't think anybody will complain—thanks, Madeline."

Hightower pivoted, and briskly made her way back to the door. Warner turned back to Dell. He decided that the FBI was putting too much pressure on the girl, when she was the one responsible for winding up the case.

"Agent," the Sheriff said, "Dell has given you the perps on a platter. This man is a known criminal, and a certain amount of force may have been necessary to escape an uncertain fate. Now I think you should stand down, and tie up any loose ends at a later date. This girl has been through a lot."

"Not this time, Sheriff." Special Agent in Charge Joiner had begun questioning the girl with Maddis, after finishing up with Billings and the CSI Team at the motor launch. "We have a lot of things to go over in this incident, including the fact that there were three homicides. The girl is going to have to come with us for further questioning." He looked around to the suddenly silent group. "It shouldn't take too long, and we will take good care of her if we have to hold her overnight."

Martin had been writing in his notepad when he heard this. He jerked his head up and peered around the room. Everyone looked at the FBI man. "Sir. There is really no need for taking Dell into custody."

Francine chimed in. "She's finally back home, and is easily reached for any further needs. I swear..."

"It's not your call, Missus Parker. If the federal government decides we need to secure a witness, or possible suspect, then that is what we'll do. Now, I understand your concerns, but we can't be hopping out here in the middle of nowhere every time we need to ask her a question, can we? So just let us do our job, and there won't be a problem. Okay?"

"Oh, I think there's a problem." This from Dell, whose tight voice barely betrayed her anger. "I'm not going anywhere for now, not unless Francie says, and if you feebs think otherwise, then there's a problem."

Everyone looked at Dell. She sat on a stool near a coffee table, dressed in rumpled jeans and a clean tee-shirt. She contemplated her hands, as they balled into fists on her knees.

Agent Maddis responded first. "Listen, Dell. You really don't have any say in the matter at this point. We think it in everyone's best interest if you would cooperate, and come with us for a certain time. We need to do a thorough investigation of this matter. It is in the national interest, and at this point we are telling you to come with us." She looked to two other agents standing near the front door. "Now I know you don't want to do this the hard way..."

Dell shifted her feet, placing them in a wider stance. "You don't know me, ma'am. My way is the hard way. Before you do anything stupid, ask yourself, who is this girl, and what is she thinking? Is she thinking she's going to be okay with someone else trying to push her around today?" Her eyes shifted up from her hands and slowly scanned the room. "You might be able to take me, but I won't make it easy. You should get that...it's not going to be sugar and spice!"

"Dell..." Agent Joiner took a step toward the girl, who rose to her feet, arms tensed at her side.

The air in the room was now electric, like an approaching thunderstorm. Francine jumped to her feet as well. "I think you should take your team and leave now, Agent Joiner!"

Sheriff Warner could see that this could easily get out of control, with unpredictable results. "Agents! Stop this! You are about to ruin the best asset you have in this case." He indicated Dell. "This girl has blocked, not once, but twice—two times—an attempt to destroy one of this country's important assets. She has blocked these attempts not for any personal gain, but because it was the right thing to do. Now that has to count for something!" He glanced around the room, measuring the effect of his words.

"Not only that, she has refrained from showing you directly what she can do when push comes to shove. And that points to her good judgement, as well as her self-restraint. Now, I think we can get an agreement here to hold a formal inquest on this matter in court in a few days, with all interested parties in attendance." He waited for reaction, and was pleased to note the nonverbal communication in the room indicated a guarded, but positive response to his suggestion.

"Damn, you are an amazing hostage negotiator, Sheriff." Planck had never seen Warner pontificate so fluently before.

"You think that was a hostage situation, Marty?" He asked this on the porch of the Parker Ranch, as they stood watching the last of the federal vehicles retreat from the drive on clouds of dust.

"Hell, yeah! Only this time, it was a case of the Feds trying to take hostages."

The sheriff smiled at that, and they turned and retreated back into the house.

Chapter 21

Peter Savior and Fred Tulley hunched in the front seat of a rented Pontiac Grand-Am, while Lonnie and Roach languished in the back. They were keeping eyes on three black SUVs receding into the billowing dust, near a faded sign that read 'Parker Ranch'.

"Those guys are all cops." said Tulley. "You think there's more of them up there?"

"That's a lot of cops. We could hang out for a while, and observe what goes on. Maybe we can catch her when she goes out. Better yet, Lonnie," Savior turned his head to look in the back seat, "we'll go back to the motel and wait, and you can come back here and see if she goes anywhere. If so, you call, and we'll take it from there."

"Aw, Savior, that's no good. I could be out here forever—I could die of thirst!"

"Yeah, Lonnie. I know you're not comfortable without a drink in your hand—tell you what...we'll get another car and take shifts watching for the twat." He grinned at the man over the seatback. "And you'll take the first two hours."

"Thanks for standing up for me there, Francie. You too, Sheriff, Martin." Dell hung her head in front of the adults, her eyes downcast. "It's just that I am really on edge. I can't relax, and I couldn't face being somewhere with no friendly faces around. I really need to just chill and stop thinking about things." Her eyes began to tear up, and she wiped them with the back of her hand. Francie offered her a tissue and she wiped her nose.

Francie, Martin, and Sheriff Warner all sat in chairs near the girl, who tugged at pillows, trying to recline on the couch. They all began speaking at once. "Listen Dell..." "We're all..." "You're going..."

Francie glanced around and started again. "You are going to

be fine, girl. I think that some time outside with the horses will do you some good, and most of them need to be groomed today. There is still a lot of time before dinner, so why don't you catch up with Jimmy and Donnie and have at those horses?"

Dell brightened at this, jumped up, threw Francie a quick hug, and banged out the kitchen door after the boys.

Warner smiled after her. "Can't figure her out—one minute she's hell on roller skates, and the next she's an eager little girl."

"She's like a lot of kids her age, despite what she's had to face." Martin shifted one leg over the other. "She'd probably fit right in with most of the kids in my classes...after she undergoes some anger-management training," he joked.

"You're forgetting Martin, she's not ready for college—she's hardly had any high school, even though she presents herself much older emotionally than she really is. I think she has never been able to be 'just a child', at least not for a long time now."

"You think she has trouble managing her anger? That may be so, Martin," Warner leaned in closer to Planck, "but the fact is, she appears to use only as much force as she needs to, to get the job done, and when it's complete, there doesn't seem to be any anger left. I would call that good anger management. Probably as good as any of my deputies' display in bad situations."

The pronouncement intrigued Martin. "You think she would make a good cop then, Vern?"

"Hah! She would have to learn a whole lot more about taking orders, wouldn't she?"

Even Francie smiled at this. "Nobody's recruiting her into the Sheriff's department just yet, guys. She needs to learn a little bit more about the world, and what she might want in life besides living day-to-day on the street."

"So how are you going to handle this girl in the future, Francine? I suppose you're thinking that you're going to make her a part of the family?" Warner raised his eyebrows quizzically at the Parker woman. "How do the boys feel about that? There going to be any tensions of one sort or another?"

"The boys just love her, Vern—and they already think of her as a big sister." She looked out toward the stables. "Maybe a little sister. Depends on circumstances, I guess."

Marty chimed in. "I think you are opening yourself up for some incredibly interesting and unpredictable times, Francie."

She pursed her lips in thought. "Maybe so, Martin. But I think we're up to it. What Dell needs right now is some stability in her life, and I'm hoping that she will agree to some kind of routine...which includes school."

Warner guffawed. "Let's hope she goes for that idea! If she doesn't want to do something, I think it might be a bit hard to persuade her, given what we've all witnessed."

Martin played the optimist. "You know, the girl's really bright, and obviously learns quickly. I think in the right environment she would love learning things about her world that she never could imagine on her own, even though she does have a powerful imagination. We might look into some self-study college classes."

"Yeah, she does appear to be able to assess situations on the fly, with very little to go on." Warner scratched the back of his head. "Maybe she would make a good cop."

Francine stood and moved to the stove. "Coffee's ready, guys. I'm hoping you'll stay for dinner, where we can all talk about this some more." She raised her eyebrows expectantly.

Martin said, "Sure, Francine, sounds like an offer I can't refuse."

Warner said, "You know I love your cookin' Francie, but duty calls, and I should be getting back, after I sip some of that coffee, of course. Besides, I think your girl there will be happier if I'm not getting myself too much in her face at this juncture."

Chapter 22

Martin helped Francie with the clean-up, after the boys clambered upstairs and Dell retired to her room. They were enjoying a glass of after-dinner wine in the living area, lights dimmed.

"I'm going to say, Francie, I think that was one of the best casseroles I've ever enjoyed. I'm beginning to wonder why I've never met you before this weekend."

"Well, you know, Marty. Things have a way of happening in their own time. I was perfectly happy here with the boys and the horses until the excitement started happening this week." She smirked at the ceiling. "Now I'm seeing that new experiences come with the unknown, if you open yourself up to them."

"I'm hoping that I'm one of those new experiences." He leaned close and kissed her on the lips, and Francine did not resist, inviting his exploration.

They embraced, and Martin began to lose himself in the essence of her breath and pulse.

"Well, okay. This is good." Martin observed, when they came up for air.

"You seemed to have swept me off my feet." Francine sat up, and tugged on her blouse. "I think I need to know more about you...where are you from...who is your family? Do you have a lot of money?" This she asked in jest, with a sly grin.

"I tell you, Francine. You are the finest, prettiest and most genuine woman that I've happened across in years. Since my wife left me," he modified. "No, seriously. You're a gem."

Francine raised an eyebrow. "So, why did your wife leave you, Marty?"

"Well, that is the question, isn't it? I think mainly that she didn't love me anymore. But she also wanted to pursue her career in film, so she moved to California, and that was that."

"You didn't go after her?"

"No, by that time, it was over. I love it out here. I love the space, the people—or lack of them." He swept his eyes over her face. "Is that a bad thing?"

Francie lowered her head and toyed with his shirt buttons. "That could be a very good thing..." She suddenly straightened. "Okay, well. Look at the time. Morning comes quickly around here. I've really enjoyed being with you Marty." She looked everywhere but at his puzzled face. "No, really. I just don't want to get, you know, ahead of myself."

"How about I come by tomorrow, and we'll talk some more? Would that be good?"

Francine thought a moment. "Actually, I need to go into Fort Pierre tomorrow—why don't we meet at our favorite Mexican place for dinner? It's called Juanita's Tequila Bar and Grill, right downtown."

"Sounds perfect—what time?"

When Martin left, Francie went upstairs and checked on the boys, who were slumbering peacefully, with Panda curled up at the foot of Donnie's bed. Dell was awake and beckoned to Francie from where she lay. Francie sat on the bed's edge, noticing that Dell's eyes were reddened.

"Are you okay, sweetie? I imagine you had a rough day?

"Francie, do you think I'm normal? I mean, am I anything like other girls?"

Francie wasn't sure how to answer this, but she was willing to pick her way through it. "I can answer that in several ways, Dell. First of all, nobody is completely 'normal'." She made quotes with her fingers. "Everyone has their quirks, and it's all how a person responds to things—the people around them, where they live, what they are taught, and so forth."

Dell rose to her elbow. "Francie, please don't bullshit me! I don't mean to be disrespectful, but you know what I mean—is there something wrong with me?"

Francine studied her for a moment. "Honestly, there is nothing wrong with you, Dell. You are a beautiful girl."

"Francie...!" Exasperated, she sat up.

"No, I mean it. You interact well with others, you know right from wrong, people can trust you...most of the time."

Dell rolled her eyes at this.

"You are willing to do your part, you are not a selfish person; you're respectful. What else...you're smart. You can figure things out, you control yourself very well. I think you shouldn't be asking yourself if you are normal, but ask 'how do I feel about myself, and do I need to improve'."

"Dammit, Francie! That's just it! I don't like myself most of the time...okay, I control myself now, but I used to be totally out of control, and I, you know, liked sex a lot. I didn't care if they made me do it, I liked it. They didn't have to give me drugs, even, like the other girls. Well, except for the Depo shot every few months. And I would just, you know, whoever paid to do me." She threw up her hands. "And I still like it, dream about it. But then, it was like, I woke up. I started to feel so creepy. It wasn't who I wanted to be. I wanted to have a normal life, but now I don't think I can ever be normal with a man. I mean, I get these thoughts, but I'm not going to ever let myself be an old man's play-toy, ever again!" Tears began to flow down her cheeks.

Francine had heard tales from abused children before, not to such a degree as Dell's, but her counsel was similar. "Dell, you are very young, and you have started to get where you want to be. I mean, look at you. You got yourself out of that life, didn't you? It was all you. And you have so many good things in your life to look forward to now."

Dell continued to weep. "Francie, every time I think things are going good, someone comes along and fucks it up for me. I killed three guys today! I didn't want that to happen. I just killed them because they made me mad. Why does this keep happening?"

Francie embraced the girl. "I don't see how you had much choice, Dell. Sometimes bad people don't give you a choice. Now, I know that most of us just sit back and let others do the hard work to keep the bad guys from taking what they want, but not you. You're one of those few who are chosen, by some means, whether it be fate or the gods, or just chance. You are a chosen one, and when the shit hits the fan, girl, you don't duck and hide—you clean up! Am I right?"

Dell wiped her cheek. "Yeah, I guess."

Chapter 23

Jimmy busied himself with Lady's mane and tail. She snorted her advice and stamped a hoof. Dell had insisted that Jonny, the stallion, should be hers to brush, since she had an obvious rapport with the animal. Jonny was difficult with anyone but Dell. Even Donnie agreed. Jonny was better behaved when Dell was with him. It must have been a gender thing, the boys agreed.

Panda looked forward to mornings. She loved dodging hooves and running around correcting stubborn horses. Being part shepherd, she couldn't help but put her nose in when she sensed some recalcitrant animal misbehaving. That was most all the time, of course.

The sun was a golden promise on the horizon when they completed the brushing and feeding, and Donnie and Jimmy were thinking about their own breakfast. Dell still lingered with Jonny.

"Come on Dell, let's go see what Irma has made us for breakfast this morning." Donnie beckoned furiously.

Jimmy turned to see what might be holding her back. "Hey, Dell..." He saw she was staring off toward the sunrise and started back toward her. "Dell, you okay?"

She seemed to be lost in her thoughts, and his closeness startled her. "Oh, Jimmy! Sorry. I was just somewhere else. My bad. I am seeing what a beautiful spot this is. With the sunrise, and everything. And you've had this your whole life."

"Yeah," said Jimmy, "well, you haven't seen the winter here yet. You may want to re-think in about seven months."

Dell brightened. "Well, I've seen Chicago winters—they're pretty horrific. You think it's worse here?"

"Oh, much worse. But I'm not going to say anymore 'cause I want you to stick around—I take it back. The winters here are like spring in Chicago—you'll love winter here!"

"Yeah, right."

Donnie, who waited impatiently for this interchange to finish, hollered, "Hey, bet I can beat both of you back to the house!"

Jimmy and Dell eyed each other, then glanced at Donnie, and took off like coyotes after a rabbit.

That afternoon, after Irma had left early, the Parkers and Dell all crowded into the pickup for a shopping excursion into the city. They rarely ventured into town on a weekday, but this was spring break week, and the boys had lots of spare time from their ranch chores and school work. Jimmy called shotgun, meaning Donnie would sit next to his mom, and Dell would be sandwiched between the boys. None of them complained about the arrangement.

They would take the opportunity to get needed supplies, maybe a new science fiction book for Jimmy and a new Lone Star Ranger book for Donnie. Francie needed nothing, but she had her eye on a new pair of Ariat boots, although her old ones were just finally breaking in after eight years of wear. Dell, curious about her new friend, Pan, wondered whether he still camped out behind the mall.

They didn't have an unlimited amount of free time, of course, since they needed to meet Martin Planck at five o'clock at Juanita's for dinner and maybe a cocktail or two.

Jimmy and Donnie said they would be happy to spend a couple of hours around that time at the Cinema, where the new Star Wars movie had been playing, and Francie said, "We'll see."

Francie knew Dell was part of the reason Martin agreed to dine with the Parkers. She hoped the other part might be he wanted to see her again, despite how abruptly she had dismissed him the night before. She told herself next time would be different, if there was a next time.

Painted predominately red and black, Juanita's featured a large backlit bar at one end of the room. At least fifteen different Tequilas sat on display in front of the mirror behind the bar.

Brass upholstery tacks dimpled the black Naugahyde bar-stools. Several Formica tables occupied the middle of the café, and a dozen booths lined the sides of the room, also trimmed in black Naugahyde. They kept the lighting subdued, to mesh with the motif. On the wall near the entrance, a list of daily specials had been printed in colored chalk. Next to the specials, a menu of mixed drinks denoted those served until two a.m. or closing, whichever came first. The all-female wait-staff strode in and out of the kitchen, outfitted in white ruffled blouses with long black skirts.

"I recommend the Chiles Rellenos—they are to die for," Francie told Martin, who perused the menu.

"Where are the boys?" he inquired.

Dell answered in a tone indicating maybe she should be with them. "They thought it would be a lot more exciting to see a movie, rather than eat."

"Now, Dell, please behave. Martin is not bad company. He actually knows a lot of people your age—he teaches at the University Center in Sioux Falls."

Slightly curious, Dell threw him a question. "Okay, what do you teach these blossoming young citizens, anything useful?"

"Well, Dell. I like to think that my students come away with a larger knowledge of the world, and how to navigate the various pitfalls that will present themselves throughout their lives. It's disguised as a journalism class." Martin smiled broadly at this.

"Oh, so you are teaching them how to best get the dirt on other people, so they can make money doing it?"

Francine interrupted with a cocked eyebrow. "Dell, that's not fair."

Martin smiled again. "You are very perceptive, Dell. And some journalism is like that, appealing to the basest senses of its audience, like, say, stopping at a car wreck to see if anyone is bleeding. 'Yes folks, one person lost an eyeball and the use of his left hand forever,' that sort of thing. That kind of journalism is colorful, maybe, but does not educate anyone as to the nature of the world they're living in. Whereas, maybe a story an alert journalist writes stating, 'Ace development company has plans to run the largest oil transport pipe ever under the Missouri River to refineries in Mississippi, and Ace has a sterling 80% record of success without mishap...meaning of course, that there's a 20% chance of something going dreadfully wrong'...now there is a story that could get people thinking and moving to protect themselves and their communities."

Dell and Francie were both mesmerized with Martin's passion.

"Sorry, I get over enthusiastic at times."

Dell was first to answer. "No, I see what you're saying. It's what you pay attention to that helps the most."

Francine noted Dell's ability to grasp the nuance. "It's like the difference between a journalist and a...a gossip."

"That's right. Both have information to share, but only one will affect your life, and give you pause."

After they finished their meal, Francie regarded it as her task to get Martin and Dell into a conversation, something that would not threaten the girl in any way, but something close to what Martin needed in the way of a background information that he could put to use. She trusted his judgement, but she would be there just in case. She would not let Dell slip into any traps.

"So Dell, do you mind if I ask some questions about your view of things? Hopefully, nothing that you will object to?"

"If you don't get mad when I tell you to go...you know."

"Fair enough. Why don't we start with any background information that you might be willing to share...Like, can you remember anything about your childhood?"

"I can remember I didn't have one...or maybe I'm still an infant. I don't know much, do I? I never had a mother's breast. Do you want to know every detail?"

"Just the things that made you aware of yourself, as a person."

"Boy, I bet you give hard tests. Okay, let's see. I was always picked on, 'cause I was ugly, with this mop of red hair. They would call me names, like lip-stick and rag-mop. But I didn't need them, and started this little world in my head. Lots of animals there. Cows, ducks, horses. Especially horses. I learned to ride in my head. The only horses I'd ever seen were in picture books. There were some in the home, but then I found the library. It wasn't more than a couple miles away, and there were books on everything there."

"You didn't have any friends growing up?"

"Actually, I did. There was this one girl, her name was Shirlee—she was almost black. She liked horses too, and we used to tell each other about our horses. Her horse was a golden Palomino, with a long blond mane. She used to ride him bareback. Mine was pure white, and he always had a big black leather saddle with silver medallions all over it. We would ride in parades, then out into the country, where we would have picnics. We actually had chips and sodas in an alleyway, but it didn't matter, as long as our horses were there."

"What happened to Shirlee?"

"I don't know. One day she just wasn't around anymore. I looked for her everywhere, but she was gone. I asked adults at the home, but they didn't know anything, or they weren't saying. So finally I just gave up. She was the best friend I ever had, and she just disappeared." Dell's eyes moistened, and a tear found its way down her cheek.

Francine put her arm over Dell's shoulder and squeezed. "It's okay, sweetie." She looked up at Martin. "Didn't think it was going to be this hard, did you?"

"I'm sorry, Dell."

Dell looked up, wiped her eyes. "It's not your fault. I just haven't thought about her for a long time. I was about twelve. I met Savior after that. I think that's when my childhood really ended."

"Can you tell me about this guy, Savior?"

Dell shook her head. "I'm sorry, Martin. I really can't talk about him. Not now. Not in a long while, even."

"Okay," Martin said, "Then why don't we..."

"You know, Francie, I need to go for a walk. Why don't we meet up after the boys get out of the movie? I just need to be by myself for a while. I'll meet you at the theater, okay?" Dell got to her feet, gave them both a farewell smile, and shot out the door of the restaurant.

Martin looked at Francine. "You told me this was going to be difficult."

Francine sat facing the door with her chin in her hands. "I should be worried about her, but how can I be? Oh, well." She focused on Martin. "At least you haven't walked out on me. After the treatment I gave you last night."

Martin smiled. "Maybe we could have a do-over on that."

Dell found herself in the gully behind the Mall, looking for Pan. Things were subtly different there. In amongst the juniper shrubs, festooned with what looked like clotheslines full of hanging clothes, toys, pots, wire mesh and whatnot, stood a bright orange nylon tent, complete with rain fly. Pan was seated cross-legged near the entrance. He was engaged with what appeared to be an electronic game, contorting his shoulders and elbows to keep up with whatever he was chasing across the screen. "Can't talk," he said, without looking up.

Well, at least he knows I'm here, Dell thought. She moved around in front of him and squatted. "Just wanted to check and see how you were doing. Looks like you are keeping the rain off your head."

"Hasn't rained." He continued to work the game.

Dell sat for a few minutes, looking around and at the ground. "I'm in town with my new family—gotta get back soon. I'm Dell, remember?"

He looked up, then back at the game, then slowly put it aside. "You're the girl in trouble."

"Not anymore." She smiled broadly. "I took care of the trouble, and things are getting good."

"Always more trouble, Dell. I spent all the money. Do you have more?"

"Not this time, Pan, but I'll get you some more soon, okay?"

"You have a good life, Dell, and stay out of trouble." He turned once again to the electronic game.

I guess that's goodbye, she thought, and stood. "See you soon, Pan."

He looked up. "Sooner than you think. Heh, heh." Then she was dismissed.

Dell knew that the boy's movie was over at seven thirty, so she had a good half hour to connect with everyone. She moved through the brush behind the mall at a leisurely pace, breathing deeply, enjoying the spring air. The sun had set, giving the western horizon a green afterglow. The first stars began to appear, and for the first time in her life she was aware of them. Where she grew up, the stars were nonexistent. She wondered what that bright one was that gleamed like an engagement ring just over the western skyline. She thought it wonderful not to have to think about sheltering for the night, or where she would find her next meal. She felt like a queen. She moved up the hill and found a sidewalk, then stopped to get her bearings. The mall was that way, and the theater complex was directly south. So she turned south along the walkway. Very few used the venue at this time of the evening on a weekday—just fine with Dell.

She took a step and a figure appeared in front of her, blocking her progress. She stepped aside, but the large man would not be avoided.

"Lookie here," he said, in a deep voice with a distinctly big city accent. "What's a little girl like you doing out here, all alone at night, with no one around to look after her?"

"I have to be somewhere," Dell mumbled, trying to step around the intruder. Then she stopped. The man was familiar. She immediately tensed, and smiled. "Oh, hello. I know you, don't I?"

"That's good thinkin', little girl. Yeah, you know me. I'm here to bring you back to where you belong. You're causing us a lotta problems, and I promised I wouldn't hurt you too much."

"Your name is Lonnie Shit-for-Brains, is that right? Seems I cracked your nuts or something, some time ago. Is that why you're here—you love pain?" Dell glanced around, certain that this oaf was not on his own. She was right. Strong arms grabbed her from behind. Her chest was encircled, her arms pinned, and she was lifted off her feet.

At this point, it seemed useless to struggle, so she relaxed, waiting for an opening.

Out of the darkness, a man strode toward her. She recognized him immediately, and the blood rushed out of her head. She felt her knees go weak, and counted it a plus that her feet were not touching the ground.

"Well, Dell. You've given us a merry chase." Savior appeared just as she remembered him—dark, handsome, and evil. His slick black hair fell over his right eye, and his even white teeth gleamed at her in the darkness.

Chapter 24

"Sweetheart, you've gotten even much more lovely in your absence. I guess the country air agrees with you."

He made a sign, and she was dropped to her feet. He stroked her cheeks. "I think vacation time is over, darling. It's time you came home where you belong. Everybody misses you!"

Savior took a deep breath, assessing the girl before him. He bent down, and kissed her on the mouth.

Dell was trembling. She couldn't think. This was the man who had directed her to the depths of depravity over the past several years. His presence threatened to close off her very sense of self. She became docile, and she had difficulty remembering who it was she had hoped to be. She felt her joy of the past few days of freedom receding into a distant dream. She was succumbing to the inevitability of her shrinking ego, and accepting the return of the life she was meant for. She, after all, was good for nothing other than providing men with sexual gratification. At a cost, of course. They would pay, but she would bear the cost as well. The cost of gradual submergence of her self as a person, until she was nothing but a sexual automaton, living for nothing other than the peak of excitement that, like a drug over time, became harder to obtain.

The vision may as well have been death. She tried to steel herself. She mentally squeezed the kernel of spirit deep inside herself, until it squeaked. She was not a slave, and she would die before she would allow herself to be dominated.

She smiled. "Who's that with you, Savior? Couldn't chance meeting me alone?"

Savior allowed himself a moment to assess the girl. "You've changed, Dell. You used to be so...willing. I sense that you have gotten yourself an attitude. You're going to have to lose that attitude, girl, if you want to be my star attraction again."

He directed Roach with a flick of his head, and looked back into Dell's eyes. "Shall we go? You can walk, if you want to."

Lonnie piped up. "Oh, can't I just whack her a couple times, and make her bleed?"

"Later Lonnie. We'll teach her a good lesson." Savior glanced around in the growing darkness. "I think we'll get her back home first, then we will give her a reason not to try this stunt again."

They moved up the walkway toward a dark sedan waiting at the curb, about a hundred feet away. Dell was now actively looking for opportunities. They hadn't bound her. She could easily slip out of Roach's grasp and run. But they would have pistols, and she would be shot, no doubt. So she would have to elude her captor, then disarm him, and use him as a shield. Maybe she could get his gun, if he had one. *Think, Dell! You only have about a half a minute—how is this going to go down?*

Savior was walking ahead, still glancing around as they approached the waiting vehicle. Roach gripped the back of her neck with his right hand, and the other was grasping her wrist. Lonnie was close behind. Do it now, she thought.

She kicked between Roach's legs, throwing him off balance. At the same time, she ducked under his arm and threw her shoulder into his chest, knocking the wind out of him, and causing him to release her wrist. The momentum of the action carried her other outstretched leg through a three-hundred-degree arc in half a blink, her heel connecting with his throat. He staggered back.

Lonnie was on her. "You tricky bitch!" His fist connected with her face, instantly bloodying her nose. She kicked at him, but he jumped back with a yell, and came at her again. She dodged another blow, going low, her arm coming around. Lonnie caught it, and drew back his fist for another powerful blow.

A loud clonk sounded, like a muffled church bell. Lonnie reeled, and dropped to the ground.

From the other direction, Roach lurched toward her as she

stared at the downed man. Another clonk, and he lay splayed on the ground. Dell saw Savior turn and run toward the waiting car. A door slammed, and the vehicle sped off. She quickly turned away from the street, toward the bushes beyond. A large, dark figure stood there, gazing after the speeding car while tapping an aluminum baseball bat into his palm. It was Pan!

He smiled, revealing large iridescent teeth. "I bought me a new baseball bat, too, thank you very much."

"Oh, Pan!" Dell went to hug him.

"Don't touch!" He warned, backing off.

"Sorry." She composed herself. "Glad you stopped by. Nice bat."

Francine and the boys hovered near a bench outside the theater, when Dell strolled toward them. As she came closer, their expectant faces turned to alarm. Her appearance was not as expected.

"Dell!" Francie was first to call out as she leapt from the bench. Jimmy and Donnie looked in astonishment. "What happened?"

"Are you all right?" "Geesh, you look like you've been fighting again!" "Does it hurt?"

Dell smiled at the boys. "I know. I've been fighting again— just can't seem to stay out of trouble." She turned to Francie, and a different expression flickered across her face, which alarmed Francie, but then Dell was herself again, sitting down next to the boys, jostling them for room. "Thanks for warming the seat for me."

Donnie shoved back. "I was here first!"

Francie said, "Relax guys, we have to get going anyway." She turned to Dell, peering intently at her face. "That looks like we need to go to the Urgent Care."

Dell felt her nose. "I don't think it's broken, just bleeding. Let's just go. I can put some ice on it at home."

Francie saw that Dell was trying hard not to cry in front of the boys. "Okay then. Let's find the truck."

"Weren't we going to get frosties before we go home?" Donnie asked, with alarm.

Francie sighed. "That's right. I promised. I guess everyone could use some ice-cream."

Dell looked cheered, and turned to Jimmy. "I could use something cold! So how was the movie?"

"Awesome!"

Chapter 25

Jimmy and Donnie hit the sack when they got home, the long day taking its toll. Panda lingered with Francie and Dell at the dining table, where they shared a hot tea. Francie could tell that Dell was upset. "What happened tonight, Dell?"

"Oh, Francie!" She finally let go the tears. "He's found me. Savior knows I'm here." Her shoulders shook with sobs, which she quickly brought under control. "I have to leave."

Francie took in her suddenly sober expression, gauging how serious she actually was. "Now, let's think about this, Dell. This Savior guy has tracked you down—okay. But that isn't a reason to run! This is where you should make a stand. I've seen how you handle trouble, and here you have friends who can back you up."

Dell was adamant. "Francie, I can't let you get involved in my problems. I have to get away from this, this...asshole. He owns me, and I can't let him get near you." She put her head on the table and groaned. "I'm as good as dead."

"Dell, look at me!" Francie spoke sternly. "You are strong. You have friends. We will make sure this guy does not get close again, I promise."

Dell looked up at her.

"I mean it, Dell! I know a lot of people in this county, and I'm going to get every one of them going on this, beginning with Sheriff Warner." She turned to the wall phone, and dialed 911.

Dell looked puzzled as the operator answered with, "What is your emergency?"

"I need to report an assault and continued threats on a person at our home by a gang of terrorists." She reached out and touched Dell's hand.

Next she called Sheriff Warner directly, then the Pierre Police Department. Then she called the state office of the FBI, reporting an attempt at kidnapping across state lines. Finally, she rang Martin Planck.

When he answered, she immediately apologized for calling so soon after their meeting, "But Marty, things are not going well with Dell's situation, and we need all the help we can gather. Now!"

"No need to apologize, Francie—I'll get back on the road here in a couple minutes. I'm still at the motel in Hayes and should be there within the hour. Then we can talk details."

Martin had actually been wondering how he would get through the rest of his week, waiting until he could see Francine Parker again. Every time he thought about her, he went off into a pleasant reverie, where the fields were covered in flowers, the Mockingbirds were always inventing new songs, and there were long pleasant afternoons on a shady deck, with glasses of cool Provencal Rose at their lips, as they traded stories about their pasts and future together. There was something about the woman that he could not shake. She was worldly, though stuck out here in the middle of the country. She maintained her good looks, youth and vitality, despite being a widow with two growing children and, mainly, she was competent, able to handle whatever obstacle or hurdle came her way. Case in point was the girl, Dell. It was like she had been waiting for her to come into their lives, with all her baggage. Francie just absorbed it, like a mother eagle, lifting her wing to allow another chick to shelter there, even though she didn't resemble any of the others.

Francie and Dell faced each other on the couch, neither one the least bit sleepy. It had been an hour since the boys had gone to bed. Dell pressed an ice pack to her injured nose.

"Dell, I think you need to go over what happened at the mall tonight with whoever gets here first, and you need to think about any detail that might be helpful to the police—description, type of car, that sort of thing."

"I can tell them exactly who to look for, and where to find

him!"

"No, we need to put him at the scene tonight, so we need any information that might lead us to him now, before he has a chance to get away."

"Oh, he's not going away. And there are a couple of guys laying there in the grass that might lead the cops to him. But he's not going away until he gets to me. That means he will come out here, if he has to."

"I don't think it will get that far. The Pierre Police Department sent units out to the Mall area, and if those guys are there, they'll find them and they'll figure out where this Savior guy is staying, and they'll get him. Meanwhile, Martin is coming out here, and maybe Sheriff Warner as well, if he can be reached, so we can get some sleep tonight."

Dell appeared to relax for the first time in hours. "So, you like this Martin guy? The school teacher? He is good-looking in a dorky sort of way."

Francie ignored the implications. "Dell, what exactly did happen to those two guys that were holding you tonight?"

She looked at her hands. "I have a friend, Francie. But you can't mention him. Otherwise the cops will hassle him, and he's, you know, kind of special—kind of weird. If the cops talk to him, he won't answer, and they'll just get, you know, how cops get."

"So this friend...?"

"Ambushed them with a baseball bat."

"How did he know you were there?"

"Oh, we met up earlier and, as usual, he didn't have much to say. But, I think he followed me afterward, just to keep an eye on me—because he, you know, has this ability to know when something's not right?"

"So, you're saying that this guy...what's his name?"

"Pan, Peter Pan."

"THE Peter Pan?" Francie raised her eyebrows. "Well, that may be what he calls himself but, anyway—your friend Pan—he knew you were in trouble?"

"He told me last weekend there was going to be trouble."

Francie assessed Dell and thought, *he knows you all too well,* but knew now wasn't a good time to say that. Instead she said, "How long have you known this...Pan?"

"Oh, last weekend was the first time. He's camped down behind the mall. He goes south for the winter, 'cause he says he's too old to stay here when it's so cold."

"Well, I guess it's a good thing you became his friend. Okay, we won't tell the police about him, we'll just say a passerby helped you out—you know we have to have some explanation as to how those fellas were incapacitated."

There was a knock on the door, and Francie answered, holding the shotgun out of sight. It was Martin.

Francie invited him inside and peered into the darkness outside just to make sure there was no one else, then she closed and bolted the door.

Martin watched her. "This looks ominous."

"Just being careful, Marty. Hi—good to see you, and thanks for coming." She nodded at Dell. "We have a problem here, Marty. Some acquaintances of hers have come back to haunt her, and we need to do something about it."

Chapter 26

Dell told them about Savior. At least, she told them what she could. Francie had already pieced much of it together. This man preyed on girls and young women, most of whom were neither smart nor talented, but they were cute, and attractive to older degenerates who would not hesitate to spend lots of money for their favors. Savior had a well-organized operation, complete with street hawkers, internet promotional experts, accountants, and enforcers. He had people also who specialized in catering to the girls' needs. Their medications, birth control, disease prevention, nutrition and drug regulation. He didn't want them overdosing on their clients' time, so he made sure that their narcotic intake was regulated. He didn't mind them using opiates or psychedelics, but made sure that it didn't interfere with their main enterprise, which was to satisfy customers.

Dell had started turning tricks for Savior when she was about thirteen years old. At that point, she was well into puberty. They gave her Depo Provera shots about every three months to stave off the worry of pregnancy. She had never had a normal period after that. She had been sexually active well before Savior snagged her.

Her first time, she just didn't know what was happening, and most would consider that rape. Then there were occasions when she would be curious and willing with an older boy. But later on, boys viewed her as an easy sex target, and several times she would be forced into sexual situations by various individuals or groups of boys. After this period she decided to take control of where and when she would allow herself to get naked with a boy, and various individuals learned quickly that it would be very painful to try and force her into anything.

She enjoyed having sex a lot. It made her stop thinking about things—things that might matter to someone who wanted more than just what the body could offer. She read books, and started thinking about love, winning, the universe, and death. She gradually realized that she had never been in love, and was never likely to have someone love her. Because sex wasn't love. For some, it was a gift of love, but she had given that gift away so many times, she didn't think she had it in herself to give anymore.

That's when she knew she had to get away from her life with Savior.

Martin asked Dell, "Do you remember where you went to school?"

The girl raised her eyes and jutted her chin in thought. "There were lots of different schools. Maybe six, before I stopped going. I would get kicked out and have to go to a different one. Swift's Institute for Special Needs Children is where I met Shirlee. My friend that I told you about?"

Francine asked, "Why were you kicked out of so many schools?"

"For fighting. I did a lot of fighting when I was little. I guess that's why I'm so good at it." There was a hint of pride in her voice.

Martin paused his recorder. "Dell, is it okay if I contact that school to see if they have any information on you that might give a clue as to where you were born, how old you are—that sort of thing?"

"Feel free—doesn't make any diff to me."

A knock on the door brought the interview to a halt. Francine grabbed the shotgun that was leaned against the wall, and peered through the glass view. "It's the sheriff!"

Sheriff Warner hung his hat on the rack. He was now familiar enough with the place that he didn't have to ask. He nodded to Martin and turned to Francie and Dell. "Hello, ladies. Got some trouble again?"

"Hi, Vern. I'll get you some coffee." She rose from the table and pulled a mug off the shelf.

After they were comfortably positioned around the kitchen table, Warner looked pointedly at Dell. "Looks like you took a licking today. What's the story, young lady?"

Dell relayed her account of the assault at the mall in Pierre, who the assailants were, and how a passerby helped chase them off.

"Why were you at the mall, Dell?"

"Oh, Jimmy and Donnie were at the movies, and I was just walking around until they got out. I guess those men followed me out there."

Francine frowned. "I don't see how they could have followed you all the way from Chicago—they must have known you were here somehow, and followed you from here."

"That's right, Francie. You can thank Marty here, for that." Warner tilted his head toward Planck.

"Sorry. I didn't know enough at the time to think there might be someone looking to get revenge on you, Dell. That story I wrote was picked up by the wire services, and they probably read about you in Chicago. Who knew they wanted you enough to come this far out to try and grab you."

"Must of been a good story." Dell smiled a little. "Guess I'll have to read it."

"Good enough to chase the roaches out of the wall." Warner leaned forward. "Listen folks, I've been in touch with the Pierre police, and they reported two injured men were found on a sidewalk near the mall. Those guys are currently in Saint Mary's in bad shape. There is no trace of who we're looking for, though. They could be at any of dozens of hotels or motels. And Francie," the Sheriff looked pointedly at the woman, "I talked to Joiner over at the FBI Agency in Pierre. He says simple assault cases are not in his playbook, so the Feds are not wading in on this one."

Dell rolled her eyes. "If I don't see those guys again, it'll be too soon."

Martin added, "What they're not saying is that you trampled

on their egos last time they were here, Dell, and they're not going to play anymore."

"So, what it boils down to now is you've got the Pierre police sniffing around over there, and you've got me and my department here in the Fort."

Francie didn't look happy. "What are you going to do then, Vern?"

The Sheriff sat straight and scratched his chin. "Okay, first we need a detailed description of these guys from you, Dell, so the cops can canvass the hotels in town. Then we need more details on exactly where they are coming from in Chicago. We might be able to catch them on the other end with the help of Chicago PD. Hell, they might even be well known to Chicago PD!"

Francie was still unsatisfied. "So, if we find these guys, then what?"

"Well, then Dell testifies against them, and we put them away!"

Dell smiled to herself. "You find this guy and I'll put him away!"

Warner tried to ignore the implications of Dell's pledge. "So, Dell. Let's go to work. Marty, would you take notes please?"

Chapter 27

When Dell awoke to the red misty light filtering through the window, she was relieved to find she was in an actual bed and not constrained in any manner. Her dreams had not been pleasant. All night she had been chased by a dark, nebulous cloud, and couldn't quite get away because of large, sticky spider webs that blocked her way. *I guess it will take some time for me to chill after the last few days,* she thought. After visiting the bathroom and dressing, she ambled down the stairs toward an animated jumble of voices. She was greeted by the smell of bacon, toast and hot coffee.

Jimmy and Donnie were eating already, and waved at her. Francie was cooking, and it surprised Dell to see Martin Planck leaning against the counter near Francie, sipping from a mug of coffee. Francie smiled when she caught sight of Dell. "Hello, sweetie. These beasts haven't eaten it all yet, so grab yourself a plate."

"Good morning, guys." Dell reached up for a plate and smiled back. "I guess I'll be seeing a lot more of you around here, then, Teach."

Martin coughed after a hot gulp. "Well, the fog was pretty thick last night, and Francine thought, to be safe, I should just...spend the night down here on the couch."

"I get it—I can keep a secret."

Francie reddened, and changed the subject. "I hope you slept well. We have a lot to get done today, starting with the animals, so get yourself some toast. Bacon's in a pile, there. Juice's on the table."

Dell sat and began eating. Jimmy sat across from her and stared.

"What?"

"Your nose—it looks...sore."

"Well, thanks for making me think about it!"

While Martin busied himself with the digging, hammering and nailing that had been assigned him, Francie took off to check the fence. The kids finished up with the horses and chickens, while Irma tidied up in the bed and bathrooms. That's when the sheriff chose to call.

When Francie returned forty-five minutes later, Irma rushed out on the porch to greet her. "Francie, Francie! You have a very important call to the sheriff!"

Francie tracked down Martin and they both listened as the call was put to Warner's office. "Hi, this is Francine Parker. I'm returning a call from Sheriff Warner. Could you put him on the line, please?"

A moment later Vern was talking to them. "Francie, it looks like we got the bastard. Two of them were holed up at the Empire, in Fort Pierre. Tell Marty and Dell."

"Marty's here. What'll I tell Dell?"

"We need her over here, to positively identify these jerks. Anyway, her description was right on, and these two we have are carrying Illinois licenses, so I'm confident these are the ones we're after."

A fine spring day materialized for a trip into the county seat. The air felt crisp, as mere wisps of clouds floated across the sky. Dell spent the time thinking about confronting the man who had held her in slavery for more than three years. She appeared to be studying the grass and farmland rolling by, but really could see none of it.

Martin realized his involvement with the girl grew by default as his fondness for Francine grew. Francie had been fiercely protective of Dell almost from the day she had met her.

The three of them arrived at the Stanley County Sheriff's office on Second Street in just over an hour. The single story building stood tall, constructed of sturdy brown brick. Its most outstanding feature being the long, narrow windows situated vertically along the front exterior, like the battlements of a medieval castle.

Sheriff Warner greeted them. "Welcome to my world, folks. The jail, where the suspects are being held, is just down the hall."

Marty appeared very interested in the building and its surroundings. "This is great, Sheriff! As long as I've known you, I've never once been invited to your place of employment!"

Warner looked at him askance. "Count yourself lucky, Marty."

Dell was counting herself lucky. She had never been in a jail office before, and didn't feel comfortable at all. The interior shone a dull light greenish color. The waiting room, furnished with sturdy hardwood chairs, faced a counter along the wall, now occupied by a female clerk who looked up without expression when they walked by. A glassed-in area covered the bulk of the counter, with a slot in the glass to allow for transfer of documents or whatnot. To the left of that stood a massive door, fitted with a small glass window at eye level, and a number pad in place of a knob. Dell wanted to get out of there as quickly as possible.

The sheriff punched in a code and led them through the door. To their right was a large, well-lit area occupied by four desks. Behind the desks, three doorways provided access to other rooms. A deputy at one of the desks looked up as they entered.

The sheriff addressed him. "Charlie, would you let Sergeant Larch know we need the prisoners in line-up?" Then, indicating Dell, said, "This is the girl I was telling you about. Folks, this is Deputy Bradford. He is holding the fort while Daniels recovers—the deputy you rescued, young lady." Once again nodding to Dell.

Dell frowned in surprise. She had not thought of herself as a rescuer of cops. She had only been dealing with the creeps threatening her friends.

Martin greeted Bradford with a nod. "Deputy."

Francine shot Dell a reassuring smile, as the deputy got on the intercom.

Warner escorted the small group through one of the doors at the far end of the room, where they found folding chairs lined up facing a long glass window. "Sit down folks, it shouldn't be a minute."

They waited in a tense silence until a light came on behind the window, and two men filed into the area, followed by two guard officers. One of the guards placed himself on one side of the room, and the other, a woman, remained near the door. Sheriff Warner turned to Dell. "Okay, Dell. Tell me if these men look familiar to you."

"Yes."

"Are these the men who attacked you at the mall in Pierre?"

Dell thought a moment as to how she should answer. "Well, one of them is. The other one is one of his cronies, and I know him, too. The dark-haired guy on the left there is Peter Savior, from Chicago. The other man is his friend Tulley. Fred Tulley. They have a bunch of young girls working sex for them in the City. Chicago." She narrowed her eyes and turned to the sheriff. "Can I go in there and beat the shit out of them?"

Francine started to say something. Dell cut her off. "I know, I know! We don't do things that way here."

Martin was studying his fingernails, a smile on his lips.

Warner responded to the girl's question. "I bet you could, young lady, but you can do something even more useful. You can help us take down their whole operation. What we need to do is get a warrant for their place in Chicago. That's where you can help, by showing us where to look. I'll have to persuade DCI to get a judge in Illinois to do that, then we'll have to arrange for a CPD team to actually do the grunt work because that is out of my jurisdiction and the Feds aren't exactly enamored with us now."

"Wait, you're losing me." Francine was confused. "DCI, CPD?"

Martin explained. "Police agencies. DCI is the state Department of Criminal Investigations, CPD is Chicago."

"Would I actually have to go back to Chicago?"

They all turned to look at Dell. She wore a grimace of disgust, and shook her head. "I'm not sure I could do that. I think someone would try and arrest me."

"Why would you think that, sweetie?" Francie's voice expressed concern.

She looked at Francie, then glanced sideways at the sheriff. "I wasn't exactly an angel when I was there."

Francie gave her an affectionate look. "Well, you're an angel now, Dell. A guardian angel."

The sheriff nodded. "Looks like you've been promoted. Don't worry, we'll make sure you have immunity from prosecution, just like any CI would get." Glancing at Francine, he elaborated. "Confidential Informant. Some like to call them 'Criminal Informants'...not that you're a criminal, but you would be guaranteed immunity from the State Department of Justice for any past infractions that might be brought to light." He informed the guards they were done with the prisoners. "Now, we'll hold these guys on assault charges for the time being, but we need to get moving on the Chicago thing quickly. I understand there will be a court hearing in Pierre on this terrorist matter on Friday, so we want to be ready to travel right after that."

Dell looked to Francie for guidance, who nodded slightly.

The girl sighed in resignation. "Okay. What do I have to do?"

"Just be prepared to leave for Illinois after the hearing on Friday. Probably won't take longer than mid-week, so bring a couple changes of clothes. We'll have someone accompany you there and back, a woman, probably an officer from the DCI." Warner led them back to the lobby. "Will you be able to get her to the court house at nine o'clock Friday morning Francie?"

"That won't be a problem, Vern. We'll see you then."

They had lunch at Juanita's before heading back to the ranch. After lunch, Dell persuaded Francine to take her to the mall for a little bit, to check on Pan.

"Okay with me, if it's alright with you Marty." Martin had no objection. "Just don't be too long. We'll wait over on that bench." Francie indicated a wrought-iron bench next to the sidewalk under a large sycamore just leafing out.

"It's never very long with Pan, you know." She walked quickly away, then half-slid down the familiar embankment.

Dell found the lines tied hither and yon, filled with debris, various pieces of ribbon, cooking utensils and whatnot, but something was missing. The orange nylon tent complete with rain fly had been removed. In its place hung a large banner tied between two saplings. The banner looked crudely decorated with rattle-can spray paint. It read—'You can fly! We see you flying! Fly far!'

Dell stared at the banner. Pan is gone, she thought. It's too early for his southern journey. It must have been the police snooping around. He's gone and I will never see him again. She felt empty. This strange man was someone she could count on. Now he was gone.

It's a small thing, she told herself. I have real friends now. But Pan was her only 'unreal' friend. She would miss him. She turned and climbed back up the hill.

Chapter 28

Spending Friday at the Hughes County Superior Court proved excruciating. As dull as week old horse-shit. As tedious as trying on dresses for the prom. Okay, she never did that, but that must be tedious. She sat in front, between Sheriff Warner and a woman from the Public Defender's office, Sugar Johnson. She looked serious enough, in her fitted black suit and white crinoline blouse, but what kind of name was Sugar?

Every time Dell went to answer a question, Johnson would jump up and declare, "Miss Dell has no comment on that at this time." The sheriff answered a few questions about evidence pointing to the asshole nature of the victims, and the crimes they were charged with committing on Dell's person, against the community, etcetera.

Dell had thought from the beginning this would be a gigantic waste of time, and now felt justified in that opinion. She kept looking back to the spectator seats, to see if Francine would stick it out with her or if she had left in disgust. Francine smiled her encouragement, and Dell resolved to continue until it was done.

For their part, the Feds had not much to add except vague suspicions and wild speculation, as Johnson would adamantly point out in her many interruptions. Two agents sat at the other table, in front of the judge, a small middle-aged man wearing dark, circular glasses, thick as coke bottles. Dell recognized the feebs from the other day at the ranch, where they wouldn't get out of her face. Agents Joiner and Billings. They kept making annoying and cutting remarks about her character, which mostly was what Johnson was getting up and down on them about.

Dell thought they really wanted to get her in a small room where they could starve her and beat her until she told them what they wanted to hear—that she loved beating up on men, no matter how innocent they were. She had planned all this because she is a loose cannon, a reckless anarchist who would go to any length to knock down what decent people have spent their lives building if it stands in her way. Okay, some truth there maybe, but so what. Her actions made things better for most everyone. As to the way she did it, what choice did she have? She doesn't have a big army, any money, or a lot of big bombs on her side. So she makes do—and makes no excuses! Dell could feel her rage growing again, and tried to put a damper on it. Just a little more time, and this'll be over with.

Finally, it was over. The Judge banged his gavel, just like she knew he would, and intoned, "No basis for prosecution of the defendant. Justifiable homicide, in all cases. Miss Dell, please try to avoid dangerous situations in the future. I would prefer not to see you back here."

"Yes, Your Honor." She told herself that he was probably right. If she could just avoid those situations she kept stumbling into, she would be a lot more of...what she could never be—cautious and careful. She would have to be somebody else, so why even think about it?

Francine came up to her and gave her a long hug. "Looks like you're home free, sweetie. I'm so glad it worked out." She turned to the PD. "And thank you, Miz Johnson, for doing a great job."

"Well, we hardly ever get cases like this one around here, so it was very interesting, and certainly my pleasure Missus Parker, Miss Dell." They shook hands and she turned to leave.

Sheriff Warner stood aside to let her get by, then turned to the two women. "Okay, ladies. I've arranged for Dell and her escort to be on their way to Chicago at around three o'clock today. You'll fly out of Pierre Regional, and will have to be at the airport around two. You all packed?"

"Airport? I'm going to fly?" Dell was dumbfounded.

Francie looked at her with concern. "You're not afraid to fly, are you Dell?"

"Well, I've never been on a plane before, but I'm not afraid. It's just...strange, that's all."

They both decided it must be 'nerves'.

Chapter 29

One last lunch in town before she had to leave, this time with Martin, Sheriff Warner, and Francie. They chose a different spot near the regional airport, the Oriel Bistro.

"Go ahead, Dell," urged Francie. "I think you'll like Calamari."

Not too sure, Dell poked at the appetizer with her fork, finally stuffing a small ring into her mouth as if plunging into an icy stream. Her eyes searching the ceiling as she chewed. "Not bad. Kinda like tough chicken."

Martin attempted to get her attention. "Dell, I have some information—would you like to hear?"

She stopped chewing, and nodded. "Sure."

All eyes fixated on Martin. "That school you mentioned, the Swift's Institute? I contacted them and got some information about you regarding your history."

Dell put down her fork. "Okay..."

Martin noted everyone had stopped eating. He read from a sheet in front of him. "You were born sometime in the summer at the start of the millennium, the year two-thousand. Exact date and place are unknown, just somewhere in Chicago, according to these records. Your full name is Adele Louise Martin. Apparently, your mother, Constance Martin suffered poor health and died that winter. No father listed."

Francie frowned, not sure what effect this would have on the girl.

Sheriff Warner smiled. "Well, young lady. That would make you a ward of the court, being nowhere near eighteen yet. Good work, Marty!"

Francie spoke. "Listen Dell. Don't worry about Vern, here. He's not going to take you in, or anything. You may not be eighteen, but you are still old enough to have a say in where you want to stay. And so do I, so don't worry about it, okay?"

Dell looked from one to the other. "Louise? My middle name is Louise? It's so funny that I even have a middle name, or a last name. After all these years. I'll have to think about that for a while. So Teach," she looked at Martin and began chewing again, "you say I was born in the summertime? I guess that makes me kinda hot, right?"

"You are a very special girl, Dell, and I hope what I've found out about you does you some good. Information is always better than ignorance, trust me."

Dell smiled. "Well, I guess I can't lie about my age anymore."

One airline served the Pierre Regional Airport. It flew a direct nonstop to Denver. Dell would fly a chartered plane, direct to Chicago.

A familiar face greeted her at the gate. FBI Agent Rene Maddis smiled briefly as Sheriff Warner approached with Dell. "Sheriff, Dell." The agent nodded. "We'll be flying together, Dell."

Dell stood askance, hands on hips, as she turned to Warner with a raised eyebrow.

Warner caught the unspoken question. "Agent Maddis here is representing the FBI in this case. They decided that possible interstate procurement of young women is something they want to be involved in."

It was Maddis's turn to look askance at the sheriff.

"Well, you know what I mean. They consider this crime to fall into their bailiwick and are taking lead in the matter. The plane you're flying on is an FBI charter."

The Agent took it from there. "We are going to be together all the way in this, Dell, so I hope we can get along. We will meet up with a team in Chicago and scope out the place or places where the warrants will be served, based on the information you will give us. Your job will end after pointing out the targets, and we will head back home while the team does the dirty work.

We'll probably not even spend the night." Again, a slight smile. A final hug from Francie. "We'll see you soon, Dell."

They grabbed their bags and boarded the little Cessna C-550 twin jet. Two rows of seats, six in all, lined the space back of the cabin, and a pedestal table surrounded by ell-shaped seating on two sides sprouted up-forward. A small counter and sink grew out of the bulkhead across from the table. The pilot's cockpit visible through an opening beyond, was accessed by a sliding door. Two pilots busied themselves at the controls. One reached up and keyed a microphone. "Prepare for takeoff, please."

Maddis motioned for Dell to take the first seat on the far side, and she slipped into the one across from it. She pointed to the front of the plane. "We'll move to the table when were air-born so we can look at the maps."

Dell moved closer the window. "I guess on a flight like this, we don't get peanuts?"

Maddis rolled her eyes.

Soon after a smooth takeoff they moved to the table. The agent spread out a detailed map. "We'll be landing here at Midway." She pointed to a spot on the paper. "It's closer to the West Garfield and Lawndale Park areas that we'll be entering, and the airport itself is much easier to get in and out of than O'Hare." She leaned closer over the map. "Now, can you see on this map any familiar streets that will get us into the neighborhood that our friend has been operating out of?"

Dell squeezed in and got her bearings. She bobbed her chin, and placed her finger at an intersection about six miles from the airport. "There. That block, I think."

Maddis appeared more relaxed, if not pleased. "Good. That'll save us a lot of time when we get on the ground. After landing, two more agents will join us. When we pinpoint the correct location, they'll call in the breach team. At that point, you and I will head back to the airport, and home." She rose and moved to the counter across the aisle and opened a cooler underneath. "You want a Coke?" She retrieved two red and silver cans, offering one to Dell, then sat opposite, and gave her a defiant look.

"Now, I have to tell you, that I don't buy this super-hero routine that your friends are peddling about you. To me, you are just a CI, and once you come through with the information we need, we're finished! After that, I'm charged with getting you home safely, and that's it. My job is done. You get it?"

Dell studied the agent's stern demeanor. She figured there were a lot of things this woman had never been exposed to, given her privileged status, and she decided not to hold it against her. "What's a CI, again?"

"Somebody who is doing the right thing for the wrong reason, that's what!" Maddis turned to her papers, giving Dell the impression she was done talking.

Dell looked at her, then sipped her soda quietly. What could possibly go wrong, she mused.

They were instructed to return to their seats for the landing, and after twenty minutes had bags in hand on the ground. As promised, two agents, identified as Lindquist and Barclay, presented themselves. They would use two vehicles, and the local guys would pilot. Maddis and Dell rode in one with Barclay, and Lindquist would follow. After winding out of the airport, the SUV's turned north. They had strapped Dell in the back seat, while Maddis sat enthroned up front with Barclay. Reflecting their differences in relative worth, Dell conjectured. She also mused that two black Ford Expeditions, barreling along the expressway in tandem, presented as not altogether inconspicuous, but the feebs were obviously too cocky to care.

They rode in relative silence, except for the roar of the all-weather tires chewing up the road. About halfway to the destination, they veered off the expressway and sped along a two lane drive through high-rise apartments looming on either side. The vehicles slowed at intersections, where stop signs controlled traffic from the side. As they plowed through the second of these, Dell noted that a large pick-up on the right was not stopping and was heading very fast toward them.

She yelled, unsnapped her belt and dove to the floor, just as the truck rammed into the side of their vehicle in a thunderous shower of bent steel, plastic and glass! Her quick action had saved her bones from injury, but slivers of glass caught in her neck and blood seeped from the small cuts.

Two doors flew open on the truck and men with automatic rifles tumbled out. Dell frantically shoved at the door on the other side. She rolled to the ground as gunfire peppered the Ford. She vaguely noticed the SUV following them screeching to a stop ten feet behind. The agent in that vehicle jumped out and joined in the gunfire with his Glock.

Instinctively, Dell yanked the front door of her vehicle open and found Barclay slumped over the wheel, his shirt covered in blood. Maddis was seated sideways, trying to loosen her seatbelt. Most of the impact had been absorbed by the rear door, although the pillar had been caved inward and Maddis was having difficulty locating the button.

Dell reached over and popped Agent Barclay's belt loose, then tugged him to the ground, cupping his head to prevent it from getting knocked too hard. The sharp reports of gunfire continued, as bullets whizzed and clanged above her. She noted Agent Lindquist still firing his weapon from the cover of his vehicle's open door. Barclay's open jacket revealed his holstered Glock, and Dell quickly grabbed it.

She rolled under the Ford, aimed at a pair of legs she glimpsed there, and fired four quick shots. The sound was deafening under the vehicle, but her target screamed and fell on his back. She put two more rounds into his side. Rolling out from under the SUV, she rose to a crouch and swung around to the rear, where she spotted the other shooter exposed behind his door.

As he whipped his rifle around to Dell, she put two shots into his chest, her Glock trying to jerk out of her hands, as the target lurched backward, slamming against his truck.

Maddis had freed herself and was crawling head-first out of the Ford. She rolled to the ground, and came up with her weapon pointed over the hood at the truck. Lindquist ran forward, and leaned down to check on his partner.

Screeching tires just then announced the arrival of another vehicle. It came out of a side street behind Lindquist's Ford, sliding to a stop next to it. Three men with rifles emerged. Maddis and Lindquist dived for cover behind the wrecked Federal vehicle as more bullets sought them out.

Barclay still lay where they had left him, not moving. The new assault had them pinned, and neither agent could take a shot without exposing themselves. Maddis caught a movement on the other side of the SUV, where they squatted. She pointed in that direction and was about to fire when she saw it was Dell. The girl stood at the rear of the first assailant's truck, the loud, rapid bursts of automatic rifle fire announcing her assault on the newcomers, catching them in a deadly crossfire.

Dell had picked up both rifles from the downed men, and they now jerked furiously in her arms, as the newcomers lunged and twisted in a desperate attempt to dodge the deadly storm. She didn't stop firing until both weapons were empty and the victims lay slumped in unnatural poses.

Lindquist looked at Maddis. "Let's get Barclay over to my car. Come on!" They both grabbed an arm, and half dragged him to the unit. Dell dropped the rifles and jogged to the Ford, flinging the rear doors open. They lifted him in, and Dell climbed in next to him. "I'll keep him still—get us out of here!"

The SUV started and Lindquist screeched a hard U-turn, the vehicle's wheels bumping over the curb in their haste. The plaintive sound of sirens wailed in the distance.

Chapter 30

Maddis propped herself next to Dell in the lounge seat after the Cessna's takeoff. She was sporting a sling on her right arm, where her shoulder had been injured. "I hate to say that this mission turned out not as planned, and by any criteria, should be considered a failure." She looked closely at Dell. "There was a leak of information, and obviously these guys were on our tail from the moment we set foot on the ground. I'm not blaming you, Dell..."

"God, I hope not!" Dell blurted. "I was there, you know, taking the flak."

Maddis groped for an adequate response. "And I appreciate what you did, Dell." She looked inward for a moment. "Actually, you were incredible. I think I may have been wrong about you all along. And thank you for getting us out of there in one piece." She reached out and touched Dell's shoulder. "I really find it hard to say this, but I think we may owe you our lives..."

Dell didn't know how to respond, so she just sat, and considered the clouds rolling by. There I go again, she thought, bailing out the cops.

After being attacked, the Feds had swarmed over the scene. Their investigators came up with dozens of leads concerning who had staged the ambush, and they were busy following up those leads as quickly as possible. That being the case, any information that Dell possessed was downgraded to follow-up status and marked for future reference. In other words, she was turned loose, and was allowed to head back to South Dakota.

Dell was thinking about the ranch and Jonny, the stallion, and how she was going to love riding him again, when Maddis intruded on her thoughts. "Dell..."

"Hmmmh?"

"Dell, since you don't have military training, mind telling me how you got to be so good with automatic rifles?"

Dell considered for a moment. "Well, they are automatic, aren't they? What's to learn?"

Maddis shook her head. "That's absurd!" She tried a workaround. "Okay...how did you get to be so accurate with unfamiliar pistols that you just picked up? To me, that indicates that you have a lot of experience with all kinds of weapons—is that the case?"

"I have lots of experience," Dell lied. "Guns were everywhere when I was growing up! You took me out there today in my territory and I just did what I have always done—that's what you deal with every day, when you grow up in a place where people are fighting all the time."

"You're telling me you've done this before?"

"Well, not this exact thing, but we were always trying to figure how to survive when the adults around us were always surprising one another. I mean, try and imagine not having a family and having to scrabble for yourself from the time you could walk. If I didn't learn quickly, I wouldn't be here...it's like being in some poor country, where nobody has any food or water, and you just have to get it however you can."

"So, how did you survive?"

"Well, most in that situation would lie, steal, fight—whatever it took. I may have done my share of that."

Maddis placed her good hand under her chin. "So, is that who you are, Dell?"

Dell's eyes widened. "I don't know who I am—I'm still trying to deal with who I'm not." She felt her nose, which was still sore. "I went along with what they wanted me to be for a long time, until I started feeling sick about it. I was dreaming a lot, like I always do—it takes me out of myself—but anyway, I was thinking about the future, and I realized I didn't have one—not like normal people. So I got tough—stopped doing it the easy way, you know, what they wanted. When I saw a chance, I went for it. That's what led me to you, isn't it? Only, now I'm doing what you guys want me to do, right?"

Maddis looked thoughtful. "I think what you need, Dell, is a plan. I mean, it's not enough to say, I 'm not going to be that person anymore. You need to envision what you want to become and work toward that. You are so young! As for today—you needed to be there, Dell. For closure. We were just there to back you up. And, of course, to follow you to the bad guys...right up until things turned to shit."

"Right. Glad I could help."

"You are so talented, Dell. I didn't believe it until I saw you doing it. Okay—how's this? Have you ever thought about a career in law enforcement?"

Dell threw her head back. "Hah! I've never thought about a career in anything. Law enforcement? That's where you make people do what they don't want to do and then you arrest them, right? Let me ask you this—you used to be a girl. How come you ended up a feeb?"

"A feeb, huh? Haven't heard that one in a while. I guess I just grew up wanting to do some good, and I kept hearing about the bad guys always getting away with...whatever. So I took criminal justice classes, and I was up there at the top of my classes, so I shot for the best, and here I am."

"So, you like shooting people?"

Maddis started. "It's not about shooting people." She considered a moment. "Well, we really don't get to do a lot of shooting, except on the range, but I think I don't like getting shot at, and when that happens, I'm happy to fight back...but I don't really like shooting people. What do you say? Do you like it? Shooting people?"

Dell smiled. "Depends on who I'm shooting, doesn't it? You know, I don't do a lot of shooting either—my ears are still ringing from today. I think if guns were a lot quieter, I would enjoy it a lot more. Especially if the person I was shooting had been trying to kill me or my friends." She stopped, and looked out the window at the cumulus clouds drifting quickly past. "You know, I don't think I would ever shoot someone with a gun unless that person needed to be stopped immediately from killing or injuring a friend or just someone who was totally innocent." She looked back at the agent. "You know what I mean?"

It was Maddis' turn to smile. "That's right on, Dell."

When the plane landed, Francie was there to greet Dell, and so was the sheriff.

Agent Joiner also. He hustled Maddis aside, and they exchanged hushed words. Finally, Maddis shot Dell a glance, indicating she would catch up with her later.

Martin Planck was waiting with the car. The three of them clambered in, and Martin made straight for Fort Pierre and the Sheriff's Office.

Warner, in the front with Planck, turned a grim face at Francine and Dell. "When we get to the shop, we're going to sit down and go over what went wrong today, then we'll see if we can do anything else or if we should just plan to let the feds do their thing."

Fatigue had overtaken Dell, who said nothing.

Martin looked back at the girl. "Dell, I'm going to have to write a story about what happened today. It'd be great if you would give me a few words to keep it accurate?"

Dell kept her eyes closed. "Later, Teach."

They crossed the long bridge across the Missouri, the water seemingly still and black. Francine knew different. There were strong currents in that river that could grab you when least expected, and drag you down, only to cough you up miles from where you had innocently entered into the shallows. She never did put her full trust into that river. The boys had always been cautioned not to go there alone. She realized her thoughts had turned dark, and she wasn't at all sure why that was.

Chapter 31

Dell thought there would be chaos in the Sheriff's Department, but it was eerily quiet. No one lurked behind the counter. Sheriff Warner punched the code into the large door, and they followed him into the depths of the building. They moved past the desks, where no deputies were in evidence, and into a room back on the left.

Warner spoke to them over his shoulder. "They're waiting for us in here." He pushed open the door to a conference room. "I hope they let you stay, Marty. It'll keep them honest."

Martin and Francine followed Warner into the room, and Dell trailed behind. She saw several familiar faces of federal agents that she had to deal with this past week, and two people she didn't recognize, presumably representing bad news. The department clerk sat in the back, notepad in hand, all business as usual.

Billings and Joiner were there, from the Pierre Regional Agency, as was Agent Maddis. Maddis gestured with her good left hand to a seat for the group.

Joiner greeted them. "This won't take long. Sheriff, this is an official debriefing—explain please why it is necessary to have guests." He indicated Francie and Martin.

Warner leaned back in his chair. "Well, Agent, Martin here is representing the public's interest in what goes on here, in plain terms, so no one can say that anyone is being railroaded or made to take the blame for something that may or may not have happened. And Francine is here in her capacity as counselor and representative for your CI there." He pointed to Dell. "She will make sure Dell's rights are not being trampled on, accidentally or deliberately." He looked around the room. "Just as a precaution, you understand."

Joiner looked as if he had swallowed a bug. "With the stipulation that nothing discussed here leaves this room without specific permission. Otherwise, I'm fine with that. Let me introduce the others here that you may not know."

Joiner turned to the man and woman seated on the other side of the table from Dell and the others. "This is Assistant District Attorney Jefferson, who will represent Illinois in this matter, and next to him is Miz Blue Dove, from the DCI, representing the interests of this state. Agent Billings you know. He and I will be conducting this, ah, debriefing."

ADA Jefferson was a black man with a shaved head, who Dell judged probably stood over six feet. The woman was almost as tall, and her skin was almost as dark, but with much finer features.

Jefferson spoke. "Good evening, folks. Let me just say that this excursion was done all above board, with full cooperation from the City of Chicago and the Chicago Federal Field Office. What we are trying to find out is why it didn't work as planned."

Dell said, "So who fucked up?"

Joiner looked at Billings, and he took the narrative. "Colorfully put. We are going to determine here if anything could have gone differently with..."

Maddis interjected. "There was a leak, and what we have to find out is how that happened."

Sheriff Warner spoke. "I think what happened was a large boner on our side. You see, the perp got his mandated phone call. That was a big no-no. He obviously had more friends in the city than we had imagined. Therefore, phone call? That should have been delayed until after this critical operation. We dropped the ball, and we suffered as a result. I take full responsibility, but I don't see how we could have done it any differently."

"Constitutional rights are good, Sheriff, and no fault on your part, except for maybe timing?" That from Blue Dove, who stood when she talked, then quickly sat.

Dell crossed her legs, shifting from one cheek to the other. She began drumming her fingers on the table.

Joiner shot her a furrowed stare. "This won't take long, Miss. Okay, we suffered one casualty at the scene." He referred to notes. "An agent Barclay, is that right?" He looked around. "I hear that Barclay was hit, but will make a full recovery. Nobody else injured, on our side, that is." Looking at Maddis, he amended the pronouncement. "Sorry, except for Agent Maddis, who has lost function in her arm. How is that coming along, Agent?"

"It hurts." Maddis rubbed her shoulder. "Listen, the simple truth is we were ambushed, and it was all because we didn't deny the perp his right to a phone call. That sucks in so many ways!"

Joiner attempted to defuse her ire. "Don't worry, Agent. It was not in vain. Those men who attacked you, now deceased, all had histories, and Chicago has various teams working the scene. So the good news is, we are clear of it. For now, at least."

Billings added. "What we're looking at now is reports on weapons fired. It seems the only gunfire on our part, was from Agent Lindquist, out of the Field Office. And they're taking care of that. So that only leaves us with how five perps actually got killed. Simple, right?"

All eyes turned to Dell. She slumped down in the chair.

Agent Maddis was the first to speak. "It is amazing to me that our CI, Miss Dell there, was able to obtain a pistol from an injured agent, then turn it on the two assailants who had us pinned down. Furthermore, when three others appeared, she grabbed weapons from the downed assailants, and took out those guys. It's as if she was programmed. We didn't even have time to do anything but dive for cover. I have to tell you, we would have been up shit-creek if it wasn't for her quick action." Maddis looked around at the assembled agents. "She didn't even have her own weapon!"

Joiner followed her scan around the room. "So what we're saying here is that only the CI was able to return fire, and they were the shots that took out the perps. And she salvaged the weapons she needed to do that?"

Maddis replied. "That is correct."

Joiner frowned. "Was she previously authorized to take that kind of action?"

"Of course not!" Maddis tried not to show her annoyance with the question. "But, as you recall, we gave her immunity from any infractions that may have been committed while in Illinois. I am assuming that included spraying bullets around the neighborhood, whether done in a good cause or not."

ADA Jefferson squinted. "Hmm...well Miss," He looked down at his notes, "ah...Dell. Looks like we owe you some recognition for your bravery and quick thinking in this operation. Am I correct in assuming that your role was only to point out the precise location for serving a warrant?"

Dell nodded. "Yes, sir."

"So you had no idea what was in store?"

"Shit happens, sir!"

Jefferson smiled. "So they say. I think that if you were operating in some official capacity, you would be up for a commendation. As it is..."

Blue Dove stood, nodding to the ADA. "There is precedent for presenting commendation to a citizen who has performed outstanding public service. I think Miss Dell can be recognized by the state in that manner." She sat.

Francine, however, had different ideas. She stood. "What Dell needs, and would like, is a two, no, I mean, a four-year college scholarship, so that she can get herself to a place where she can be even more valuable to her community. It is not enough that she be recognized, then left once again to her own devices, where she may or may not struggle to some form of successful public achievement. She needs all the help the community can give her, so that her talents can be realized, and her contributions to the public good can be maximized. So, how about it, folks—what'll it take to recognize this young woman in that manner?"

Dell shrunk into her seat even further. She didn't want anyone to know she never finished school—and now Francie wants her to go back.

Jefferson nodded. "A good argument, and I think Miss Dell would deserve all of that, if it were mine to give. What I can do, is ask the people I know, who may be more cognizant than I am about available scholarships, and I can put in a good word for her from this office."

Blue Dove stood. "There are State Justice Department scholarships available in this state, for talented students who want a career in law enforcement. With the endorsement of all present, Dell would be an excellent candidate for one of those scholarships. The only catch would be that they are for criminal justice studies, not for English or art majors." Her mouth turned downward.

Martin stood. "There is a great criminal justice program at University Center in Sioux Falls, where I teach classes. I know several of the lecturers there and could help grease the wheels, if needed." He looked at Dell, slumping in her chair. "And, should Dell be willing to take hold of this opportunity."

Dell just wanted to go ride Jonny.

They left the sheriff at his office, and with Martin driving, headed back toward the Parker Ranch. Warner had cautioned them that the man who was after Dell could only be held until tomorrow. His charge was simple assault, and unknown attorneys had bailed him out.

So, he would be free tomorrow, Dell was thinking. Did that mean that he would come after her again? She hoped so. Because it was the only way she would have an opportunity to be rid of him. Savior had to die. But she couldn't just go out there and kill him, could she? It had to be self-defense. *So the sooner, the better,* she thought! Maddis said she needed a plan. Well this would be her plan. Wait for him to come get her, and get him first!

The boys were still up when they arrived. Jimmy and Donnie

both rushed toward Dell, giving hugs and asking questions. Panda danced around like it was someone's birthday!

"You went to Chicago? Did you get to fight anybody?" This from Donnie.

Jimmy had questions as well. "Did they hurt you, Dell? How come you're so late? Were you scared?"

Dell took them both in her arms, and they twirled around. "I'm back! That's enough for now. Now tell me about the horses—did Jonny miss me? Is Lady getting fat?"

"Gad, you should see what I found yesterday by the lake..."

"There's a turtle in the watering trough!"

Chapter 32

Dell peered into the murky water of the trough. "I think I see him!"

Donnie held a dog biscuit over the tank. "I can get him to come closer—watch!" He dropped the morsel into the middle. A large muddy looking form appeared at the surface for an instant, then was gone in a splash.

"Wow, is he ugly." Dell pulled her head away from the surface of the eight foot oval tank.

Jimmy laughed. "Better not get too close—it's a snapping turtle."

"Do they bite?"

Donnie answered. "They'll take your hand off if you're too slow."

Dell backed up a foot. "How'd that thing get in there? It can't climb up the walls can it?"

Jimmy thought on this. "I don't think so—but it must have done something."

Donnie rubbed his hands together and whispered loudly. "It's supernatural!"

Jimmy picked up on this. "Yeah, it's like, a Ninja Turtle!"

Dell looked puzzled. "What's a Ninja Turtle?"

"You know, Teenage Mutant Ninja Turtles?" He raised his eyebrows at Dell's ignorance. "Seriously, you have to Google a lot more."

Donnie answered for her. "Ok, we know—what's Google?" He punched his brother in the shoulder as they tried to contain their mirth.

Dell screwed up her lips, pretending offense. "Having fun with the dumb kid now, I see. Is that the way gentlemen act?"

"Sorry, Dell," Jimmy answered after his laughter subsided. "We just forget that you've been, I don't know, out of it, for a long time?"

"Yah, you're the best, Dell, but sometimes it seems you're from another planet."

"I am! I'm from the planet Grunge! And we eat little boys like you after you've outlived your usefulness, so you'd better behave!" She stood on her toes, and raised her arms, trying to look fierce. Both boys turned and ran, with Dell chasing them. She tackled them in the dirt at ten yards, and had them both in headlocks, begging for mercy, after a minute of rolling around in the mud from the trough.

All three lay on the ground until Donnie sat up and pointed at Dell. "You are so dirty, you look like a girl Golem."

Not to be outdone, Dell countered, "Well you look like a wet rat that just crawled out of the sewer." She pointed at Jimmy. "And you are...very dirty." She covered her mouth to keep the laughter in.

Jimmy picked up a soft clod, and the tossing began, each ducking and tossing, until they couldn't possibly get any muddier.

When the action petered out, Dell looked around, then toward the ranch house two hundred yards away. "Maybe we should clean up for lunch."

This caused another round of contagious giggles.

When they arrived at the house, they found Francie and Marty, sipping Chardonnay on the deck. Francie spotted them and stood, looking sternly at her boys, then Dell. She didn't say a word except, "Leave your shoes outside, please." Then she sat, and resumed her interest in Marty and her wine.

The day warmed with high clouds, and temperatures hovering in the eighties. Irma served lunch outside on the back deck. She produced the usual Saturday fare, roast beef sandwiches with cheddar, lettuce, tomatoes, pickles and sliced onion. The onion optional.

The boys resisted onions, and Francie long ago gave up fighting with them about it. A frosty pitcher of lemonade stood in the center of the table, and everyone helped themselves.

Noting Marty seemed to be a regular at the table, Jimmy and Donnie figured him fair game. When trying to enlist Dell in a series of secret signals out of the man's view, they found she had turned serious, and resisted their attention.

Marty caught on that they could not remain still. "So, some dirty shenanigans this morning, guys?" His gaze drifted from Donnie to Jimmy and back.

Jimmy answered. "What do you mean, Mister Planck?"

"Well, I noticed that you were very muddy after spending the morning in the field, and I'm wondering if you were on some kind of adventure, or if someone came along and sprayed you with dirt?"

Dell smiled, and put down her half-finished sandwich. "It's my fault, Teach. We sort of got in a tussle at the water tank." She looked at the boys. "It involved a snapping turtle, and we were lucky to get out of there alive." She devoured the rest of her sandwich.

Francie smirked. "So you were attacked by a snapping turtle and got covered with mud, but managed to escape with your lives—how resourceful. I'm glad you all made it back in one piece."

Dell changed the subject, after gulping down the last bit of roast. "Francie, Mister Planck—I need to talk to you about school." Martin and Francie exchanged glances at the formality, simultaneously catching on that she was no longer joking around.

"You know, I have been getting more clues lately about how clueless I really am when it comes to knowing stuff." She threw a glance at the boys, then turned again to her empty plate. "And I'm wondering if there's a chance that I can catch up somehow. Maybe there are some special classes I can take for dummies, or something."

Francie squinted in thought. "Dell, sweetie. Don't sell yourself short—you are no dummy. That's why I brought up the subject of schooling yesterday. I think that would be a good next step."

Jimmie added, "There's a lot of stuff you don't know, Dell, but you know a heck of a lot about stuff we have never even thought of."

Donnie added. "Yeah, like jujitsu and stuff."

"And Dell," Martin put in, "there is a difference between being dumb and not knowing about things. I think we have been around you enough to know that you're very adept at picking things up. What I mean is, if you are interested in something, you learn it very quickly."

"So, how do I get caught up? I want to know things. Like Peter Pan, you know! I didn't know that name until I googled it—the boy who took kids to Neverland, where he promised they would never have to grow up."

She looked at Jimmy. "Yeah, I found out about Google when Francie lent me a phone at the mall." She smiled to herself. "If I spent all my time going on Google, I could probably catch up, real fast."

Francie remarked, "If you spent all your time on Google, you wouldn't have much of a life."

Dell frowned, but refrained from saying that she didn't have much of a life anyway, up to now.

Jimmy finished his sandwich, and turned to his brother. "Just one more day before school starts, again. So we'd better go work with the horses some."

They understood that meant 'let's go riding', so after bussing and rinsing their dishes, they grabbed hats and clambered out the door.

Francine looked fondly after them, and turned to Martin. "They are having such a good time these days. I think Dell has been a very positive force in our lives."

Martin scratched the back of his head. "She is a force, alright. And I'd hate to think what might have happened this week if she wasn't around. We can't depend on her fighting bad guys all the time to keep her busy, though, so I think this school thing is past overdue."

Francie agreed. "And she seems to be warming to the idea of school, but I think dropping her into high school, with all the dynamics going on there, is not the right answer, at least, not right away."

"Agreed, and that's why I think your scholarship idea is a good one. I think we can get a special curriculum planned for her at the college level, designed to catch her up, and be a challenge as well. I'll start the ball rolling on Monday, by talking to the UC administrators and counselors there. Meanwhile, you can have the sheriff introduce you to some of the state people who might be open to a scholarship plan for the expenses. See if he'll talk to that DCI woman, who came up with the idea of DOJ money."

Francie looked out to where the horses were voicing their excitement. "That sounds like a good place to start. If things work like they should, we could have her enrolled in a month, when the summer session starts."

Martin was pensive, resting his chin on his hand. "So, I have to be back on Monday, but we still have tomorrow, if you would like to spend it with me exploring various extracurricular activities."

Francie fluttered eyelids and smiled girlishly. "Let me check my calendar...oh, and while I'm at it, I think I'll give Irma the rest of the day off."

Chapter 33

That evening, when the house was quiet, Dell and the boys conferred quietly in the living area. Donnie kept looking upstairs to see if they were being observed. Their mother had gone up with Martin. Donnie could only speculate how this new development would affect their routine. Theoretically, the idea of Francine having a boyfriend was thought to be long overdue. However, the reality proved a bit unsettling. The bedroom door, traditionally always kept open, now stood closed. Francie had instructed the young people to settle any problem or incident that might arise on their own, excepting what she might term the direst of emergencies. Until breakfast.

Dell said, "You need to be here for your mother, guys. This is something I have to do. If something goes wrong, you have your instructions. Remember what we talked about?"

Jimmy answered, as he picked dirt from his nails. "You'll be down by the corner fence past the road. We flash three times every hour to make sure you're okay. We stand two-hour watches, so one of us will be up at the right time. If you don't flash back, we wake Mom and call the sheriff."

Donnie looked puzzled. "How will we know you just didn't fall asleep?"

"Because I'll have the phone alarm, OK? Look, chances are these guys are done with me and all we'll lose is a little bit of sleep."

"What are you going to do if they sneak up on you?" This from Jimmy, who still looked dubious.

"They are not going to sneak up on me because they won't know I'm out there. And besides, they are big city dorks who will be crashing around in the bushes like gorillas. We'll do this just tonight, 'cause I've got a feeling that if they do show, it'll be tonight."

Donnie yawned. "Why tonight?"

Jimmy looked at his brother. "Because tomorrow is Sunday night, and nobody does anything on Sunday night when they have to get up Monday. Get it?"

Dell made herself comfortable in the darkness. The crickets and cicadas had picked up again, after going quiet when she first settled in. She leaned against a fence post, her neck cushioned by a pillow she had brought. She also carried the HK semi-auto pistol, retrieved from under the mattress where she had hidden it before flying to Chicago. The pistol rested in her lap, a round chambered, with safety on. She had a clear view to the house, a hundred yards away. The night sky shone brilliant, black punctured by millions of bright pinholes. She had never witnessed anything like it in the city. Back then, an occasional bright prick of light would emerge above the skyline, and maybe she would make out three stars in a triangle, but never anything like this! Fascinated, she tried to find the patterns. When her phone beeped, she waited for flashes from the house. There they were, a comforting acknowledgement that she was not doing this alone. She flashed three times back, and settled in for another hour of solitude.

Her phone beeped again, bringing her out of semi-consciousness. She saw three flashes, and returned the signal. She chastised herself for falling asleep. Anything could have happened in that time. She pinched her breast. *Ow! Don't do that again.* She scooted up straighter and made a game of deciding which stars were really stars, and which were planets. She knew the planets were supposed to be brighter and wouldn't twinkle like the stars. She had read that to be really sure, you had to look at them night after night, and see which ones moved in relation to their background. If they moved, they were planets, orbiting around the sun just like the earth was. But you couldn't see them move in just one night, because they were going so slow. Just like this night.

She found herself wishing she was lying in her soft, warm

bed, with nothing on her mind except when breakfast would be served. Her phone beeped again. She looked for the flashes, and there they were. She returned them in kind, and considered the pistol in her lap. If you cycle it by pulling on the slide, a bullet is moved into the chamber and the gun is cocked. But if you just pull back the hammer, it will be ready to fire, but there won't be a round in the chamber and it can't be shot. So it takes some practice to get the weapon ready, especially if you're using it for the first time. She learned this the hard way a long time ago, and it was something one could not forget, if the gun was to be reliable. A crucial lesson, that—the person most familiar with their weapon had the advantage.

Savior would come, she told herself. They released him today, and she knew him. He always took immediate action. He never forgot an insult, and he would view running away like she did the most unforgivable action she could have taken.

Others had tried in the past, and Dell always heard about the unfortunate accidents that cut short their lives. Like poor Lupe, who had fled her country, El Salvador, somewhere below Mexico, only to end up in Savior's snare. She knew she didn't have to end up trading sex for money, when she could work in an office or a hospital. So she walked out, contacting some organization that promised to help. Only she never got that far. She was found with her throat cut in an alley, and the police didn't know who she was, so they moved on. Savior was never suspected, but Dell knew. And she knew that it would not happen to her, or anyone she cared about, ever again.

What was that?

Dell sensed something different in the air. The crickets and cicadas had stopped talking again. A slight breeze blew the odor of gas fumes across her nose. A soft whirring over there, then the crunch of something heavy, rolling on gravel. All her senses were on full alert. She rechecked the pistol in her lap, and slowly moved from sitting to a crouch.

The gravel crunching continued, then she caught sight of a dark vehicle, rolling up the drive. She was right! This bastard could not control himself—he knew where she was, and he was coming to get her. She originally thought his plan would be to cut off any power to the house, then enter and make a quiet search, but he wouldn't be that dumb. Before he found her, someone would wake and the whole house would be alerted. So then she decided his only option would be to kill everyone in the house, before they knew what was happening. That would mean a bomb, or a fire. Probably a fire, because it could be made to look accidental—at least an idiot would think so.

She kept still, straining to detect other signs of something unusual. Not wanting to be surprised by tricky stuff, she listened. Soon other subtle sounds and smells crept into her hyperaware senses. Savior had brought a back-up team! Unknown numbers. Dell would concentrate on the second vehicle. It should be disabled first, so as not to alert the folks in the first unit.

The car moved very slowly. She kept pace at a distance as it rolled through the brilliant dark. Two people sat in the front. *Not too much trouble.*

She loped along the drive to the back of the car, a cottonwood cudgel in her hand, and delivered one swift blow to the trunk, then rolled aside, into the tall grass. The vehicle suddenly stopped with a squeak of springs and doors flew open. Two dark figures emerged, looking to the rear, weapons in hand.

Dell waited for them to get close and heard rustling beside her. She turned her head slowly to the sound. A large black snake was uncoiling next to her face. Without thinking, she grabbed the creature behind its narrow, yellow head, causing it to hiss and snap its mouth as it coiled around her arm. She rolled to her feet, shuddered, and hurled the animal at the backs of the two men.

One of them yelled in surprise when the five foot long snake slapped his shoulders. It quickly plunged to the ground, and slithered away through the grass. The man continued twirling in a panic, as his companion tried to see what had attacked them.

Thus distracted, they missed the slim figure in dark clothing rushing toward them until it was too late. A hop, a flying leg, and a round-about boot to the side of the face announced Dell's presence. The man's head ricocheted with a sharp crack into that of his nearby companion, and they both toppled like timber struck by lightning.

The first vehicle, an SUV, had stopped near the house. Dell slinked toward the driver's side, then crouched in the grass, waiting. The car stood idling, apparently waiting for some signal. Nothing happened. It seemed an eternity, when the engine stopped. Then, four doors opened simultaneously and one person emerged. The man shifted his gaze warily, jerking his head from side to side as he made his way toward the back of the car. The rear hatch popped open. The figure withdrew a large container, which appeared to be a five-gallon gas can and, by the way he strained, it seemed full.

Dell wanted to be sure, but there was no way to gauge one hundred percent if this was the threat she thought it to be. Okay, there was the following car, which she had already dealt with, so in all probability this was not a late-night delivery to the ranch house that Francie had neglected to tell her about.

What was wrong with her? She was second-guessing herself at every step. Was she losing it? Or was it something else, something one of those cops had planted in her brain? She was listening to too much bad advice. Just do what is needed!

The answer came when the dark figure began emptying the gas can next to the house.

Dell didn't bother to shout a warning. She stood up, and with both hands steadying her sight, she aimed at the animated figure, then squeezed the trigger. The gun jerked twice. Both bullets hit the target, dropping the man with the can. The reports reverberated, destroying the peace of the night. As she dove into a roll, the air burst into gunfire, several bullets impotently kicking up dirt where her shadow had stood a few seconds ago. Doors slammed and the idling vehicle lurched into motion, wheels spinning in gravel.

Dell pulled the trigger countless times more, loud missiles barking at the car, until it swerved out of control and crashed headlong into a nearby Cottonwood.

Lights came on in the house.

The girl cautiously approached the smoldering SUV, pistol still ready in a two-fisted grip. Unseen hands pushed open doors with groans of protest. A man wrenched himself from the rear door nearest Dell. As he struggled to raise his pistol, Dell shot him between the eyes. The bullet jerked his head backward in a spray of dark mist.

On the other side of the cab, a figure emerged and Dell swung around to confront him. It was Savior. He was attempting to pull a gun that snagged in his belt.

"Couldn't leave it alone, could you? We're done!" Dell's rage turned her snarl into a scream as she aimed her pistol and pulled the trigger.

Click. Glancing at the breech, she saw it was open—no more bullets.

Savior grinned, blood dripping from a cut on his forehead. "Oh, you changed your mind. Well, I don't want you back now, you bitch!" He raised the weapon he had managed to drag from his waistband, and aimed carefully.

"Goodbye..."

She squeezed her eyes shut, feeling suddenly empty. This man who had taken her childhood was now going to take her very life. She tried to think of something that mattered to carry with her to whatever or wherever nothingness she would end up in, and all she could think of was the life she had here, with Francie and the boys, and Jonny and Lady, and Panda, and that damn snapping turtle. Her ears roared from the gunfire, but she thought she heard murmuring.

"That's enough, now."

Her eyes flew open!

Savior's hands were being cuffed behind his back by the Stanley County Sheriff. A scowl creased the criminal's face, as

Deputy Daniels pointed his service revolver at his head. Martin Planck stood to one side loosely holding a shotgun. Francie waited on the porch, her arms around her pajama clad boys.

Sheriff Warner gently took the empty pistol from Dell's lax fingers. "We're all done here, young lady. Let's get yourself inside."

Dell floated, as if from too much coffee and too little sleep. "How come you're here, Sheriff?" She smiled a little. "I mean, not that I'm unhappy about it."

"Oh, we headed out here soon as Francie found the boys flashing signals at you. Figured something serious was up. Put two and two together, like the excellent lawmen that we are. Rolled in right as you started shooting."

Martin put his hand on her shoulder. "Vern will take care of this mess. Don't know about you, but I've had enough excitement for tonight, so let's get you kids to bed."

Francine arched her eyebrows at Martin as she embraced Dell, who was beginning to shake. "Sweetie, I think you can rest easy now. Is there anything I can get you?"

Dell looked at Francie for a long moment, then her gaze fell. "You can get me that last bullet."

Jimmy looked at her sheepishly. "Mom said to keep watching for you, like we arranged, but she called the Sheriff."

"She told him to get his butt out here again!" Donnie was wide eyed.

Francine directed her flock to, "Get to bed now and we'll talk this over in the morning."

She and Marty watched from the dining table as everyone tromped upstairs.

"Marty, I think Dell is not in a good place."

Marty reached to touch her hand. "What—do you think she's been traumatized?"

"No, it's beyond that, Marty. I think her whole life has been one large trauma after another, and this fiend coming after her hasn't helped balance things for her. I don't think she will ever feel at peace without some sort of resolution with this guy."

"Well, the sheriff seems to think that they have him on pretty solid ground to put him away for a long time. It's not just assault this time. It's attempted murder, arson, conspiracy to commit mayhem, and lying in wait. I don't think he's going to wiggle out of this one!"

Francine nodded indulgently. "That may be true enough. And it may satisfy the justice system, but Dell is not going to be able to let her guard down. There will always be a part of her on the edge."

"Maybe that's a good thing. I can't picture her hanging out in the mall with friends, but I can picture her focused on some trajectory to bring some happiness or fulfillment to her life in the future. I think going after criminals in a professional capacity, as opposed to a futile chase after one elusive character, just might bring her closer to self-realization."

"That may be true, eventually, Marty, but let's be real—she killed two people tonight, and she was prepared to shoot a third, wanted to shoot him! That means to me, that a lot of healing has to be accomplished before any competent decisions about life goals can be made. I think she has to stay away from any conflicts or involvement with criminals for a long while."

Marty stroked his chin. "I'm sure you are on the right track, Francie, but the details of what you're proposing are crucial. The whole thing depends on what Dell may think about our suggestions. If we can offer alternatives that she'll find attractive, then she may be able to find her own path, without putting up a fight. That's why I think college courses in criminal justice will get her moving in the direction she wants to go. And she'll be dealing with these bad guys on a safe, theoretical basis only. At least, for a while."

Francine was soon won over. "You're right, she is a fighter. And to put her on a plane above street level probably is good policy. So how do we get started?"

"Let's go into that tomorrow—right now all I can think about is how good it feels to be in a particular bed upstairs—for sleeping purposes only, of course."

"Of course," Francie agreed, with a sly grin.

Chapter 34

The rest of that night was wasted on Dell. She lay in her bed, wondering if sleep would ever come again. Maybe Savior was going to jail, but he would still be out there and someday he would be back for her. She would always have to watch her back and worry about those people she now cared about dearly.

She agonized over staying put or moving on. To leave would be devastating and would take all the courage she could muster. But she had to decide, and she had to be resolute.

If she stayed, her friends would be in jeopardy. If she left, she would be running the rest of her life, until something or someone brought her down, *like a deer in hunting season—just a matter of time. Or,* she thought, *more like a bear. Because I will not go down easy.*

She needed help with this decision, but who could she talk to? Who would not have a stake in whether she stays or goes? Francie's advice would be predictable. She would say that together we can support one another and not be afraid of anything.

The Teach would be just as supportive. He would go along with whatever Francie says, and would try to get her into some program or another, to give her credentials in whatever future she might choose to pursue.

The boys...well they haven't really had a lot of experience, so they would want her to stick around just because they like her, but would understand if she chose to leave because she had to. Not much counsel, though.

But, what about Sheriff Warner? He doesn't have an emotional attachment to her, and yet knows her pretty well. She thought about the sheriff. *I guess he has come to like me well enough and respect what I can do, but he won't really be sad to see the back of me. He knows what's going on pretty much, so he might be just the person I can get some straight answers from. God, why'd it have to be a cop that I'm thinking of trusting my future with?*

So, Dell caught some sleep. When she awoke, a few hours later on Sunday morning, she dressed and took the stairs two at a time. She found Francie at the kitchen stove, putting on water to boil.

"You're up early, sweetie. Couldn't sleep?" She eyed the girl's disheveled demeanor, and made the obvious conclusion.

"No, I slept great, Francie. I guess I was in a hurry to get down here." She moved to the stove. "Is it too much to ask? Could I talk to the sheriff today? I need to ask him questions that only he can answer." She pleaded with her eyes. "Can you get me in to see him?"

"But he was just here, Dell. He's probably sleeping it off today. Can't this wait?"

Dell yawned. "Yah. I guess it can wait a few more hours. I just need to talk to someone who doesn't really care about me. I would talk to you, but I know what you're going to say. You understand? I think I know what your boyfriend will tell me, too. So that's no use."

"Sounds ominous. What is it, sweetie?"

The girl flopped into a chair. "It's just my whole life!"

Francine stepped back from the stove, and studied her. "So, you know me that well? Wait...if you know what we are going to tell you, then does that mean you don't want to listen to what we'll say?"

Dell crooked her lips. "Don't put it that way, Francie. Of course, I'll listen! I just want a second opinion, Okay?"

"So, what I tell you—and what Martin says—will be essentially the same thing, you think?"

"Of course! It's the viewpoint. And I need a different one. Can you understand that I am really, really screwed up here?" She took a deep breath and her bottom lip trembled. Francie could see that she was facing a real dilemma, although she hadn't a clue what it might be.

"Look, Dell. We're going into town today, just like on a normal Sunday, and you're welcome to come with us. So before we go, we'll give Vern a call, and see if he'll agree to meet up with us at some point. Will that be okay?"

"I guess that will be all right, but tell him it's important, okay?"

Martin had declined to make the Sunday ritual, giving the excuse that he had family business to catch up on. Francie and the boys would attend church after dropping Dell near the mall as she requested. "The sheriff has agreed to meet with you at two o'clock, at Memorial Park on the waterfront. Do you want us to pick you up at the mall after church?"

"No thanks, Francie. I can be at the park by two—it's not like I have a lot of other appointments to keep. And I don't think this'll take more than an hour, so if you could get me there at three, I would be grateful."

"Fine, three it is, then. And please stay safe, Dell."

Dell threw her a shrug, pivoted and strode away toward the mall. She had other business before meeting with the sheriff, and she had time. She noticed not many people were about on a Sunday. Most of those she saw appeared ragged or homeless. Many were on bikes, usually dressed inappropriately for the sport, and always ignoring traffic laws. She didn't care, as long as they stayed away from her.

She guessed that those who had homes were in them this morning, or in their cars. Or maybe at Church, like Francie and the boys. *Some churches made room for the homeless, but many were just for the well-off,* she thought. And she could see how people needed to get together somehow. It wasn't like the big city here, where everyone was out on the sidewalk night or day, going to some rendezvous or just hanging.

She knew that she could never be a church person. Most people there would not like to be around her, once they found out what kind of life she had. That's what made Francie so puzzling. She was a church-goer, yet she didn't judge her at all. She just expected her, or anyone for that matter, to treat her with honesty and respect. Didn't require or demand it, just expected it. That's why she was so easy to love.

Dell had walked straight down to the gully in the open space area behind the mall. She was hoping to see Pan again and wondered if he had returned or was gone for good. She clambered down into the bushes, checking every disturbance or pile of debris for signs of habitation.

Rounding a large growth of thick Lilac, she halted. Thirty yards away was a flash of bright orange, partially obscured by a gray covered bin, which appeared to be a cargo container. A metal container, the kind they load onto ships to carry stuff across Lake Michigan. The only lake around here was Lake Oahe, and she didn't think there were large container ships running up and down there at all.

As she approached, a movement caught her eye. A huge black man with a bush of kinky, ruddy hair fiddled with a stick. Pan!

He sat in a camp chair and picked at his boot before looking up. "You came again, still with a bad nose."

Dell reflexively touched her face, where the bruising hadn't yet faded. "I was back here a couple days ago, and you had gone."

Pan just looked blank.

"What happened?"

"Too many cops. They never leave me alone. So I leave until they are tired of looking."

"Well, I'm glad you're back. I need some...advice." Her eyes wandered over the site, as she sought a place to sit. "I need to know what to do about my future."

Pan examined his shoe again. "Future. There is no future, only now."

She settled on an overturned paint bucket. "Come on, Pan! I'm really trying to decide on what I'm going to do in the next day or week. I am looking for all the help I can get."

Pan bobbed his head around, then looked Dell in the eyes. "Did you fly? I knew you would fly, you bet. When you fly, I fly, and dodge police. That's the way things work. You go. Then I go, second star on the right. I'm back, now."

Dell glanced up, but it was mid-afternoon, and hard to visualize stars. "I've seen a million stars out here at night."

Pan grinned. "Right—so hard to choose. Maybe, sometime, you come at night again, and we can look for the good ones."

"That would be nice. But, Pan. I have a decision to make, and I think you can help."

"Decisions. Not so good at those. But we'll see, and decide later. What do you need to see?"

She crossed and uncrossed her legs, settling in. "Well, I'm kind of a magnet for trouble, as you might know. And, I don't want to get the people I care about hurt in any way. So, what I'm thinking is, maybe I should move on, and just keep dodging trouble from now on. Or, should I stay and try to keep those close to me from harm, even though they'll be in danger because of me?"

Pan looked confused. "I'm thinking, you are leaving, then people will be okay? That's not right. Trouble comes. It doesn't look for you, it just comes. That's the way it's always been. Trouble is trouble. You can't help, if you're not there. You have someone? You stay, in case there's trouble."

Dell digested this. "I get it. So if I stay, I can help, but if I'm gone, then I can't, and things will be bad anyway. So, you don't think I'm a trouble magnet?"

Pan grinned. "Hah! Magical thinking. You maybe are a witch?"

"No, of course not! How 'bout this, then—lots of people are saying I should become a cop, that I would make a good cop?" She stated it as a question, unsure of the concept.

Pan frowned. "No! You could not be a cop. Cops are ugly. And tricky, heh, heh. They are unfeeling. You could never be a cop."

"So, that's not a good idea?"

Pan reconsidered. "Wait, maybe...you could be a pretty cop. Might be nice to have a cop friend. I could stay here instead of run all the time. Maybe you should be a cop, and tell all those other cops that...'this is not the one you're looking for'..."

"You think I'm pretty?"

Pan squinted and cradled his chin in his hand, appraising her. "More so than most cops. If you were a cop, you'd be the prettiest one."

"So I'm not ugly, but I might still make a good cop because I'm tricky and unfeeling?"

"I think you are feeling. You are the most feeling person I know. You could be very tricky, and pretend to be unfeeling. You are tricky enough, I think."

Dell liked the idea that she was tricky. She'd just never thought about herself, and the various ploys of survival she'd used in that way. *Tricky Dell Louise,* she mused, and immediately pinched herself for the self-indulgence. *Stay alert,* she thought, looking around just in case.

The large cargo container drew her attention, looming near the campsite.

She pointed at the object. "What's that?"

Pan caught her movement and slowly followed the line indicated. "Ah. You found my secret. We have to keep it secret." A mischievous grin spread across his face. "That's where I keep the treasure."

Dell tilted her head to see if the box would change at a different angle, but it remained there, occupying a significant amount of space. "That is not a secret. It's too big for a secret."

Pan stopped grinning. "It's the treasure that's a secret."

"You keep treasure there? What kind of treasure?" A wild thought flittered by, about pirates leaving their treasure here for Pan to find.

"Don't know what kind—it's a secret."

Dell was losing patience. "You mean it's a secret, even from you? Well, how do you know if it's treasure? There could be garbage in there, if you've never seen it."

Pan's grin re-appeared. "Nobody would put such a big lock on the door, if it was garbage! Look!" He stepped to the front of the container, and lifted a lock in his hand that was as big as a toaster. "See. It's treasure."

The logic was impeccable. Dell, however, was not satisfied with the conclusion. "So, that is not your lock, I take it?"

Pan just stared at her, blankly.

"Stupid question. Okay, did you see how this got here, or who left it?"

Pan continued to stare.

"Right." Her gaze drifted beyond the box, as she looked for some clue pointing to its origin. She moved around to the back of the container, which was about twelve feet in length, and as high as she could reach. Heat seemed to be radiating from the metal, and when she placed her palm there, it was immediately withdrawn, as if of its own volition. The thing was hot. Probably from sitting in the sunlight all day, she thought.

Broken juniper and greasewood shrubs marked its path to the spot, and when Dell examined the area closely, she discovered deep tire tracks. Large tracks—something bigger than an ordinary truck.

She turned again to Pan, who had taken his seat back near his tent. "Somebody brought this here to get rid of it. Probably would be too expensive to take it to the dump."

A be-bop tune sounded on her phone, reminding her of the appointment with Sheriff Vern. "Pan, I have to go, but I need to tell someone about this box. It may not be the treasure you hoped it would be, and it may even be dangerous. I'm sorry, but they will probably be coming here to look."

Pan coughed, turned away, and spat. A smile crawled up his face. "How much you give me for it then?"

Chapter 35

It took Dell a half hour to walk the three miles or so to Steamboat Memorial Park where she was to meet the sheriff. The Stanley County SUV was parked conspicuously in the lot near the Memorial Building when she rounded the corner. She knew he had probably arrived way early so he would be sure to gauge her arrival. She strode to the vehicle, pulled open the passenger door, and slid in.

Sheriff Warner eyed her up and down, then peered forward through the windshield. "You gave me a start, young lady. How're you doing?"

Her face turned toward the Sheriff, and she drilled him with a steady gaze. "Thank you for meeting me, Vern." She turned to look out the window to the distant river, where his attention had been fixated. "I feel we know each other enough for you to give me some good advice. It has to do with everyone around us, so I think you will maybe feel connected, and tell me truthfully what to do."

Warner was immediately intrigued with what this remarkable girl might need his advice on, and just nodded. "Go on."

Dell braced herself. "Okay. First, there is something going on that is entirely unrelated, but you, or somebody in charge here, in Pierre, might want to investigate further." She looked at him again, then turned back to the window. "A large, mysterious container has appeared in the gully behind the mall, about three miles from here. I think someone should be sent to investigate."

"A large container? How large?"

"Well, it's probably big enough for a couple of cars, one on top of another. And the reason I think it should be looked into is because, number one, it wasn't there last week. Number two, it couldn't have been just thrown off a truck. And number three, it is locked with a very intimidating piece of hardware, that no one could ever be expected to crack open unless they were trying very, very hard, and possessed all the right tools, of course. Or maybe explosives."

Warner furrowed his brow in thought, while Dell continued. "I was down there looking, and to me, it seemed like a large equipment hauler had dumped it there. There were signs that this big truck, or whatever, had come off Dry Creek Street, behind the mall."

She shifted position, bringing her arms around her knee, then resting her head to look at him sideways. "Just in case you want to notify someone."

A slow grin spread across his face. "You have to know that I'm going to ask how you just happened to be 'down there looking'."

Dell straightened, dropped her leg, and sat back in the seat. "I'm thinking that is likely going to take this conversation along a whole new path, and it doesn't really matter, anyway."

Warner opened his mouth to react, but didn't get the chance, as Dell blurted, "Okay! I was there to see a friend. He's kinda strange, and spooks easily, but he's a good person. I've told him someone might be coming around, so he won't be there anyway. Besides, I've less than an hour here, and haven't even got to what I need to talk to you about."

The Sheriff digested this, then relaxed. "Okay, young lady. I'm all ears."

"All right. Thank you for coming. Here's the deal. I can't talk to Francie about this, 'cause I already have her answer in my head, so I'm talking to you because I think maybe you can be more...objective. Is that right?"

"I am the picture of objectivity, if that's what you need."

"Okay. Here goes. I am a trouble magnet. I've made friends here, and I don't want them to be endangered..."

"By your magnetism?" Warner couldn't resist.

Dell tightened her lips. "I'm serious. I don't want my friends to get hurt by my being around them. So as far as I can tell, I have two choices. Leave, so the bad things that follow me will not affect them." She gave Warner a small smile. "You, even. Anyway, the other choice is to stay and figure out a way to stop this stuff from happening so everyone will be safe, and I can start to live like a normal person."

Warner waited. "Is that it?"

"No, it's not a simple question. If I go, then I am really going to keep on going and going, because I can't stay and be with people and develop attachments, only to have them be targeted because of me. I will have to keep running forever."

"Or until your time runs out, which may be sooner than that."

"Yeah, but if I stay, stay here, with everybody, it won't be happily ever after. Not like in the stories. I'll have to figure out a way to keep everybody safe."

Warner stroked his chin. "Listen, young...Dell. Listen carefully. You already are keeping people safe. We just happen to be those people and we are grateful you are here. Now, as for being a trouble magnet, as you put it—well, I don't think you are a magnet as much as a finder. You find trouble. Like this big bin you want us to look at. You are just out there, girl. If there is trouble around, that's because it's always around but no one else notices. You are tuned to it—you see the difference? We need you, hell, anybody would need you to be on their side, but you are here and we sure as hell don't want you to leave!" He pointed his index finger straight to her sternum. "Now, I know for a fact girl, that you don't run from trouble. So I can't figure why you are thinking about it now. Fact is, we have kind of grown used to you around here and, although I know some federal law enforcement folks who may argue, you have come to be one of our secret assets here in the heartland."

Dell started to respond, but Warner's finger spread to a blocking hand. "Wait, before you say anything, listen. I, for one, do not want to keep your presence a secret for us to hide from the world. Absolutely not. I think what needs to happen now is for you to commit yourself to further studies in fields of knowledge that you may not be familiar with so that you can be cognizant of what makes everything tick. Including yourself. Haven't you asked yourself why you do certain things, or react certain ways to what people say or do? There's a world of people out there who have studied those very questions, girl, and you should chase after them."

Dell remained silent for a bit. Then, "You sound just like the Teach. I really don't know much about anything. I mean, I can read and do arithmetic and all, but there is so much I don't know, that I wouldn't know where to start." Her eyes began to mist, as she tried to gain control of the emotions welling up. "Sometimes I feel so out of it, I could scream!"

Warner smiled indulgently. "So, I'm guessing not too much attention was paid to your schooling when you were growing up."

"You got that right. I was on my own a lot. When I did learn something, it was because I was interested in it. Taught myself to read with picture books. Learned a lot about horses that way." Her expression relaxed with the recollection. "Then I started reading everything I could find, but a lot of that just didn't make any sense, except when I was able to figure out a word here and there, then it was like victory. But learning words is not the same as learning stuff. I wish I could know things—things like you were talking about. What would I have to study to figure people out? I mean, right now, I just know good people from the bad ones, but it couldn't be that simple, could it?"

Warner could hardly believe this girl didn't understand how much she really knew about people. He tried to make it simple. "I believe, Dell, that you are really good at reading people. You couldn't have lasted this long without knowing what people were going to do before they do it. Reading people is understanding who they are, and how they will react in any situation, without having to think about it. You just know, like you knew I was going to keep my word and meet out here with you. The same way you knew Francie was a person who would offer you a safe haven. Also, you can judge when talking is no good anymore, and the only way to get people to behave is to challenge them. Or stop them, when that becomes necessary. Also, there are different kinds of learning—that which deals in abstractions, and that which teaches the body various skills and physical reactions. Now, you're really good at physical skills, but combat, which you excel in, is just one of many physical skills that can bring you satisfaction."

Dell was getting mixed up. "Okay, stop! What are abstractions?"

"Well, I guess those are things that exist only in your mind, which may or may not correspond to real things outside your head."

"Oh—like dreaming. I'm good with that."

"That's part of it, yes—dreaming, day-dreams. Then there is mathematics—you know, arithmetic. You play with the abstractions to eventually solve physical problems. A simple example—you want to move a chair into another room. Will it fit through the door? You measure the chair with your arms. Then you measure the door. Whoa, this door is way too small! You didn't just try to stuff the chair through right off the bat, and get frustrated. You were using your head, using abstractions."

"You'd have to be pretty dumb."

"That's right, and because you are smart, you know this. You use abstractions without even thinking, like when you are fighting, and you swing your leg around and connect with the guy's jaw. You are calculating timing and distance in a split second. You probably have practiced it so often, that your head is no longer involved. What I'm trying to tell you is you are smart enough to find out about things that you need to know, or that interest you. You just have to go for it. And I know people who are more than happy to help you get started."

Dell stretched her arms, and straightened her legs up, placing her feet on the dash of the vehicle. She spoke to the rearview mirror. "Do you think I could ever become a cop?"

Warner pursed his lips. "Depends. Cops, or law enforcement officers, as we like to call them, don't just clobber bad guys. We also try to mediate disputes peacefully, which is the best way. We try to stop any violence from happening before it starts. We help people in distress, or in need of rescue. We make sure people are following the law, and we fine or punish those who ignore or disobey laws. We also investigate criminal or suspected criminal activity, and through research, knocking on doors, interrogation and observation, try to determine who did what crime, and whether or not there is a victim or victims."

Dell brushed a lock out of her face. "How could there ever be a crime if there aren't any victims? Why would you arrest someone if they weren't stealing from a person, or hurting someone in some way?"

Warner responded patiently. "Well, it's like this. People break laws all the time and don't hurt anyone, just because they are lucky. Those laws are designed to protect people, like traffic laws, for instance. If someone runs a red light, that is a crime, even if no one is hurt. It would be a greater crime still, if they crashed into another car or pedestrian. See what I mean?"

"What if someone was waiting at a red light late at night and no cars were coming, and the light didn't change to green? If I drove through that light when I could see no one would be hurt, because there was nobody there...would I still be breaking the law?"

"Good question. That's where the training and judgment of a law officer comes into play. You could be ticketed because you ignored the red light, or the cop could let you go with a warning. If you were ticketed, you would be able to contest it in court, since questions like that fall into a gray area. Disputes like that are gradually changing the laws all over the country."

"That's just stupid. Any driver should be able to go through a red light, if there is no danger in doing it."

"You have the right to hold that opinion and you can work to change the law, but if you are a cop, you aren't hired to do

that. You are there to see that everyone is toeing the line."
Dell's old ire against cops bubbled to the surface. "So you tell people what to do even if they don't want to do it, like you know their situation better than they do."

"Everything's a judgment call, Dell. A lot of times there are questions, but in many cases, decisions have to be made in a fraction of a second. Sometimes those decisions are wrong and, that being the case, there are usually consequences for the police as well as those wronged by the police."

Dell looked skeptical. "You mean 'sometimes' there are consequences. I've seen cops beating up on people for no reason other than they were in the wrong place, and I didn't see any cops getting in trouble for that."

Warner scratched under his chin, buying a little time. "You're right—'sometimes'. I imagine you've seen a lot of things we don't get privy to, and I can see that, once again, you're no dummy." He studied her for a hard moment. "I'm amazed at how you have kept yourself out of the hands of the law, living out there on the streets as you have for all these years."

Dell stiffened at that, and Warner quickly amended. "Not that I think you have been breaking the law, but youngsters out on the street usually come to the attention of police, sooner or later, for this or that reason."

Dell's face became stony. "You want to know the truth, I've been breaking laws for sure, but tried never to hurt anyone. Sometimes I stole things to get by, and I suppose that hurt somebody, but not much. Once I took a coat from a store because the guy didn't want us anywhere near his place, for no good reason. Besides, it was getting awfully cold then, and I didn't have a job." Her brow furrowed in recollection. "Then Savior started giving me money, and I could get some things. And I didn't really mind what he was paying me for—at least not at first. It was something I was used to. I suppose that is one of those crimes, even though no one is being hurt?"

"It is a crime, Dell. A serious one—and I think you know who the victims are."

Dell didn't have to think hard on that one, and answered, looking down at upturned palms. "The girls." She turned sad eyes to the sheriff. "But not all the girls were like me. They had no problems with what they were doing—didn't have to answer to anyone, got all the booze and drugs they wanted, and it was easy. Why is it a crime to do sex work if it's what you want to do?"

Warner just lowered his chin and lifted the brim of his hat, to eye her skeptically. "Most of those girls around your age, Dell?"

She considered. "I don't know much about anything, do I? Much less what I want to do with my life, except for not that! Those girls really have no choice about what they're doing, do they?"

"Yeah...we call that human trafficking, and that's a big crime. It is pretty much the same as slavery."

"So, I'm a victim, then?"

"Well, you were, certainly—but you were able to get yourself out of it. Most aren't able to do that and need law enforcement investigators, like the FBI and such, to arrest the perps and free those slave girls so they can find themselves happier circumstances."

Dell coughed. "Yeah, maybe, if they are lucky." She thought of Lupe and what had happened to her. "I think most of them will just go to jail, though. Don't you think?"

"Why would that be?"

"Well, 'cause by the time you get at them, they're drug addicts and whores. Most of them just get in and out of jail, on and on. Don't you think that by the time they get too old to save, you should just let them alone? Who's the victim, when they're old enough to decide for themselves who they want to be, or are satisfied being?"

Warner smiled. "You've got a point, young lady. And that's a fight that has been going on for ages. I'm sure not going to be able to give you an answer, and as a law enforcement officer, I once again have to defer to the law, as it stands today. But, I'm curious. And I'm just asking as the person trying to give you informed counsel, here—why weren't you given drugs to keep you under their control?"

Dell had no problem sharing anything with Warner at this point. "Oh, they gave me all kinds of drugs at first, but I couldn't control my dreams with drugs. I had no control at all! The dreams were all strange, and weird, and scary. So, I just hid the drugs and threw them out, or gave them to whoever wanted them, until I was back in control again. I had nothing in my life but my dream worlds, and the sex. That's what I was addicted to. After a while though, it became strange and painful. There wasn't anything good about it anymore. Too many men were always looking to hurt me. I guess I was too big and old to attract the ones who were paying good money to pop cherries, so I was given the really bad ones who were looking to do some damage. When one of those assholes wanted me to bleed, I made him bleed instead, and told myself it was time to leave this life. Now I want to help get rid of all those guys. They are going to regret meeting up with me!" She glanced over at the sheriff, looking a bit sheepish. "Sorry. Guess I can get a little preachy."

Warner stroked his mustache. "I can't fault your judgment where it concerns the bad guys, Dell, so I'm not going to caution you about being too quick on the trigger. You've shown you can make the right decisions when it counts, so I'm hoping that you'll make the right decision this time, and stay with us for a time. We really do want you to be happy and get on with your life. We'd be saddened if you were to run out on us for no good reason. You have a home here, Dell."

Once again, the girl fought to keep her emotions at bay, as tears filmed her eyes. She impulsively leaned close to the lawman and planted a kiss on his cheek, the same instant that he noticed a bright flash from the trees a hundred feet into the park.

The windshield glass shattered with a loud crunch, as a hole appeared directly in front of where Dell's head had been a second before.

Warner wrenched the door open, and rolled to the ground, Dell tumbling out with him. They scrambled around to the rear of the vehicle as another shot thumped into the open door. Warner had his service revolver out in his right hand, and reached down to retrieve another small automatic from his boot. He handed it over to Dell, as they crouched with their backs against the vehicle. As she took the weapon, the sheriff observed a trickle of blood creeping down her cheek. "Damn! That was close, girl!"

He caught a breath. "I'll take a look and see if the shooter is still there."

"Be careful!"

Warner popped his head over the top of the door, and a second later another bullet slammed into metal as he ducked back. He threw a glance at Dell, who had jumped into action when the shot was fired. He cursed under his breath as she sprinted to the nearest building, about forty feet from the parking lot. Another shot splintered wood at the edge of that building as she dived from the shooter's line of sight.

Warner could see her, however, when she signaled to him as she moved around the building. He lay prone at the side of the vehicle and, when another shot came, he threw two slugs back, with huge explosions, to where he determined the sniper to be.

Dell crept toward the sniper's position, and darted from tree to tree through the thinly forested area. Warner fired another two shots, and the sniper returned fire, aiming his long rifle toward the sheriff's SUV. As Dell came near to where she thought the sniper had to be, she was disappointed. He had slipped away. She kept to the path, eyes darting back and forth. He must have bolted, she thought, trying for the road, and a possible escape vehicle. She veered toward the edge of the park and spotted a shadowy figure, clad in a dark tee shirt, carrying a rifle. The short, dark man appeared to be breaking a trail as he crashed through the brush in front of her. Her pace increased, just as the man reached a small, tan-colored car. The rear lid lifted, and he tossed the rifle into the trunk. While in the act of closing it Dell changed his plans.

She launched herself into a twisting jump, swinging her long legs into an arc, boots adding to the momentum like a gaucho's bola, until connecting suddenly and painfully to his ribcage. The blow tossed him to the ground, but he rolled and sat up, grabbing a gun from his belt.

The weapon went flying, as Dell kicked it aside and landed butt first onto his chest, pinning flailing arms beneath her thighs, one hundred and forty pounds of downward force knocking his breath away. Holding the small automatic very close to his nose, she advised, "Stop!"

The struggling ceased, and as he tried to catch a breath, she yelled, "Sheriff! Over here!"

A small crowd began to gather, as Warner and Dell forced the handcuffed man into the SUV. He stood shorter than Dell, and his features were well covered by at least two week's growth of black hair.

As he slumped in the cage, Warner turned to Dell with fire in his eyes and growled at her. "That stunt you pulled while under fire might have gotten you, or both of us killed!"

She allowed a crooked smile. "Don't fret, Vern. I was sure, by the pattern of the shots, he was using a bolt action rifle and I had a good three or four seconds to get to the building before another shot came. It worked out okay, didn't it?"

Warner grudgingly conceded the point. "Well, you were cutting it pretty close, young lady. But okay—as long as you had a plan." He walked around the vehicle, studying the damage, then turned back to the girl. "All right, what say we get this guy back to the shop—see if we can find out who he works for, and what his gripe is."

When attempting to start the SUV, they got a loud coffeegrinder sound. Raising the hood, Warner discovered one of the fan blades had been pushed back into the water pump area, and the bullet that did it had torn through the radiator. He grimaced at Dell. "I guess we'll have to call for a tow, and," he added loudly for the benefit of the prisoner, "we're going to have to add destruction of county property to the charges."

Tires screeched as an old Ford truck rumbled into the parking lot and halted in a busy cloud. Doors slammed as Francine and the two Parker boys jumped from the vehicle. Francine took in the SUV with its hood up, and a bearded man lounging in the back cage. Jimmy and Donnie rushed up to Dell with questioning looks. Jimmy surveyed her dusty, disheveled visage and asked, "Are you okay? How come there's that blood running down your face?"

Donnie whined, "Delllll..."

Francie just shook her head. "Sundays are just like every other day now, I guess."

Chapter 36

The prisoner was a local, and they weren't able to get much from him, except that he had been carrying a lot of cash for a part-time worker. He told them his name—Steve Karamotsov, and he did occasional road work for the state. When someone approached him with a lot of money, and told him to get rid of this meddlesome orphan girl, he accepted the job happily.

An easy-in, easy-out assignment, he thought. Nobody would miss her, after all. They didn't find anything on his person to relate him to the Chicago crowd, their first area of investigation.

They charged and booked him, then put him away to await trial. Sheriff Warner had taken second on the case, in deference to the Hughes County authorities, where the attempted crime had occurred.

Hughes County Sheriff Wallace Jenkins was a 'by the book' man. He looked at the attempted assassination as an unwarranted discharge of firearms in his county. There could be no excuse for the breach of civic harmony, and if he and Sheriff Warner hadn't been well acquainted, he would have seen to it that everyone involved did at least some community service.

Warner tried to placate the guy, even inferring Dell had been appointed a special deputy, skilled at curbing this big city gangland virus spreading into the Dakotas. He told Jenkins they were hot on the trail of human traffickers out of Chicago who would stop at nothing to protect their precious properties, valued in the millions.

Jenkins remained unimpressed. He warned Vern to stay on his side of the river, and keep his dirty laundry and sleazy operations over there as well. No matter that the FBI had been involved on some level. They were meddlers, who had no business delving into the affairs of this state except where U.S. interests might be involved. And that was hardly ever.

Why, even now certain federal agencies were trying to cap

the growing uranium mining industry out here, with proposed regulations certain to guarantee a massive loss of revenue if the feds had their way. Think of it. A great alternative power source for the country and it's all right here in South Dakota. The state would not be sidetracked into any sordid human-trafficking boondoggle. Resources were scarce enough already.

Now late in the day, Francine anxiously attempted to get her brood home. School would start tomorrow, and everyone needed to get plenty of rest. *Dell has apparently finished what she needed to accomplish with the sheriff, and then some,* Francie thought. Dell looked worn out, as well, staring blankly at the wall as the two sheriffs verbally circled around each other.

"You ready to head back to the ranch, Dell? It's going to be a big day tomorrow, what with the boys off to school again. And we need to make some plans about getting you situated on a regular basis."

Carefully vague about what she thought Dell should be doing with herself, Francine knew there were still many discussions to be had with the girl before anything would be settled. Though concerned about Dell's future plans, she remained unsure how much of the conversation Dell was in on. She had to find out what the girl thought about all of it.

Warner, apparently his business finished here, joined the Parkers and Dell and he shook his head as they passed out of the stark cement slab building. "I'll never figure that guy out. Sometimes I don't even know what he's talking about."

Dell matched steps with him, as he headed for a sedan brought over the bridge to sub for the disabled official unit. "I just wanted to thank you for all your help with my problems today—you gave me a lot to consider, and I think you're awesome." She threw him a toothy smile. "But today's trouble makes it even more apparent that changes are coming, whether I want them or not."

Warner stopped shortly and turned to the girl. "You know,

young...Dell, things are never going to be ideal from day to day. We had a glitch today, but we got through it. Don't let the details spoil your momentum—you are destined for great things, and you just have to keep moving forward. And guess what? We want to be there with you, wherever the adventure takes us." He let his eyes linger on hers for a moment. "Just do us all a favor—go easy on the wild stunts, okay?"

She smiled, with eyes downcast, and turned back to Francie and the boys. "Let's go home."

Purposeful chaos reigned the next day. Irma had returned. The boys rushed to ready themselves for school. Backpacks were stuffed. Breakfasts eaten on the fly. Lunches bagged. Panda danced around like she once performed in the circus.

It was a circus, as far as Francie could see, and she the ringmaster. The boys juggled, making improbable moves while keeping impossible numbers of items in motion. Dell, the princess of the high wire, flew off to fetch needed items without tripping or falling into the abyss. Irma calmly worked around the periphery, keeping everything orderly and scheduled. Then Francie cracked her whip, putting the whole show on the road to the bus stop.

Back home at his Sioux Falls apartment, Martin Planck prepared for the two classes he instructed at University Center. Working through half the night, he tried to keep his mind drifting off wantonly toward Francine—her face when he teased a dimpled smile, her devotion to those close to her, the way her hips swayed when she walked in her boots, the way her eyes flashed after he kissed her, how...*come on Planck! Get a grip! There's work to be done, and other things to occupy the brain other than Francine Parker.*

He needed to be fresh for class tomorrow. Francine and Martin would get together for sure at the end of the week. That promise made, he plowed into the outline with renewed determination, a pit bull puppy with a new slipper.

He also knew he had to devise an agenda for Dell's re-introduction to the educational system. It was apparent to both him and Francie that she would benefit from a combination of home schooling and hands-on formal lab work. Details would be worked out as they went along, depending on her progress, and where her skills lie. He figured she could earn a GED within a year, while going on to more specialized college level training at the same time.

No doubt she could handle it. They just had to convince her to embrace the regimen, unsure at this point of how much incentive she might need. What or where does she see herself being in the next few years?

The next few days settled into a pleasant routine for Dell. She spent mornings with Francie, tackling the unending maintenance and repair jobs which cropped up. Francie asserted these were a normal part of an operating ranch where the animals in residence were not responsible for the wear and tear they caused.

Ever-changing weather conditions also posed maintenance problems. It was still early in the season, so weather had not yet settled into the hot, still summer ahead. Wednesday afternoon, a heavy hail storm arose from the north and tore part of the roof from the chicken coop. The horse stalls, built a bit sturdier to put up with constant equine abuse, escaped unscathed.

The next afternoon, all four of them worked until after sundown to get the coop functional again. Meanwhile, the chickens took up residence with the horses, and there they stayed relatively safe from the raptors and other predators.

That night Sheriff Warner called the house.

After several minutes of pleasantries with Francie, he asked for Dell. "It'll just be a minute, Vern. I think she is reading in her room."

Dell was reading the 'Golden Bough', by Frazer, a compilation of human mystery and religion. It fascinated the girl. She reluctantly took the call on the phone extension. "Hi Sheriff, what's up?"

"Dell, I thought you'd like to know. We, that is, the Hughes County Sheriff's Department, have investigated that cargo container out near the Pierre Mall. They found a huge amount of illegal radioactive sludge. It apparently was unloaded there because whoever created it was at a loss as to how to dispose of such a mess. They have also arrested a black man out there who would not give them any information as to how the waste was deposited."

Dell became immediately enraged. "No! That's Pan! He's entirely innocent! Not only that—the only reason he was there was because he was expecting to be paid for the container. He considered it his, since he found it. It's totally wrong."

"Tell you what, Dell. I'll send Daniels out there to pick you up first thing tomorrow, and we'll straighten this thing out. That sound okay?"

"I'll be ready, Sheriff!"

Dell jumped down the stairs, to where Francie was relaxing. "Hi. Sorry to disturb you, but I think I have to go with the sheriff first thing tomorrow, so I won't be here to get things fixed as usual. Sorry."

Francie looked up. "That's okay, Dell. I'll carry on." Francine harbored feelings of happiness when Dell showed signs of having a life of her own. The more outside influences pressed in on her, the better she'd be able to develop a sense of what was really important. The more independent she became, the more able to realistically deal with the world, an important achievement for anyone on their way to adulthood.

On the other hand, she would miss the intimacy of her continual presence.

Deputy Daniels arrived at half past seven, well after the time he was expected. Dell had been able to collect the day's eggs and give alfalfa flakes and water to all the horses before he showed up. The boys were long gone, and Francie had already gotten to somewhere on the other side of the ranch inspecting fences.

Daniels used a cane to mount the porch. Dell greeted him, wearing the same black straight-legged jeans and plaid shirt he had last seen her in. She also wore a sports cap, imprinted with the local school logo. That was new.

"Hi, Greg. How's the leg?"

They traded small talk to pass the time, more than an hour to the sheriff's office in Fort Pierre. Dell made good use of the time, grilling Daniels on everything he knew about the sludge they found. Daniels expressed gratitude to Dell for her quick action with the terrorists, and she said it was ancient history.

"What we have to figure out is how to get Pan out of the clutches of the Hughes County Sheriff." She liked the word 'clutches'. It came from a book she had taken with her new library card. She now checked out books digitally, from the Stanley County Library.

The great thing was, she didn't even have to go there—all she had to do was borrow them from the 'cloud', and download them onto a tablet which Francie had given to her after upgrading to a newer version. No big sacrifice, she assured the girl. And what Stanley County didn't have, they could get from the other counties around the state.

The amount of reading she could do now, all without leaving her room, amazed her. So 'clutches' was one of her favorites, garnered from the Sax Rohmer "Fu Manchu" books. She knew those were considered 'trashy' pulp fiction, but a heck of a lot could be learned from them.

So, Sheriff Wallace Jenkins—basically inflexible to a fault, took everything at face value, not believing in any sort of gray areas. "What do you think, Greg? How can we get Sheriff Jenkins to release Pan? And then pay him some money—at least a hundred dollars. I think Pan will settle for that."

"Well, miss," Daniels theorized, "I don't think you can persuade Jenkins to do anything he doesn't feel is right. Unless, maybe you can persuade him this man, Pan, is the key to some investigation that maybe is being undertaken to..."

"I know!" Dell got a flash. "We'll tell him Pan is an undercover agent, put there by the authorities to flush out those miscreants on the payroll of the industry, wanted for the illegal dumping of toxic waste throughout the state, because the mining industry has not bothered to devise other provisions for getting rid of this waste."

She studied Daniels, who did not take his eyes from the road. "Does that sound bull-shitty enough? I mean, for anyone to believe?"

Daniels chanced a glance at Dell. "I think you are chasing phantoms there, Miss. Sheriff Jenkins thinks mining, especially uranium mining, is good for business and shouldn't be curtailed or hampered in any way."

"So why is Pan being held?" She pounded the dashboard.

Daniels cheek displayed a tic. "It seems simple. The guy is the only one there where an illegal dump has been made. So he must have something to do with it."

"So we convince the sheriff the dump was not illegal, that it was planned at the state level as a temporary or emergency stop, and the sheriff just got left out of the loop. And Pan was there to ensure local officials get notified of what was going on with this temporary drop-off that might have been on its way to somewhere permanent, say, in Wyoming."

Daniels glanced again at Dell. "I don't know if that will work, Miss. Sheriff Jenkins is pretty hard-ass."

Dell examined the heavens for inspiration. "It will work, Greg, if everyone is in on the scam. We tell this to Jenkins, and you and Vern say it's true. How could he not believe it?"

"We couldn't do that, Miss. It would be a breach of professional ethics."

Dell appeared frustrated. "I bet it's a breach of sanity to think that Pan is responsible for any of this!" She looked out the window for any other ideas that might float by. "So, what we have to do, then, is figure out who really dumped that container there, and prove that Pan had nothing to do with it. Not too hard."

Daniels couldn't argue with that one, except for the 'not hard' part. "How do we go about doing that, Miss?"

"I don't know." A note of irritation in her tone. "I guess we have to go there and look around some more. It was really easy to spot the tire marks, where they came off the road. Now we just have to figure when that was—a little harder, maybe. Then we do a survey of active mining operations in the vicinity and go there and see what big trucks they're using, with what kinds of tires and what sort of containers they have for holding the tailings, and what they usually do with them, and what scheduling they have for those operations, and who might have had a reason for not following the protocol. Stuff like that."

"That sounds like a lot of time and work to do all that, Miss."

Dell was about ready to lose it with Daniels. "Well, how would you guys go about it? Just find some poor schmuck nearby and arrest him because he can't tell anyone where he was last week? And stop calling me Miss!"

Daniels said nothing, just concentrated on the road.

Dell was immediately contrite. "I'm sorry, Greg. Didn't mean to snap at you. But we have to do something, and it'll take some time." She relaxed a bit. "And, please call me Dell."

Daniels expression softened, as he turned his face to her briefly. "You got it, Miss Dell."

Chapter 37

Warner and Dell shuffled through the mud, the aftermath of the recent storm, looking for something, anything, that might lead them to whoever was responsible for the container. It still stood there, not quite blending in with the juniper and sage dotting the sodden area. Authorities had plastered the entire circumference of the bin with yellow tape. Then it had been staked and surrounded with orange plastic temporary fencing, blocking access to within five yards.

The tracks had been all but erased, some nondescript ditches the only remnants of what, a few days ago, had shown impressions of tread and distinct heritage. Now they could determine only the general direction of origin. Fortunately, Dell had retained a picture in her head of their exact design and dimensions.

Sheriff Warner did not doubt her powers of observation for a minute, but the Hughes County deputy accompanying them had reservations. Deputy Chong was also a wise-ass. "I suppose you can also remember the exact moment of your birth? How you suddenly saw the light?"

Dell appraised him with interest. *This guy is hard to convince and needs more than opinion to make a judgement. That's probably why he excels at his job.* "Deputy Chong, is it? What's your first name?"

"It's Frank, Frank Chong. Why?"

"I'm sorry, I'm just uncomfortable dealing with people on a 'last name' basis. I'm Dell. I have an advantage over you in that I have no last name. So, Frank, what would convince you that I know what I'm talking about?"

Chong drew a straight line with his lips and wrinkled his brow. "Draw me a picture!" He pulled a notepad and pen from his vest and thrust it toward Dell.

She smiled, nodding slightly, and without hesitation, began

marking the paper in light and dark designs. After a moment, she returned the pad and explained. "The dark lines indicate deep impressions, while the lighter ones are not so deep. The design looked to be an industrial tread, for on and off road use, with uneven ribs and knobs and long sipes for all-weather traction. Your pad is small, so it's drawn to quarter scale."

Chong studied first the drawing, then Dell.

"Approximately," she said, hedging.

"Okay, Dell. This is a lot better than what we had. We'll get this over to the research guys and see what they come up with." He started to turn away, then turned back, his lips turning up in grudging admiration. "And thanks for the help."

Sheriff Warner had observed the interaction with amusement. "Looks like you might have a new convert, Dell."

She brushed off the comment. "Vern, we have to get over to the jail and see about Pan!"

"I'm with you. We'll head over there now and see what kind of nonsense they're holding him on." They waved at Chong and made their exit.

The Pierre Police Department and Hughes County Sheriff's offices occupied different parts of the concrete slab building complex on the same law enforcement site on which the Department of Corrections was situated, near the southeast edge of the capitol. It was hard to imagine anyone venturing into that part of town unless they had really serious business to take care of.

Warner and Dell, who he referred to as Deputy Dell, if anyone asked, were directed to the Department of Corrections directly across the quad, where they should be holding the prisoner. Senior Deputy in Charge of Corrections, Lars Wilson met them there. When told who they were looking for, Wilson disappeared into another alcove full of monitors, with access controlled by sliding electric doors.

Since no record of a recently incarcerated 'Peter Pan' could be found, they had to furnish a detailed description of the man. Dell had to provide that, since Warner had only the vaguest idea of what the man might look like.

"He is black and large, with reddish kinky hair, worn without any style. Let's see," she pondered, digging into her reddish curly hair with a finger. "He usually wears black coveralls with no shirt, and maybe a canvas coat, and just some rubber slip-ons for his feet. Oh, and he is clean-shaven, too, although I don't know how he does that."

Wilson re-appeared with an eight by ten B&W photo, which he held out to Dell. "Is this the man?"

Dell studied the photo of a disheveled, dispirited African man, whose eyes shifted away from the camera. He was dressed in a light-colored jumpsuit, standard corrections issue. "We booked him as a 'John Doe' since he refused to give us any personal information."

Dell fretted over Pan's appearance. "That's him. When can we see him?"

Wilson looked surprised. "Oh, you missed him. He's gone. Only held overnight, then he was released."

"Released?" Warner put a cautionary hand on her arm, in reaction to her surprise. "Where was he released? He wasn't where he usually is."

"I don't know about that. We release them with their belongings and give them a bus ticket to help them on their way. Can't say where he chose to go." Wilson's tone was dismissive. He turned back to some paperwork he had been dealing with.

Warner thanked the deputy and steered Dell from the facility.

On their way back across the bridge to Fort Pierre, Dell broke the silence. "Well, at least he's out of there—but where?"

Warner did not appear concerned. "Probably wherever he goes, he'll be in good shape, that is, if he can stay out of the way of the cops. The way he looks, they're liable to shoot him, in any case."

Dell shook her head, wondering if the sheriff was serious. "So...'Deputy Dell'? What's that all about?"

Warner appeared slightly befuddled, one eye twitching. "You understand. Here I am, on duty, traipsing around with a young woman at my side—there had to be a logical explanation, and the best I could come up with is you're my deputy."

He gave her a thoughtful look, with furrowed brow. "So, maybe we should make it official—make you an official deputy, with irregular hours. We'll put you on the payroll. Hell, I'm the Sheriff, and I can put anybody on the payroll I want to!"

He checked her reaction to the proposal. "What do you say? Want to join the Stanley County Sheriff's Department?"

Dell's eyes opened wide and blinked several times. "Wow! You want me to be a cop? That's a whole lot of spit to swallow...but, you know, lots of people have been bringing it up lately...so I guess it's not a totally crazy idea!"

"I know. There are problems with it, such as some recent past behaviors, but I think, that with how you've excelled recently in bringing the bad guys to justice and your keen sense of observation, it would be very hard for me, as a sheriff, a law-enforcement official, not to recognize the value you would bring to the department."

His head bobbed side-to-side as he considered. "And I wouldn't always have to explain your presence. Now, some details would need to be worked out, such as your obligations to Francine and your future schooling, but there would be a paycheck involved, and that would be a good thing, allowing you some economic freedom with less dependence on others for your well-being."

"But, isn't my age going to be a problem?"

Warner pursed his lips. "Well now, how old did you tell me you were?"

Dell was dumbstruck, then delight crawled across her face. "Going on nineteen! Can I still call you Vern?"

He stiffened, and nodded curtly. "You can call me Sheriff

Warner, Deputy."

Chapter 38

A Friday afternoon and Martin toyed with speed limits on his way back to the middle of the state and Parker Ranch. He wondered how this thing with Francie would work out. He had not been affected to such a degree by a woman in a long while, and it was disconcerting, to say the least. Not unwelcome, but a distraction nevertheless and detrimental to his work as an instructor and a journalist. He could think of nothing else but how his body would tingle all over when he connected with her again. Certainly a problem, but a euphoric one. How to handle it? The main thing is try to stop thinking about his failures as a teacher and writer and savor the weekend, when he didn't have to consider such nonsense. His students would forgive him, of course, as most of them were going through similar angst, albeit at a much more convenient time in their young lives.

The ranch appeared the same as always when he arrived, but the atmosphere seemed different somehow. Francie stepped out to the car to greet him with kisses and an embrace. Her gait had an extra bounce. Even Irma was happy to see him.

She produced a couple of beers, which they took out onto the rear deck. "There's been some interesting news this week, Marty," Francie remarked when they had settled next to the railing, "and it all has to do with Dell."

Marty immediately became intrigued. "I guess with Dell, it could be either good or bad news now, couldn't it?"

"Well, this week the news is good—Dell has gotten herself employed by, get this, the Stanley County Sheriff's Department!"

The news surprised Marty, mostly with how quickly it had happened. "No shit?"

"No doo-doo involved, Marty. She came home earlier today and told us that Vern would deputize her, and start paying her for what she had been doing anyway since she's been here."

"She must be really excited."

"Yeah, she is walking on air. It's the first time she has had a regular, you know, salary for doing any kind of work. She says she is to go in Monday and get familiar with the paperwork involved. It's not just..."

Marty interrupted. "I know—it's not just about catching the bad guys."

"She is so excited, Marty. She can't talk about anything else, well hardly anything else. She is still worried about her friend, who was arrested the other day. So that is something that's still on her mind. But she'll tell you about that. Meanwhile, Vern said she has to get some schooling in at the same time."

Marty nodded. "So we have work to do. I've roughed out a curriculum that we can go over. It involves some college work, and home schooling at the high school level. She'll mostly be on her own, and I hope it won't be too much for her, what with this new position she's acquired."

"The girl is a dynamo, Marty. I don't think we can overload her. Right now she's down with the boys, looking after the animals, and they're also feeding the newest addition to the stock, this large snapping turtle that found its way into the water trough."

"That thing still there? Those are dangerous, I hear."

"I think the boys are old enough to not be stupid, and since when was Dell ever worried about danger?"

The after dinner topic in the kitchen revolved around Dell's new position in law-enforcement.

Martin congratulated her and asked for details. "How did you talk the sheriff into hiring you? That must have been some employment interview you scheduled last week!"

Dell became defensive. "I did not schedule an employment interview. I simply asked for advice, and I impressed him. He impressed me as well. Not your typical cop, as I have known them."

"Sorry, Dell. Just my attempt at humor."

Jimmy jumped in. "I'll say you impressed him. Last week you were under suspicion in a man's death, and now this!"

"Please, don't remind me, Jimmy."

"Is he giving you a police car?" That was Donnie.

Francie, amused at the way the conversation ping-ponged at random, also thought about how Dell would get around to her new job, assuming she continued to stay with them at the ranch. "I think Deputy Daniels is going to start resenting you if you don't get your license in a hurry."

Dell smiled and relayed her other news. "I already have my permit!"

"How did you manage that?" Marty couldn't figure how the girl had acquired the necessary paper trail. "You told us you were a waif without resources."

Dell almost punched Marty, but just smirked at him. "Listen, Teach. It was you who found me out, so I had all the information. We just went 'unavailable records', with the sheriff as a witness, and there you are. 'Adele Louise Martin' is now permitted to drive." She flipped her hair with a little motion of the neck. "Vern even said they would round up a car for me, after I checked out on it, in the next few days."

Francine shook her head. "Well, aren't you the grown-up."

"Good going, Dell!" That from Marty.

"Yeah! Good going," echoed Jimmy.

Donnie asked, "You gonna give us a ride in the new cop car?"

Dell looked serious. "Maybe after I've been working awhile. You don't want me to mess up and get tossed out on my can first thing, do you?"

Donnie shook his head in disappointment. "I guess not."

Francine took over. "Anyone for tea and cookies?" She always let them enjoy tea on Friday nights.

Later, the boys opted to get the jump on their homework for the weekend, and they headed upstairs.

Francine's eyes followed their departure. "That will be you in a couple weeks, Dell. We'll have regular assignments for you."

Marty added. "Absolutely! We've come up with a course of studies for you, required stuff and other subjects you can add for credit just because you might be interested in a certain topic—psychology, astronomy—things like that. Sound okay?"

Dell felt her eyes misting again. "Thank you for this. It sounds wonderful. But how will we know if I've learned enough to, you know, move on?"

Francine answered this one. "We'll give you examinations, where you have to answer questions or talk about what you have learned, and every couple of weeks, a counselor from county schools will be out here with a checklist."

"The University Center will be a bit more formal." Martin liked this part, he being instrumental in setting it up. There are class materials you will be assigned and you'll be on-line regularly with an instructor for questions and direction. Then at the end of the class you'll be tested and evaluated. You'll be given a pass or fail grade—pass is what we're expecting and after two years you'll graduate."

"From both high school, and college," Francie said, beaming.

Dell twisted her lips into a dubious look. "Well, hasn't happened yet, so don't get too happy about it."

Marty and Francie exchanged glances.

Dell continued. "This is all good, and I'm sure it will surprise me in the end, so I'm not going to worry about it. What I am worried about right now is something I can't get my head around, and it has to do with today, not the fabulous future."

Francine's smile disappeared. "What's on your mind, Dell?"

Dell sat back on the couch. "You know that big container out there in Pierre, behind the mall?"

Martin answered for both of them. "We know. They don't know quite how to handle that, and are taking their time coming up with a plan to get it out of there."

"Well, I can't figure out why they dumped it there in the first place."

Francine knitted her brow. "We're with you, sweetie. Nobody knows who, or why they did that."

"It's not that they dumped it. Just, why that spot? It would be obvious in a very short time that someone would discover it, as we did, and would have to deal with it. If they just wanted to get rid of some toxic sludge, why didn't they pick a more remote spot?"

Martin had a ready answer. "They were probably in a hurry to get rid of the stuff, so they dumped it where it would definitely be someone else's problem."

Francie tuned to the girl's angst. "I guess your gut is telling you something different, sweetie?"

Dell smiled. "My gut is enjoying the cookies and tea. But I'm still wondering—why did they dump it there? In Pierre." She mused another minute. "Six miles from the Oahe Dam..."

"I don't see how that sludge could affect the dam or the river since, even if it were leaking, it would contaminate only a very small area, it being so far from the waterway."

"You are probably right, Teach, but my tea and cookies are telling me somebody should deal with that thing soon, or sooner." She looked from one to the other. "If it's alright with you, Francie, I think I will make the trip out there again tomorrow."

"That's fine with me, sweetie. Maybe you should tell the sheriff your concerns." Francie nodded toward the kitchen phone.

Being a deputy now, Dell got through to the sheriff, even though he was at home...with his family...on a Friday night.

"Dell, this had better be urgent."

"Well, I think it's urgent, Vern. I would like to get another look at that cargo container site by the mall—tomorrow, I think. There are some things that don't make sense about it. I should be able to scope it out on my own, but I wanted you to know what I'm doing, just in case?"

There was silence for a moment, while the Sheriff digested this. "Okay, Deputy. You head out there first thing in the morning, and if you find anything you didn't want to, let me know, okay? Do you need to be picked up?"

Dell gave a pleading look to Martin, and whispered, "Can you give me a lift?"

Martin nodded silently.

"I'm all good, Vern. I should be there at around eight. Do you have anything you wanted me to check out?"

"It's all on you Dell. You should contact Hughes County, however. It is their jurisdiction and they may want to know that somebody is snooping around."

"Thanks, Sheriff. I'll see if I can get Chong out there, as well." She hung up, and turned to Francie. "I hope he's not having second thoughts."

Francie appeared puzzled. "Second thoughts? You mean the sheriff?"

The girl flashed a worried frown. "About his new deputy."

Chapter 39

The next morning saw Martin, Francie and Dell on the bumpy road to Pierre. Jimmy and Donnie would tend to things at home, having elected to stay and get caught up on some back-burner projects.

They would drop Dell off close to the site, and Francie would accompany Marty on errands he had to complete. One scant month remained to tack down all the details for the Planck family reunion, and Francie was pleased to help. Martin could use all the direction she could lend him. He knew he was not the most coordinated of social planners.

Dell inched her way down into the ravine. She followed a sandy wash to where the object stood, now festooned with orange and yellow raiment. Still early, the sun had not yet popped out from behind the Penney's building looming in the distance. The area appeared somehow festive, with colorful bits of clothing hanging from the orange plastic barrier.

She did a three-sixty of the entire scene, and spotted an orange tent off to the left, partially obscured by a small scrub juniper. Approaching carefully, she caught sight of the man she sought, enthroned on an overturned Home Depot bucket.

He studied a smooth stone held in one hand while peering through a short black tube grasped in the other. He spoke as she came close. "I think I'm rich. This is solid jasper." He nodded to her. "They didn't pay me anything, so I came back. I have to recoup my losses."

She knelt next to him. "I'm so glad you're okay, Pan."

The black man allowed a small smile. "What's not to be okay about?"

"Well, they did put you in jail, and we came looking for you, but you had been released."

He smiled again. "There's no jail that can hold me, heh, heh!"

Dell was suddenly serious. "Did they tell you this container is full of radiation? I don't think it's healthy for you to be near it."

His gaze drifted across the object. "They say anything to keep from paying me." Then he hunched down, as if someone were listening. "It's not right, you know."

She immediately tuned in, and lowered her voice. "What's not right, Pan?"

"This thing here. It doesn't stay quiet at night. Hums like a washing machine."

"It hums?"

"That's what I say. And sometimes squeaks, but that may be the mice. Lots of mice here at night—they like my cookies."

"So, it hums only at night?"

"That's when it hums, alright." Pan was suddenly alert. "Nice to see you. You got a boyfriend, I think!" Then he was up and gone.

Dell stood suddenly, and swung around. She heard rustling in the distance, then spotted the khaki-clad figure of young Deputy Chong approaching.

He caught sight of her at the same time, and waved a greeting. Stopping to brush dust from his ankles, he smiled at her warmly. "Dell! Dell, who has no last name? We have to stop meeting like this..."

She looked at him blankly. "Like what...Frank?"

"Sorry, just an old movie line—humor, sort of. Forgive me. So what brings you out here on a Saturday morning, when you could stay in bed watching cartoons?"

"Got chickens and horses to feed, Frank—they like to eat first thing." She glanced around for Pan, but he had disappeared. "I had a feeling that we weren't dealing with this container in quite the right manner so I came out here to have another look. Sorry I interrupted your cartoons."

Chong kicked at a clod next to his boot. "I hardly ever sleep in. So, what exactly are you looking for?"

"Really, I was just wondering why this thing was dumped here, of all places, and not somewhere that we wouldn't find it right away. Also, it hums."

The deputy frowned. "What does it hum, the 'Star Spangled Banner'?"

"No. My friend says it just hums at night, real soft. I can't hear anything, maybe it only hums at night."

Chong screwed his face in thought. "Maybe if we had a screwdriver. There is a toolbox in my unit, and there might be one there—I'll be right back." With that, he turned and trotted back up the hill.

Dell again surveyed the scene. It was pretty much as she had left it a couple days ago, except for the use of barrier fence as clothesline. She wondered where Pan had got to. It looked as if there was a breach in the orange fence, which had been casually concealed with a tee-shirt. She wondered if Pan was responsible, or if some animal did it.

The sound of sliding and tramping brought her attention back to Deputy Chong, now kicking up a cloud of dust as he navigated his way down the embankment.

He approached with a grin, holding up a tool. "I found a screwdriver. We may be able to hear something with this."

Dell squinted at the tool, puzzled by Chong's reasoning. She saw it was a little over a foot long, with a clear plastic handle. Chong brandished his toy and followed as she led him through the cut in the fence straight up to the giant container. She scratched her head as he placed the sharp end of the screwdriver hard onto the wall then leaned in, ear pressing the plastic handle.

Holding the position for about half a minute, he turned to Dell. "Here, Dell. You try it, and tell me what you hear."

She took the tool, examined it, and studied his face. "You're going to tell your friends later that you got me to put a screwdriver in my ear, right?" Then, without further comment she placed the screwdriver onto the metal and listened. Then she smiled. "It's humming. Just like Pan said."

She turned back to Chong. "So why do you think it's humming?"

He thought hard. "Wait, this is a test, right? There is something in there besides sludge. Because sludge doesn't hum! So..."

"You want to know why I think it's humming?"

"Okay, shoot."

"It sounds to me like a machine that can't quite turn itself on. A bomb, maybe."

"Dell, that's...scary."

"Don't worry, just a wild guess...but now I'm thinking—what would be even scarier? What kind of bomb, if it is a bomb, might be hidden in a container of 'radioactive sludge'?" She marked the air with finger quotes.

Deputy Chong paled. "Oh, come on. You're not telling me...you can't be serious!" He turned away, then spun back. "That's just too far-fetched. It's not a nuclear bomb—it couldn't be." He looked up at the container wall. "Maybe we should start moving away from here."

"Not so fast, Frankie!" She glued him to the spot with a fierce look. "We've got a few things to do, yet. First get on the phone to your boss, quick like. Tell him we may have a nuclear bomb arming itself. There has to be an evacuation. Probably, the whole town."

"Dell, I can't do that on just speculation."

She stared at him, thinking of a response. "You're right. Can you get a team down here that can probe this thing? Like, twenty minutes ago?"

"Bomb squad! We have a bomb squad, just sitting around most of the time, like firemen. Basically, the only time they're busy, is when they're blowing up stuff for fun."

Dell gave him the look. "Not funny, Chong."

"I'm on it." He pulled the radio up to his mouth, and it squawked. Chong talked into the device hurriedly. Dell cast her eyes around, checking for Pan's whereabouts. She had a feeling he wasn't far.

"And, it would probably be a good idea to alert the military, or national guard—somebody who has a large, large...helicopter. A helicopter should be able to get this piece of garbage out of here."

Chong kept talking. Then they waited. Dell looked at the ground. "You know, Frank. I don't think we're in much danger right now, so we might as well relax."

"What makes you say that, Dell?"

She gave him a half smile. "Just a hunch. If whoever dropped this thing here, when, several days ago? If they were planning on blowing things up, they would have done it by now."

"Ah...so you don't think it's a bomb, then? False alarm?"

"Oh, no—it's a bomb alright. I just think they aren't very good at this sort of thing. Didn't study hard enough in bomb-making class. That'd be my guess. We still need to get it the hell out of here, though."

Chong looked at the container and spotted a movement on the far corner. "There's someone here."

Dell used her hand as a visor. "Pan!" she shouted. "It's okay. You can come out!" She put a restraining hand on Chong's reflex action to draw his weapon. "He's that friend I was telling you about."

Pan stood at a distance, seeing them, and casting his gaze around for others. Satisfied there were only two of them, he approached slowly. Deputy Chong was startled by the man, who stood well over six feet. He wore dark coveralls, and sported unruly orange hair.

Pan's expression remained neutral. "Did you bring me some money?"

Chong looked to Dell for guidance. Dell looked amused. "Pan, you'll get some money. Just relax." She waved at her partner. "This is Deputy Chong. He's okay."

Pan surveyed the Deputy. "He's a cop, okay. Not a pretty cop. Maybe you going to pay me. I have to get going, now. Been told this is not an okay thing, so maybe I should go. But you pay first, okay?

Dell nudged Chong. "You got some money on you?"

The Deputy frowned at her. "Usually. You mean I have to pay this guy?"

"Give him what you have. I'll pay you back."

Chong pulled out his wallet and took inventory. "...forty, sixty, seventy and three dollars."

"Go ahead. Go give it to him."

"All of it?"

"Do it!"

He glared at Dell but held out the money. Dell, in turn, gave it over to Pan, who grinned. "This will do. You can have that thing, but get it out of here—it's too noisy at night!" He stuffed the bills in a front pocket then about-faced and walked away, disappearing into the brush.

Chong still glared at the girl as she turned back to him. "You took all my money, Dell. And you know what's worse? I let you do it! How are you going to pay me back, and why are you even here? Please explain that—we just released that man from jail, and now we're out here, giving him money!"

She tried to calm the Deputy, speaking softly. "Look, I told you I'd pay you back. And you know where you can find me."

"Yes, you said you'd pay me back. I'm sorry. But why are you even involved in this?"

"I'm here because nobody else even bothers with the fact that there is a bomb here."

"Yes, but..."

"And if it wasn't for Pan, we wouldn't know it was a bomb, because he's the one who told me it hums."

"Ah, so listening to this big box was not just a whim, I get it. But you're still just guessing that it's a bomb! I mean, why would that be the first thing that pops into your head?"

"Tell you what. I'll bet that when the experts get here, they'll find that it's a bomb. I'll bet you...seventy-three dollars."

"Does that mean, if you're right, I don't get my seventy-three dollars back?"

"Yes," she giggle like a school girl, "and if you're right, you get it all back!"

Chong curled the corner of his lip. "That doesn't seem quite fair, somehow." He became serious. "Okay, Dell, thanks for pointing me in the right direction, but you should leave before the troops get here...wouldn't want you to get in trouble for lingering at a crime scene."

Dell's eyes widened in surprise. "Wait, are you saying you've been indulging me all this time?" She stamped her boot, raising a small cloud. "You think I'm just some kid off the street?"

"Look, Dell..."

"That's Deputy Dell to you, mister."

Chong hesitated. "Deputy? As in Deputy Sheriff?"

"That's correct!" She tossed hair from her face. "I am investigating this incident in an official capacity. I am not a groupie!"

"How could you be a Deputy? You are just a...okay, forget I said that. You're in law enforcement, for real?" He straightened up, tilting his chin. "All right, show me your badge, Deputy."

Dell shot him a cold smile and held open her flannel shirt. The gold Stanley County badge had been pinned high on her tee, just below the collar bone, where it wouldn't interfere with her movement. "Now, can we get back to business?"

"Sorry, Dell. I guess you're a lot older than you look."

"You got that right!" Then in a softer tone, "So you'll get your money back right after I get my first paycheck, okay?"

Chong smiled at her. "Ah. So, not too long on the job, then?" He turned to the container looming near. "Right. Back to this guy—why, if there is a bomb, would they put it here?"

Dell rested her hand under her chin, tapping her lips with a finger, as she formulated an answer. "Here's what I'm thinking. These are the same bunch of numb-nuts I had to deal with a week or so ago, when they insisted on blowing up the dam from upstream. Now they are hoping to do it from this side, with a much more powerful explosion. I'm thinking it would be a lot harder to sneak such a bomb up there on the road than it would be to just hide it in plain sight, which is what they've tried to do down here. They didn't count on anyone snooping around here, hanging with the local homeless resident."

Chong thought about that. "You could be right, Dell. But it's kind of hard to imagine. Nothing like that ever happens around here. And not likely to happen either. So let's wait for the specialists, okay?"

"Yah, well, what else are we going to do at this point?"

Another twenty minutes creeped by until the sound of many large vehicles interrupted the peaceful ambiance of the area. Trucks rumbled to a halt above, and the chug-thump of rotors overhead announced the arrival of at least two helicopters from who knew where. Maybe the military, but more likely the Hughes County Sheriff's Department putting to use equipment they'd fought so hard for in county budget hearings.

One of the choppers came down noisily in a hurricane of dust permeated with the smell of diesel fuel. After relative quiet returned, a door opened on the side and a uniformed figure emerged. He stepped into the area just outside the orange fence, and surveyed the surroundings for a moment.

Deputy Chong immediately recognized his superior, Sheriff Wallace Jenkins. He turned to Dell. "Uh, oh. Jenkins is here. We no longer have opinions, okay? Just follow my lead."

Jenkins strolled to the pair, huddled like field mice amidst the corn. "Deputy Chong. What's going on here?" His distant gaze fell on Dell. "Haven't I seen you somewhere, girl? What are you doing out here?"

"Stanley County Deputy Dell, Sheriff. I'm the primary on this site. You were called in as a courtesy."

Chong mentally cringed, thinking *now she's done it!*

"What kind of shit are you spewing, girl? You're nobody's primary in my county!"

Dell, hardly ever cowed by bluster from a cop, immediately jumped to the challenge. "This is not your county, Sheriff. This belongs to the people who live here, and I might add that these people need an official right now who will act on their behalf. Which means, Sheriff, you have responsibility for defusing this situation that could blow up at any minute taking a good portion of the county with it! So don't give me your misogynist bullshit about who's in charge here, and let's start figuring some solutions to the real problem we have."

Misogynist. That was a word she picked up from reading Simone de Beauvoir, in her furious attempt to catch up with the world of thought by devouring every unfamiliar book she came across.

Jenkins eyed the girl. Then looked at Chong. "Deputy, maybe you can tell me what's going on here."

"Well, sir. It looks like we have some sort of bomb here, disguised as nuclear waste that could go off at any time. Bomb squad should look at it, sir."

Jenkins leaned back. "So, a bomb. And exactly why do I get called about a bomb in this," he pivoted his head around, "in this relatively isolated area?"

Dell took over. "We told you Sheriff. This one has a potential of taking out a good part of the county, including most of Pierre—it is a suspected nuclear bomb—and we have to move it to an isolated site, right now!"

Jenkins studied the girl, her casual clothing, her youth, her gender. "You say you're a Deputy? From Stanley County? Does Warner know you're here? And what the hell do you know about nuclear weapons?"

"Probably about as much as you do, Sheriff. But I'm not willing to take the chance that you apparently are."

"I don't think I like your attitude, Deputy Doll. And I don't believe you have a reason for being here any longer. We'll take it from here." Jenkins turned his back on Dell, and studied the road above.

A group of five individuals in black outfits jogged down the hillside next to the parking lot. They carried equipment, serious equipment, weighing substantial amounts. Much of the equipment was borne two-up. One of the group approached Jenkins.

The man appeared to be in charge. "Commander Boswell. Where should we set up?"

Bomb Squad members were state employees from the DCI. Hardly enough bomb threats in the entire state to justify the expense of each county having a team, they traveled as needed, spending most of their time in training for worst-case scenarios.

Jenkins and Boswell shook hands. "Good to see you, Commander." He indicated the nearby large container. "Supposed to be in there, but be aware, they found it full of radioactive sludge."

"We are aware of that Sheriff, and came fully prepared. You might want to get all unnecessary personnel well away from the site, sir." Boswell then turned to his second. "Let's move that stuff over there. We'll take it up top!" He again addressed Jenkins. "What info do you have on the device? Who called it in?"

Jenkins looked around, spotted his deputy, lingering a few yards off with Dell. "That would be Deputy Chong, there with the girl. I'll start moving people back."

Boswell waved at Chong and Dell and moved to introduce himself. "Commander Boswell. I understand, Deputy, that you called in the alarm. What can you tell me?"

Chong looked at Dell. "Not much, Commander. Deputy Dell, here, first heard about the humming from inside the container, and we speculated that a remotely controlled device was trying to arm itself."

"Just speculation at this point," Dell added, "but it's based on the fact of some very bad folks are continuing efforts they started several days ago to do harm to the regional dam and power plant, which are near enough to be affected, should this turn out to be nuclear."

Boswell stared at the girl. "You are with the Sheriff's Department?"

Dell smiled. "Stanley County. Not a whole lot to choose from over there, so they picked me."

He shrugged off his misgivings. "And what, Deputy, makes you think nuclear?"

"Well, the distance to the dam would make anything else just an exercise, wouldn't it? These guys may not be the pick of the litter, but they aren't that dumb." Dell spotted a familiar figure carefully edging down into the ravine. "And, Commander, you might want to go over the intel with the FBI. I think that is feeb Agent Maddis making her way over here."

They waited while the agent carefully picked her way through the mud. Sheriff Jenkins followed, several feet behind.

Dell spoke as they approached. "Agent, I hope you didn't wear your good shoes out here."

Jenkins stopped and pointed a finger at Dell. "You! Dolly! I told you to get on out of here!"

They both ignored the sheriff, as Maddis greeted Dell. "Don't talk about me! Looks like you're the one put her foot in it again."

Dell glanced at her feet and smiled. "I been telling everyone I'm a trouble magnet."

Introductions were made, and Jenkins kept quiet while Dell filled the agent in on what she thought might be the situation. Commander Boswell looked to Maddis for confirmation of Dell's assessment.

The agent spoke quickly. "I don't know whether Dell's right on this one. She has been in the middle of it as long as I've known her, and always managed to come out on top. So, I would say let the bomb guys do their thing, and let's all move back until we get an answer from them. That will determine our actions at that point. Have at it Commander!"

Boswell moved back to where his men had set up their ladders and equipment, while the others fled back up the hill to the parking lot.

Chapter 40

Jenkins assaulted Dell the minute they reached the pavement. "I've had it with you, girl. If you don't remove your carcass far from here in the time that I can spit, then I will have you escorted to the nearest jail, and your friends will have a hard time getting to you there."

Dell was torn. Ordinarily, she would handle bullies the way she always did—throw them on their ass. This time her tormentor was ostensibly one of the good guys, and if she beat the crap out of him as every muscle in her body was now focused on doing, she knew she'd regret it. There would be drawn out consequences, legal shit hitting the fans, and her friends would be drawn into the morass. She decided not lose it. She would remain impassive, conquer her rage and wait it out.

"Sheriff Jenkins. I'm not sure what beef you have with me. I am here as an official representative of Stanley County and as such, cannot allow you to bully me with petty territorialities. I have been charged with a mission, which I must see through to the end. If you want me to deviate from that mission then you will have to take it up with my superiors. Sheriff Warner will be in on Monday. If you like, I will take him a message. Meanwhile, I will remain at my post, which is here at the point of..."

"Oh, can the bullshit!" Jenkins was obviously not buying it.

Maddis came to the rescue. "Sheriff Jenkins, I'm afraid this has become a federal issue, with a federal facility serving several different states now in jeopardy. Consequently, the FBI will be taking over the investigation. You and your men will consider yourselves under FBI command and control. Is that clear?"

Jenkins looked at her blankly.

"The first item of business is to stop harassing our Stanley County liaison, Deputy Dell here. She serves at the behest of the FBI. Deputy Dell is to be considered an asset, and her input will always be seriously considered. Is that clear, Jenkins?"

Jenkins couldn't believe his ears. *These fucking women—always taking over where they have no business. Next thing, she'll put a couple drag queens on the team, because there isn't enough drama in the situation already.*

"No problem, Agent Maddis."

"Good. Have your men clear everyone out of the immediate area who's not absolutely essential. We'll consider evacuating the mall, and surrounding area, after hearing from Boswell's team. Move, people!"

As the locals fanned out to cordon off the area, Dell leaned close to the female agent. "Thanks, Rene, he was starting to get me crazy." Maddis followed the retreating sheriff with her eyes. "I've seen my share of those arrogant assholes, including some of the ones I work with. You'd better keep an eye on him whenever you drift to this side of the river." She then ran her eyes up and down over Dell. "Deputy Sheriff! I heard about that. I guess that guy, Warner, knows a good thing when it hits him in the eye. How is it working out?"

Dell allowed a smile at the praise. "It's good. I'm only irregular hours—mostly on call, for now. They're putting me in school, and when I've completed criminal justice training, I'll probably sign on full time...if I make it."

She gave a little shrug, and Maddis waved her hand. "No reason you can't do anything you want to, girl—just stick it out, okay?"

Dell nodded. "So, where is the rest of your team, Rene? Agents Joiner, and what's his name?"

"Oh, nobody thinks there's a real crisis over here, but they couldn't just ignore the call, so I was elected to check it out. How certain are you about this device?"

Dell wasn't at all certain, now that she had time to think about it. "Well, I get it, that it's pretty far-fetched. Especially with all the flack being tossed at me, but I'm still certain it's not something that can be ignored, and thinking about the worst thing that could happen might prepare us for when it does." She squinted hard. "Does that make sense? On the other hand, if it's good news, then we'll be all the happier, won't we?"

It was Agent Maddis' turn to be skeptical. "Okay...looks like we'll just wait and see what the bomb guys turn up." She walked away to a dark-grey Chevy Impala sedan parked nearby, yanked open the front passenger door, leaned in, and pulled out an oversized pair of long-lensed binoculars. She returned to where Dell stood, then peered through the magnifiers toward the large container, where Boswell's crew waited. One of the men used a large hammer-drill up top. The sound could be heard where they were standing on the ledge above the ravine, a distance of approximately one hundred yards.

Maddis handed the lenses to Dell. "Looks like we're not leaving here anytime soon."

Dell put the binocular's strap over her head, then looked through them for a long moment. "It can't be easy, working in that get-up. Looks like it'll get real hot, too, if they don't finish soon."

The crew-man at the top of the box was decked out head to foot in a regulation anti-blast suit, designed to give some protection from a regulation type explosion.

It was nearing noon when Commander Boswell climbed up out of the ravine. His crew was still involved in wrapping up their work at the container site. Maddis, seated in her sedan, worked the cell-phone. Dell napped in the shade of a nearby sycamore.

When Maddis spotted Boswell, she climbed out of the car. "What do you have for me, Commander, good or bad?"

"Which do you want to hear first?"

"Give it to me."

"Okay, well the good news is it hasn't gone off yet."

Maddis' hand flew to her mouth. "Oh god! Dell was right!"

Boswell continued. "The bad news is we can't get to it to defuse it. We would have to drain and carry away the sludge, which is highly radioactive, and that would take at least a month. We can't afford to have this thing hanging over us that long."

Dell had awakened at the sound of conversation. She listened as the commander finished his lament. "Is it a nuke?"

He studied her for a moment. "We can't say for sure what it is, Deputy. The sludge is keeping it from us, and hiding any radioactive signature. We did manage to get an x-ray probe near it and got an idea of its size and shape. If it is a nuke, it is not a military weapon. Looks to be home-built, and the size indicates it is pretty crude, not something that would fit on a missile. I would recommend getting the military out here to deal with it ASAP."

Maddis was on it. "I've already contacted my agency, which is working with the National Guard as we speak. Probably what they'll do is haul it out of here with a big military chopper to the nearest mineshaft. Thousands of abandoned mines lie west of here."

Chapter 41

After hours of searching, they located a machine big enough to haul the box away in Winnipeg, Canada. A fire agency there had an Erickson S-64 Air-Crane not in use at the moment since fire season had not yet started in that part of the world. The U.S. Army Corps of Engineers didn't even have one of those they could put their hands on quickly. The Air-Crane was just that, a six-bladed, twin turbo-engine helicopter with a big winch where the cabin would normally be. It could haul twenty thousand pounds of cargo fairly easily, although, fully loaded, gas mileage would suffer considerably. It would arrive in Pierre sometime early tomorrow.

Agent Maddis explained this to officials gathered a safe distance from the site, or at least, what they considered to be a comfortable distance for those who didn't grasp what the possibilities were.

They met at the State Attorney General's office, situated about a mile and a half from the mall, on Highway Fourteen. Sheriff Jenkins, representatives from the DCI, the South Dakota Department of Environment and Natural Resources, the FBI, and Colonel William Mathers from the Dakota National Guard attended, as did others. Stanley County Sheriff Warner had been alerted by Dell, and he had rushed over the bridge to back her up.

Maddis explained that the local FBI office was to confer with the DENR on getting the container suitably situated, somewhere deep underground in the western part of the state. A lot of ifs remained. One unknown—if everything went as planned, the crisis would be averted and they could get back to normal business.

A question came from the doorway at the back of the conference room. "Agent Maddis, can you say how long this container has been there and how did you determine there was a bomb inside? Also, what steps are being taken to find out who did this?"

The agent shaded her eyes and spotted Martin Planck leaning against the doorframe, notebook in hand. "Mister Planck. This is a closed meeting."

Sheriff Warner twisted around and spotted Marty. "Oh, he's acting as liaison with Stanley County, Agent, and it's important that he be here."

Maddis thought a moment. "Your department keeps expanding, Sheriff. Alright Mister Planck. You can stay."

"Shall I repeat the question, Agent Maddis?"

"No need, Marty. There will be a press conference tomorrow, after the danger is past. Meanwhile, if you would, this has to be kept under wraps to avoid general panic."

Marty found an empty seat near the door. "I should point out, Agent, should you be unaware—there are two TV mobile units parked at the container site and two more outside this building, as we speak. They will be giving reports all night on whatever suits their fancy whether it be based on fact or not. I am a print reporter. Let me set the record straight, for publication no sooner than tomorrow."

"Mister Planck. If you should need more details before the press conference tomorrow, I'm sure you have resources that will fill you in." She looked pointedly at Dell. "As to who is responsible for this potential disaster, we are working on information provided by the Hughes County Sheriff's Department, which will hopefully lead us in the right direction."

Martin and Dell arrived at the Parker Ranch just in time for dinner. They were greeted with shouts and hugs upon entering the house.

Francie embraced Dell. "I hear you had a rough day, sweetie. Something about a bomb scare?"

She looked to Marty, who hung his hat on the rack, and took her face in his hands, planting a kiss on upturned lips.

Dell hugged Jimmy and Donnie, pounding backs and ruffling hair. "Animals been taken care of yet?"

"Waiting on you, Dell." This from Jimmy, who had busied himself with chores all day, and now needed to get into the field for a romp in the saddle. Donnie seemed more interested in the big snapping turtle and the chickens. The turtle was like a dinosaur, an eating machine who lurked and ate whatever came his way. Chickens were similar, in that they would eat whatever looked like food, but they would recognize their keeper and follow him around, coming when called. Donnie liked being depended upon.

When Dell and the boys rushed off to care for the chickens and horses, Francie led Marty to the kitchen, where a simple chicken and dumpling stew was being prepared. Marty took to slicing veggies for the salad, since he was the expert with the knife.

"Do you want to talk about it?"

"It was pretty crazy out there today, Francie. Cops and military everywhere. Kind of hard to keep things quiet, like the FBI wanted. TV news got ahold of the story, and they're still out there. Sure glad I don't work for those guys!"

"What about Dell?"

"Oh, she held her own. Was actually the reason everyone was there. Dell, and her friend out there, found out this big container was making noise, so the bomb squad got involved and said it was definitely a bomb. Tomorrow they're going to take it somewhere in a big chopper and make it disappear, hopefully."

"I assume you will be going back there early tomorrow."

Martin smiled at her. "I will. Shall we meet up for lunch at Juanita's?"

Chapter 42

The Erickson S-64 made enough noise to fill the entire city. The noise drowned everything else out. People could not hear themselves speak to one another, as the big air crane struggled into the air with its load. Selected officials picked the distant spot where it would be unloaded, but the destination was not made known except to a select few. All that could be said was an abandoned mine shaft would serve as the final burial spot for the device, and that a platoon of National Guard engineers would cover it over, making it look as natural as the surrounding prairie dog towns.

Dell watched the noisy machine and its cargo until it disappeared into a distant cloud. Deputy Chong was with her as she turned to face a crowd of information hungry reporters from all over the country. Only a few had caught on that Dell was part of the story, and not just there as another bystander.

One man from the Rocky Mountain News asked if she was the person who discovered that a weapon of mass destruction had been planted right here in the Capitol of the State? And was she that same person who last week foiled a plot to destroy the Oahe Dam and power plant, and would she comment on how these two events were related?

A female reporter from Action News 54, dangled a microphone an inch from her nose, and demanded to know how she happened to stumble onto the nuclear bomb, and why was she able to say what it was? Dell batted the mic away and turned to Chong, who held his arms up. "That's enough for now folks. There will be an official press conference on this incident at ten this morning, in front of the Capitol building. See you all there!"

Dell threw him a grateful glance. "Thanks, Frankie. I didn't know whether I could keep myself from swinging on those people or running away from them. They're like hungry rats, ready to chew on whatever meat might be left over."

Chong led her away from the crowd. "We still have an hour or so 'til the press conference. Want to grab a Starbucks?"

A Starbucks Coffee shop stood close by in the mall. Dell ordered a grande double mocha-latte with whipped cream, and a raspberry scone. Deputy Chong had a large house blend with cream. They sat outside, where the crisp morning air had just started to warm. Dell drank the lukewarm concoction in greedy gulps. Chong sipped his, and imagined the girl to be some half-wild creature who would bolt if he moved an inch. She looked up at him. "What?"

"Oh, I'm just daydreaming. Like, what brought you into law enforcement, Dell?"

Dell swallowed a large bite of scone and smiled coyly. "I had a choice between apprehending bad-guys, or winding up in jail myself. I chose the former."

"You saying you're a bad girl?"

Dell stopped chewing. "Actually, I'm very good. Probably better than anyone you're ever likely to meet again if you wanna know the truth. How about you Chong? You don't really look Chinese to me."

Chong almost sprayed his sip of coffee and put the cup a safe distance away. "Never had anyone ask about my heritage in such a direct manner before, but I know we're speaking 'frankly', if you'll pardon the expression."

That pulled a chuckle out of Dell.

"So, yeah, I'm sort of half-Chinese. The other half is Lakota. My mother. Father was a mining engineer for one of the big mining companies before he retired. Met my mother at a protest rally near Pine Ridge, and here I am."

Dell observed Chong anew. He had deep set eyes, separated by a prominent nose, narrow where it might've been broad. He wore his black hair short, probably so he never had to mess with it much. His dark, nearly hairless skin invited her gaze to linger, and his lips curled easily into a pleasant smile. "And there you are."

"So, what about your folks, Dell. Do you have a good story to tell?"

Dell tensed up, not used to being open with just anybody and not sure if she should start now. Then she relaxed. Frankie seemed a good sort, fun to be with and not too much older than her. She kind of liked him.

That didn't mean she would tell him things, though. "I recently found out that I was born in Chicago, many years ago. My mother had an Irish surname, so I guess that makes me mostly Irish. Don't have a clue what the other half is, so you have one up on me there."

"How many years ago?"

"Well, I've been here long enough to learn how to take care of myself, but you'd better not invite me out to drink anything stronger than coffee."

"Okay, mysterious. Maybe just dinner and a movie, then?"

Chapter 43

FBI Agent Maddis led the press conference. She had convinced her colleagues at the Agency she was the logical choice to take the lead since she'd been there from the beginning,.

At ten in the morning the lawn in front of the Capitol building crawled with dozens of news organizations. A half dozen television camera trucks lined the street in front of the Capitol grounds. Microphones had been set in bunches behind a podium to one side of the Capitol steps, where several law enforcement officials huddled. Apparently this story had grown bigger and more interesting than officials might have imagined yesterday. Who knew that rumors of a nuclear bomb in the heartland would be blown up so large?

Such thoughts might have run through Deputy Chong's head, but not so Agent Maddis. She had a distinct job to inform the public, without panic, and to reassure the masses the danger had passed. She asserted the FBI and local authorities were doing everything possible to track down those responsible for such a wanton terrorist act.

Maddis praised the local Sheriff's department as well as the Stanley County Sheriff's department for their assistance in pinpointing the danger. Especially worthy of recognition was one Stanley County Deputy, new to the department, who brought the whole episode to the forefront with her astute powers of observation and deduction.

She meant, of course, Dell. Those who did not know the girl now made it their crusade to get all the information they could on this mysterious young woman. The agent introduced Dell to the assembled crowd and urged her to go before the mic with her version of the story. The idea being, she could furnish details about what she knew and when she knew it that otherwise might fall through the cracks of history.

Dell had never spoken in front of a large group before and it looked to be more than a hundred people in front of her. Officials of various agencies and reporters from numerous regional news outlets made up a good part of the group. They quieted when she approached the podium, her recently cropped red hair still wildly out of control.

She made to bend down, and someone appeared to raise the mic for her. "Hi. I'm Dell, with the Stanley County Sheriff's Department. It was early yesterday when me and Deputy Chong there, found out this big box was more than just a nuisance. It made noise—a horrible humming sound. Now, that may not sound so bad to you folks, who were safely tucked away in your homes, but to the homeless man sleeping there at night, it was really bothersome.

"That man clued us into the fact that this wasn't just a box of neglected sludge. What we found sounded very suspicious, and possibly dangerous. I only thought so because I had a run-in recently with a group of dumb sh... excuse me, terrorists— working on blowing up the dam, and it seemed awfully coincidental that this device was placed inconspicuously close to that very same dam. So we got it taken care of, and we can thank everyone involved, including the fire-fighting organization in Winnipeg, Canada, for supplying the big chopper to haul it away."

Dell had obviously finished, and hands waved as others shouted questions. The girl stepped back to the podium. "Okay. Can it! I'll take a few questions, if you behave." She pointed to one hand in front. "You there—go!"

A disheveled blond woman with a mic and a camera man, spoke up. "Who is this homeless man? Does he have a name?"

"Everyone has a name, don't they? Next question."

"Wait, do you know his name?"

Dell smirked at the woman. She was making it so easy to dismiss her. "Yes, I know his name, but I'm not telling. I'm not telling because he has chosen to live alone, and won't answer your questions. So, move on."

She pointed to another raised hand. "Are you that same deputy who took out a group of terrorists single-handed, then were kidnapped by the same group before taking them down, and then had to fight off human traffickers from Chicago, who you used to be held by?"

Dell had to pause a couple of seconds. This was getting too close. "I was not a deputy at that time. You there!" She pointed at another waggling arm.

"Do you think this suspected bomb was planted by the same group that you had encountered earlier?"

"That's a no-brainer, at least from my point of view. This group apparently has a lot more supporters than we originally thought, and right now they are fixated on getting their job done. What we have to do is make sure that doesn't happen. So, we need the vigilance and commitment of every one of our neighbors to keep these shit-bags, oops. I mean, criminals. To keep them from destroying what we value most. And that is, our freedom to be ourselves, without any interference from those who would decide what we should or should not be concerned with."

"Are you still talking about terrorists, here?"

Dell smiled at the questioner. "Are you talking about subtext here?"

Maddis stepped in at this point. "Thank you Deputy Dell. If there are no further serious questions, that will be it for now. I look forward to seeing your reports."

Chapter 44

Dell refused all interviews and contacts with reporters after that. Too many people were calling at all hours. Sheriff Warner instructed his entire office to direct all inquiries to the newly appointed press liaison who would assign a number to the news agency or reporter, then promise to get back to them in turn. This solution satisfied no one, and the calls soon stopped coming. The problem continued, however, with reporters jamming the parking lot and front lobby of the Sheriff's Department hoping for an interview or even a glimpse of the newest Super-Deputy, Stanley County's own Wonder Woman!

Dell hardly noticed her ascent to fame in the community. She concentrated her attention instead on Deputy Chong, who made himself available whenever she had free time. She still loved spending time at the ranch—afternoons with the boys and evenings with Francie. She felt she could talk openly with the woman on any subject, her personal regrets or her new found interests, such as that certain Hughes County Deputy.

How, she wanted to know, should she handle her attraction for the man, when she couldn't tell the difference between hormones and emotions. Or vice versa. It may have been a typical adolescent complaint, but in Dell's case, the complications made it anything but routine. She definitely did not want to jump into a relationship, based on the flabby notion she missed having regular sex.

Francine could understand, and sympathize with many of the problems girls ran into in their struggle to become mature women but she had never encountered any of the issues Dell had to work through. The girl never had the opportunity to be guided through childhood. Her situation was rare, if not unique, and Francine often had to improvise her response and counsel on the fly.

She regarded Dell as a strong and bright spirit undaunted by most obstacles and set-tos, but maybe connecting spiritually and emotionally with another person was something she needed help with. "Dell, I think you have to take it very slowly. But you know that. This person has to know and accept the very essence of who you are and what you've been through, and then say, 'that's okay', before you can trust yourself to succumb to his favors. You know what I'm saying?"

Dell knew. "I can't bullshit him, in any way, and he can't do that to me, either. I get it."

Thanks mainly to Francie's guidance, Dell knew how she had to deal with Frankie Chong, but she wasn't at all sure Frankie would go along willingly with the plan. She felt he was curious about her, but maybe not enchanted by her. Was enchantment necessary? How did she feel about him, then? Was she enchanted, or merely curious? That was a hard one. Francie seemed to think she would know after a period of dancing around with the man. Figuratively, of course. So, dinner and a movie, then.

They chose an intimate café in Old Town, Benny's, where the pace was leisurely and the music, live. They chose a later hour, close to closing, so as to minimize their chance of being noticed by anyone who might spoil the moment. Chong ordered an IPA on tap. Dell asked for a cola.

"How did you ever convince Jenkins to give you a night off?" Dell knew Jenkins.

"He doesn't work us twenty-four-seven. Occasionally we get some time to ourselves, despite the fact that we are understaffed and we're operating on a shoestring."

"Maybe with this new publicity, the county will cough up some more money for the department." She mimicked a gruff department head. "Look what happens when we don't have enough deputies to look under every rock and stick. The terrorists are everywhere!"

"You got that right, not to mention the usurpers from the next county."

Dell smiled. "Well, you should thank the stars that we were around, especially with all that shortage of money and manpower."

Chong allowed a serious moment. "I'm very happy you were around, Dell, and happy you are still around. I consider myself so very lucky to have met you and hope you will continue to visit our county, despite that stiff prick I work for."

Dell rolled eyes. "I don't know, Frank. That guy is awfully scary, and I wouldn't want to cross his path accidentally in a dark alley, without backup. I mean, really!"

"Now, Dell. You can't possibly be afraid of him."

The girl grimaced. "You're right there. I'm actually afraid of what I might do if he pushed me too far. I would need someone with me to keep me from stopping his clock. He just won't let up, and one of these times, I will forget he is who he is, and show him who I am."

"Yeah, I think that would be a mistake, so whenever you find yourself on this side of the river, just give me a heads up and I'll make sure I'm there to run interference. Okay?"

"I'm down with that, Frank." Dell peered at him closely. "So, say I need to find you real quick. Where do you live, anyway? Can you take me there tonight?"

It was Chong's turn to smile. "I can probably show you the way. Maybe we can stop at my place for a drink or two?"

"Or something, maybe. You know I don't drink."

Deputy Chong resided in a modest one bedroom apartment on the north side of town. It was a downstairs unit, with unassigned parking, so Dell had no problem with finding a space close to the apartment. Frank keyed the door open and allowed Dell to enter before him. The place was sparsely decorated, with a framed 'Star Trek' poster above the couch, which faced a forty-two inch flat screen television. An array of speakers surrounded the TV, and these were interspersed with plastic models of various dinosaurs, stegosaurs, triceratops, and other unidentified critters from the Pleistocene.

Chong explained. "These are members of my immediate family—don't make any sudden moves..." He went to a thermostat on the wall near the kitchen and made an adjustment. "So, what can I get you? Soda?"

"Is this where the movie happens? You promised a movie, you know."

They sat close together on the couch, as 'Quest for Fire' played out the last scene, and credits started to roll.

Dell looked at Frank. "I guess there must have been a time when men didn't regard women as people. Do you think that has changed a whole lot?"

Frank thought a moment. "I think it's really hard to know what men think in relation to what women think because," he paused for a second, "they are like two continental jet-liners passing each other in opposite directions, aware of each other at some point but, ultimately, on a totally different flight plan."

Dell appeared confused. "Meaning?"

"Meaning, the whole sex thing, I guess. Men don't have it in their nature to create a child within their body, and so need other things to keep them occupied. They pursue conquest, both sexual and geographical, I would guess, while women create worlds within—their children and home, securing one for the other."

"That's kinda deep thinking, for a deputy. Are you into the conquest thing?"

"I think, eventually, men and women settle down to having the same goals—it's probably a maturity thing."

Dell looked thoughtful. "I don't think I've ever considered having a child, or creating a world for that person. Does that mean I am somehow not a complete woman?"

"Well, you are obviously not ready for that yet—like I said, it's a maturity thing."

"I'll give you that. I am far from being a mature person. By mature, I mean someone who finally gets it, has no more uncertainties."

"That's a tough standard." Chong paused to sip more beer. "I think if that's the measurement, then there are very few of us who reach maturity. Do you know anyone like that?"

Dell didn't have to think hard to answer. "Actually, I know of at least two people who have reached that point, and that is probably why I love them so very much! What about you, Frankie? Do you know anyone who is mature enough to set you straight most of the time?"

Chong laughed self-consciously. "You mean, present company excepted? Sure. I've had coaches who have shown me the way out of difficult situations. My mom and dad, of course..." He suddenly looked away from her. "Sorry, guess I've had it a lot better than you have in the past. But you've managed to do pretty well on your own, right?"

Dell studied this young man, as she tried to assess her achievements. "I guess you could say I have been able to gain some ground. My sense of self has been on hold for so many years that I feel I've been playing catch-up like crazy for the last few weeks."

"You don't look like you're playing catch-up at all, Dell. In fact, we seem to be playing catch-up to you."

"I know it looks like I can tackle anything, but if I start thinking about it, then I start to mess up! I guess I should stop thinking about things so hard, but sometimes I just can't help myself, and that's why I need people I can trust to be there when it becomes too much and I start going in circles."

"I'd like to be there for you, Dell."

Chong reached out and took her hand. They put their foreheads together and stared into each other's eyes for what seemed like a springtime.

It was Dell who broke the spell. "Are you looking for a conquest, here, Frankie, or are you getting creative with me?"

In answer, Frank placed his hands on the back of Dell's neck, and drew her into a kiss. A long, hungry kiss, the kind that rang bells somewhere and made the stomach do flips. Dell drew away with an inhaled breath, paused, then rejoined the embrace, doubling its intensity. They continued enjoying each other's touch, hands lightly caressing, with breasts pressed together, for several moments. When it no longer seemed possible to continue without progressing further, Dell pulled back.

She was apologetic. "I'm sorry, Frankie. I just can't! Not now anyway. Can we just give it more time?" Without waiting for Frank to assess what had happened, she jumped up from the couch and looked around for her coat. "I've gotta go. It was fun. Please call me again." And with that, she slammed out the door.

Chong sat in stunned silence. He had thought the evening was going so well. He eyed the closed door, rose from the couch, and walked to the fridge. He snagged himself another beer, then opened it and chugged. He was suddenly in need of a good buzz.

Dell's heart was pounding as she headed toward the ranch. What could she have been thinking? She obviously was not directed by conscious determination. It was something else. And she could not control it. Was she afraid—afraid of making a very intimate connection with someone she liked and admired? She wasn't entirely sure, only that maybe some kind of self-preservation thing had kicked in.

That was it! She knew she would not go back to her old life, under any circumstances, and this kind of thing, the sex thing, was still too close to mimicking her former life. She needed more time, was all. But, meanwhile, would Frankie be willing to give her more, or would he just brand her as a psycho, and move on. *That's what I'd do, if I was in his shoes,* she told herself.

Then she decided she was analyzing way too much again. Frankie wouldn't just up and lose interest in her, because of one whacky incident. If he did, he wouldn't be worth pursuing anyway.

It seemed a satisfactory outcome to her quandary, so she told herself to start thinking about something else now. Like the amount of time she would devote to the studies Martin and Francie had prescribed for her. That would keep her occupied, and she looked forward to getting started.

Chapter 45

Dell sped through town past the Fort Pierre city limits when she caught a glimpse of a large unlit vehicle racing toward her left side at alarming speed. She reacted instinctively, slamming on the brakes, twisting the wheel hard to the right, making the tires screech like wounded cats! The attacker smashed into the rear of Dell's Chevy Impala, with results similar to a freight train ramming a lunch truck.

The impact was a direct assault on Dell's gas tank, which exploded into flames like the Hindenburg, engulfing the entire Chevy. The ramming vehicle noisily backed off from the explosion, then lurched forward and sped away up the road.

Dell's car continued to burn violently, throwing off black, billowing clouds, the flames finally dying down to crackles and pops in about twenty minutes when most of the fuel had been consumed.

The ruined auto smoldered in the middle of the road until a passerby noticed and reported it to the authorities. A short while later several fire trucks and ambulances arrived at the scene. Deputy Greg Daniels arrived just after the firefighters, and Sheriff Warner followed twenty minutes later.

Deputy Charlie Bradford accompanied him. "Charlie, you and Greg try and get me a play-by-play, with the skid marks and such. I'll talk to the fire captain. Warner headed toward the captain's pickup, then stopped, and shuddered as his eyes took in the scene.

Fire Captain Grimaldi studied the wreckage and the surrounding area for more than an hour before allowing himself an assessment. "There's no sign of the vehicle's driver. That person must have vaporized on the spot or been thrown clear, in which case we just haven't found them yet. It's yet to be determined who this vehicle belongs to, and the damage is so great it'll take several days to sort it out."

Deputy Daniels asserted that it might have been one of their cruisers, since they were issued that particular vehicle, although a few other Chevy Impala models circa 2014 ran in the county.

He reported the news to Warner. "Sheriff, we authorized Dell, Deputy Dell, to take such a vehicle last night and she cannot be located at this time."

Warner shook his head. He didn't want to hear news like that. "Daniels, have you checked everywhere a victim could have been thrown from the vehicle?"

"They've checked a considerable area, Sheriff. But I'll recheck, and we'll comb the areas that might not have gotten the once over. There is a large ravine alongside the road here and it could be someone was thrown into it, and possibly made their way further along. I'll make sure it's been searched..."

Warner now speculated Dell might have been attacked on her way home, and maybe didn't make it through this time, as she had done so many times before. There were no skid marks indicating any braking of the vehicle that crashed into the Chevy, meaning it was probably deliberate, and it would have to have been a large truck to pull off the stunt without injury to the perpetrator.

The Chevy had skidded around, presenting its tail before impact, thereby assuring the eruption of the fuel tank. At the same time, however, the maneuver may have prevented a direct impact on the driver of the car, leading to a possibility of escape before impact. A remote possibility, Warner thought, but it was Dell. He kept his fingers crossed.

The door of the cruiser had flown open as Dell hit the handle going into the skid, and the sudden impact catapulted her backward. She somersaulted into a tight ball, rolling and bouncing along the ground away from the flames. She counted six turns before straightening her legs and arms and cartwheeling into an upright position on the side of the road to the rear of the assault vehicle. She spat mud and debris, as it backed toward her, away from the searing explosion. Then, with a grinding of gears, the large truck lurched forward, swerving from the destruction. In that instant, between reverse and forward momentum, Dell jumped on, holding fast to the truck railings as it fled from the scene.

She had experience with T-bone assassination attempts, having survived a similar situation in Chicago just ten days ago, and she had been unconsciously rehearsing and refining her reactions to such an event, should it ever occur again. Time well spent.

The cold, rough wind cut through her shirt, and already her skinned-up hands ached. She eyed her surroundings and struggled to change position, trying to secure a better perch in the truck bed, keeping her body low to avoid detection. It appeared to be a large tow truck, fitted with a winch and wheel ramps for transporting up to truck sized vehicles.

Hopefully, the operator would lead her to the asshole who ordered this hit. The Department had not given her a service weapon yet, as she had not had a chance to qualify, and she wished for the semi-automatic the Sheriff had taken from her last week. She would improvise a way to defend herself, she mused, when this monster truck finally stopped somewhere.

The sound of the road changed from a low rumble to a high pitched whine, and Dell knew they had started across the long bridge. The air grew chillier, and the wind cut deeper. Then the rumble returned, and the air became tolerable again.

The truck lurched to a halt and after a long pause began to move once more. It swayed during several turns, taken much too fast, then the ride smoothed out. About ten minutes elapsed before it slowed, the driver gearing down, then turning onto a gravel drive. In another minute, the vehicle stopped and the engine died.

Dell heard the door open, then slam, and the crunch of boots on gravel, and voices.

"Got it done, Boss. Whooee, you should have seen it blow—

must have had a full tank!"

"Sure you weren't followed?" A familiar voice.

"Hell, no! Not a soul around anywhere."

Gravel crunched, the voices faded, and Dell stiffly climbed off the truck. She stood very still, flexing her palms to get the feeling back. She only had a vague idea of where she might be—most likely on the outskirts of Pierre. She had left Chong's around eleven, so it must be well after midnight now, though just a guess.

A pole light illuminated a small area in front of the truck, and the front of what appeared to be a commercial garage. A sign over a closed garage door read 'Grady's Service—Air Conditioners—Towing'. A light glowed weakly from somewhere along the side of the building, where her attacker and his buddy had gone.

Dell needed to see into that space. She looked around for anything that would be of use. Other commercial type buildings stood nearby and some lights shone, but no people visible anywhere. Everything appeared buttoned up for the night.

She was on her own, without backup, or a means to contact anyone. Moving to the side of the truck, she peered into the cab. No keys in the ignition, but the door had been left unlocked, opening with slight creaking.

She wormed her torso through the partial opening and wriggled onto the seat. From there she explored the dash, glove box, center console, and sun visors. The keys came jangling down into her lap. Okay. Find the right one, put them on the seat for easy access—not in the ignition, because of the ding ding ding—and go see who's in the office.

Dell eased back down from the truck, and tread lightly back toward the light at the side of the garage.

A glass pane encased on the upper half of the door afforded her a clear view as she peered in from the bottom edge. Nothing but a desk covered with paper-work could be seen. On the wall above hung a calendar, sporting a photo of a smiling, half-naked woman, her lips colored blood-red.

A lighted room lay beyond. She tried the door. Unlocked. She glided through to the room, where light flickered on the doorframe, light and images projected from a large screen television. Three men relaxed on a couch, drinks in hand, talking and laughing. The sight of one of them brought the bile to her throat.

Savior!

Dell felt sick, even though his presence was not entirely unexpected. She carefully backed away from the door. Then she turned and rushed through the office, easing out the opening leading to the pathway beyond.

Breathing deeply, she leaned against the wall. Then knowing what she had to do, she stepped carefully over gravel to the tow-truck. Not much planning involved at this point. Just instinct.

Clambering into the seat, she shoved the key into the ignition and started up the big engine. Then, throwing it into reverse gear she backed the vehicle up about fifty feet, selected drive and floored it!

She reasoned it was mostly empty space between the garage and the offices, and by the time the truck stopped, it would have plowed through most of the building.

She guessed right. The large vehicle came to an abrupt halt after blasting through most of the outer wall on the other side of the building. The noise pummeled her ears. Dust and debris rained down in chaotic abandon. Dell had strapped herself in and though shaken, had not been injured by the forces around her.

She jumped out of the vehicle after it ground to a raucous halt and readied herself for unknown threats, her eyes darting to small movements as the wreckage continued to settle. She realized she was in the room where the TV had been flickering. It was now lying on its side in a shower of glass and sparks.

Moving cautiously through the now dark area, Dell kicked aside debris. Her boot encountered the yield of flesh and bone. She saw Savior, dragging his legs up as he tried to avoid her. Blood seeped from a wound in his neck, where flying shrapnel had cut a long gash. Dell glanced around for the others, but didn't see them. No matter. Savior appeared to be nearly dead or dying, and that was all she wanted. She nudged his head with her boot, and he looked at her.

"You bitch," he murmured. Then he closed his eyes. Dell stood there a moment, her emotions in turmoil. Then she turned and scrambled out of the wrecked building.

Outside, she got her bearings with the stars and began a steady trudge south, toward town.

It was dark and cold, but Dell didn't notice. Distracted by conflicting emotions, she tried to sort her feelings. Relief? Triumph, maybe? Or might she be afraid of who she had become in this long struggle with the devil? She walked for half an hour before a vehicle approached, slowing as it came near.

A familiar voice called to her. "Hey, Dell. That you, girl?"

She recognized the Hughes County Sheriff's patrol car, driven by Deputy Frank Chong. She stopped and turned with a slight smile to address the deputy. "You just couldn't let me walk away, could you, Frankie?"

Chapter 46

Chong leaned down to examine her through the window. "Girl, I was up all night, looking for you! Ever since we got the news that it may have been you in that wreck. The whole area is looking for you. We've been running up and down, looking everywhere. Why don't you get in the car?"

Dell appeared disquieted. "Okay, I'm okay, Frankie. It's been a long, long night. Get on the radio and let everyone know, you found me. I just wanna go home..."

Chong didn't have to be asked. He had connected with this woman on many levels, and was relieved he'd found her okay. It had shocked him when he heard news of the collision, knowing it had to be Dell.

He didn't know how she had survived, but tried to keep from overwhelming her with questions that could wait. "Hughes County unit twenty six to station. Attention—that 10-65, Stanley County deputy, located. Appears fine. Am bringing her in." He floated on a sea of euphoria and would accept anything she told him now.

Dell climbed into the patrol car and glanced over at the deputy, happy he had come by. Maybe things would work out after all. Chong caught the glance. "So, are you going to tell me what happened?"

"I don't know, Frankie. I think I may have complicated things. But I don't think that gang is going to be bothering me anymore." Dell looked at Chong, and he made no move to start the car, waiting to hear if she had more to say. And she did. "This guy who tried to kill me today—I used to...work for him." She took a deep breath and told him everything. All the sordid details.

Sheriff Warner got off the radio and gazed at the people

around him. "Dell is okay, guys. But it looks like we have a situation north of Pierre which may involve a certain Stanley County Deputy, so even though it is Hughes County territory, we'll have to send a rep. Any volunteers at this time?" Daniels was senior to those who volunteered so he was elected and prepared to head out to the address provided.

Shortly before three a.m. Dell was dropped in front of the Parker Ranch house. She made her way up the steps where Francie waited. She embraced the girl in a strong hug, and asked no questions. The house was soon dark and quiet.

Dell slept, but knew she was in for it. Another death, and she had not called for backup. What had she been thinking? Or not thinking.

In the morning everything looked different. The sun broke through the mist, renewing the countryside. Mockingbirds resumed inventing new songs. Francie fried meat on the stove. Jimmy and Donnie rushed around, making ready for another day of classes.

Dell found it hard to move. She could feel the effects of last night's extreme stress now, more than when she had been in the middle of it. She lifted her legs over the bedside, then stood. Pain intruded into muscles and joints, but she soon stretched through it.

She threw on clothing, making ready to join the others downstairs, unsure whether she had missed breakfast. The aroma of meat drifted upward.

The voice in her head said, *you didn't give those guys a chance.* She tried to shake it off. *They didn't deserve a chance. They were out to get me, and I got them first. The law of the jungle—kill or be killed.* If she hadn't done something to stop them, she would not have gotten a second chance.

But why didn't she call for backup, and let the law handle it? She shook her head. *There was no backup out there. Just them or me, and I had to act.* So she acted, and now she was the winner, wasn't she? At least she was alive, a victory of some sort, wasn't it? *Golly, that bacon smells good!*

Deputy Daniels was bone tired. He had been at the scene in North Pierre for more than half the night, combing through a mass of destruction and rubble. They found one dead body and telltale signs of occupancy, but no more cadavers had turned up.

The deceased had Chicago identification and a record of affiliation with prostitution rings. He apparently had been killed when the large truck had rammed the building. They weren't certain at this time who had been driving the vehicle, but found evidence that Stanley County Deputy Sheriff Dell had been involved. Her fingerprints were all over the interior of the truck.

Daniels figured Dell had somehow survived her ordeal and turned the tables on her attackers. Beyond that, he had no indication of what might have taken place, and had to defer to investigators from Hughes County.

Those detectives had concluded, based on the evidence alone, that Dell had hunted down these men and exterminated them. They recommended a warrant be issued for her arrest.

Warner called Dell the next day. "Dell, you need to come in today. I'm sending Charlie out to get you, since you totaled your vehicle."

"Vern!"

"I know, just kidding. But, seriously, things are happening here that we need to take care of. You'll get here as soon as you can, okay?"

"Will do, Sheriff."

Bradford arrived on time, and the trip back to Fort Pierre was uneventful. Dell had plenty of questions, but the deputy had no answers, and they mostly didn't converse on the ride to the shop, leaving Dell to stew.

She knew she had fucked up. She was a sworn officer of the law now, for Christ's sake! She had no idea what was going to happen, except she knew that Hughes County Sheriff Jenkins would try to crucify her. He did not like her, and her actions were further proof that she was not to be trusted to uphold the law, or with anything else.

What could they expect, she being only a kid? *Cut the bullshit! Stop feeling sorry for yourself and think of some way to justify your actions.* She knew it seemed right at the time. And, by god, she had been in the middle of an assassination attempt on her person! She had put an end to it. End of story.

When she arrived at the Stanley County Sheriff's fortress Warner stepped out into the parking lot to greet her. "Hey, Deputy, happy you got here so soon." He cocked his head toward the entrance. "We have a room full of people in there, and some of them you are not going to be happy to see. But stay calm, and we'll get this taken care of."

Dell dropped her chin and blinked, feigning innocence. "What's going on, Vern?"

The Sheriff shifted his eyes around, everywhere but Dell's. "There are Hughes County Deputies in there to arrest you. It's just a formality, though. So don't get upset. They are convinced you executed someone last night, without going through proper procedures. They'll take you, and book you, but you'll be out of there in no time. Sugar Johnson, the attorney, you remember her? She is going to walk you through it, and you'll be out of there in no time."

Dell felt her blood begin to pound, but managed to keep her growing rage from showing. "Doesn't sound pleasant, Vern."

"I know, it's not going to be fun, but you'll get through it, then will only have to show up for a hearing sometime in the coming weeks. Sugar will be representing you then as well. We'll get through this, Dell."

Dell was unconvinced. She had a bad feeling about her actions right after the adrenaline had stopped pumping, and couldn't help second-guessing herself. Not surprising that some observer would consider her actions wild and above the law, especially if that observer was Jenkins, *that self-righteous, ill-tempered, son-of-a-cocksucker!*

But she liked Sugar, and looked forward to seeing her work again. With a name like Sugar, the woman had to be extra sharp, just to keep her head above the fray.

"Lead the way, Sheriff."

Dell marveled at her own reaction to the mess she faced. A month ago she would have caught the first ride out of town, but today, even though convinced she had not acted rashly, she knew she could face anything they threw at her. She might have made a big mistake, but it was a mistake she could live with. There would be fewer of those in the future.

They put her through the formalities of booking and finger-printing, then made her surrender her badge and, finally, released her on her own recognizance, pending an appearance next week.

Sheriff Warner and Sugar Johnson met Dell outside the Sixth District Courthouse.

She greeted them with a featureless expression. "Sheriff, Sugar. I wish I could say I'm happy to see you again..."

Vern smiled encouragingly.

Johnson grimaced. "Nobody's ever really very happy to see me, but you'll be glad I'm on your side before this is over. Now let's go somewhere we can talk."

The next few days passed quickly, with the girl wrapping herself into the comfortable familiarity of ranch work, keeping the animals happy and good-natured tussling with the boys. At night, she would talk quietly with Francie, and Martin, when-ever he was there, which was usually Friday and Saturday nights. They always talked about her future, as if her upcoming hearing would end quickly, in her favor. The future looked rosy in their view. But later, after she had gone to bed, she would lie awake and think about all the bad stuff that could happen, and how she might deal with it if it did. She would be fired from her new job, which, she had to admit, she quite liked, and could be imprisoned for years.

When finally released, there would be no one left that she could count on as a friend—well, maybe Francie would welcome her back, and the boys would be excited to have her around again. But the Sheriff, and Chong? They would not want to be seen with an ex-con, so would politely drift away. Her scholarships would be withdrawn and she would end up...what? Not in her old life. Never! She would throw herself into the river before that would ever happen.

Dell found herself tearing up, and wiped her cheeks with the backs of her hands. Maybe she would be able to stay on at the ranch, ending up as a tough old spinster cousin to the boys and their families.

Hell, this maudlin speculation was so useless! Why couldn't she just stop thinking all this crap! She knew she was much better off when she just 'did'. *Well...usually. Oh, there I go—second guessing myself again.*

Martin savored the thought of another Sunday afternoon with Francie. This woman was a saint! Okay, maybe he was being a bit over-enthusiastic, but no. She was more genuinely creative and caring, and so together with her family, and attentive to the needs of anyone she cared about, including him, that there was never a negative incident. How could the woman handle all the complications she was saddled with, and never drop a stitch or whatever she was juggling at the moment. He was in awe. He was in love!

"What are you thinking, Marty?" Francine busied herself with sorting name cards of people she had pegged to help with the high-school commencement dance next month. Who was going to do what, and what was essential, and what was wishful thinking.

"Oh, was I that obvious? I just drifted into another dimension for a moment. Nothing to lose sleep over."

"I bet you were thinking of your family reunion that's coming up in a couple of weeks. I know it's making you nervous."

Marty looked off into the distance. "Yeah, that's part of it. I was also thinking about how to make our lives more congruent, what with living half way across the state from each other."

She looked up at him and smiled. "Do you wish we'd never met?"

The man gulped, then returned the smile. "Now, you know that's no longer possible. Once two irrepressible spirits have come together, and collided like galaxies in the cosmos, there is no separating them, ever again." He became inspired, and gestured to the horizon. "Their essences, in effect, will combine into a third distinct pattern of consciousness, so that, while the individual spirits still exist, their paths are subtly altered to such a degree that they will undertake a journey over a course that could not have been predicted before the cataclysmic event occurred."

Francine cocked her head and thought a moment. "So, Marty. You want to move in with me, and help out with things around here?"

He took her in his arms. "I think that's probably what I was saying. I really love you, Francine Parker!"

Monday morning, nine o'clock sharp, Dell found herself sitting in the courtroom next to her attorney, Sugar Johnson. Johnson had dressed to the nines in a Kelly green skirt and blazer, with a bright yellow crinoline blouse underneath.

Dell had borrowed from Francie, black slacks and a long-sleeved white shirt with pearl buttons.

This courtroom, nearly identical to the one she had been in before, gave her a sense of déjà vu. The feeling intensified when the judge strode into the room. His round coke-bottle-like glasses were unmistakable. This was the same judge who had presided over the hearing a couple weeks ago. Well, of course it would be. There couldn't be that many judges on the bench in such a small county. The bailiff intoned, "This court is now in session, the Honorable Ron Jenkins, presiding."

Dell was not sure she heard right. Jenkins? Could the judge be related to the sheriff? A feeling of dread crept across her chest.

The judge sat, banged his gavel and selected a stack of papers in front of him. "This is a preliminary hearing to determine if the defendant should go to trial on a felony warrant. Defendant's name is...Dell." He looked up and into Dell's eyes. "Who represents the defendant?"

Sugar's turn. "I do, Your Honor. We find the charges spurious, and fraught with prejudice."

"Okay, Miz Johnson, you'll get your turn." He turned to the prosecutor's table. "ADA Payne, please state your case."

Assistant DA Roy Payne stood, and read from a prepared sheet. "The defendant, known as Dell, now working as a Stanley County Deputy Sheriff, lay in wait and stalked the victim to the north limits of the city, then brutally executed the man, known as Elliot Jankowski, under the color of authority..."

Dell suddenly stood! "Jankowski?"

"Sit down young lady! Counselor, control your charge!"

Johnson put a hand on Dell's arm, and the girl sat back down, looking dazed.

"Can we proceed, Miz Johnson?"

"Yes, Your Honor." She threw Dell a quizzical look. Dell was shaking her head. "Your Honor, may I have a moment with my client?"

"A short moment, Miz Johnson."

Johnson leaned over to Dell. "I thought you told me everything, Dell," she whispered. "You knew they were charging you with killing this guy, right?"

Dell whispered back, "It's the wrong guy! I didn't see him there. I only recognized one man, who I thought was dying, and it wasn't that guy."

"They didn't tell you the victim's name when they booked you?"

"They only told me I was under arrest on a charge of manslaughter."

This changes everything, Johnson thought. "Your Honor, we're ready to continue."

"Thank you, Miz Johnson. Mister Prosecutor, you may continue."

"Thank you, Your Honor. As I was saying, she executed the man, under color of authority, then fled the scene. She was later picked up by a Hughes County Deputy Sheriff, who brought her in."

The judge was by the book. "How do you plead, Miss Dell?"

Johnson answered for Dell. "Not guilty, Your Honor."

"State your case, Miz Johnson."

"Your honor, my client, Deputy Sheriff Dell, was ambushed by the victim, and she retaliated in self-defense, pure and simple. No thinking person would concur that Dell had any other choice than to eliminate the threat to her person."

It was the ADA's turn. "Given that these men made an attempt on the life of the deputy, but that attempt was over. It was a failure, and she was no longer in danger. They had broken off their plans, and were safely ensconced in their domicile. Dell determined where they were sheltering, and decided to ram the building with an oversized tow-truck, which was guaranteed to rain destruction on the men within. At least one of those men was killed."

Johnson answered. "I do beg the court's pardon, but that was not the case at all. Dell was peacefully headed home in a police cruiser, when it was rammed in a furious manner. Dell anticipated the collision, and was able to exit her vehicle before the crash, then while her assailant backed away from the assault, she attached herself to that truck. She rode on the back of the truck, until it stopped at Grady's Service. She trailed the assailant into the building, and was unable to call for help, or defend herself upon discovery. The only option she had, was to disable the attackers with the only weapon she had available. That was the truck itself. The same truck that had been used to try and kill her with a broadside attack. She used the truck to ram the building, and disable her attackers.

We contend that it was self-defense, because Dell was continually engaged in the attack, as were the attackers, who did not stop until they reached home-base. The fact that they were unaware that Dell had survived, and was in hot pursuit, is irrelevant to the fact of the assault and its aftermath. It also does not mean she was out of danger, since these men have made attempts on her life on at least three different occasions. They have never quit trying to assassinate the defendant!"

The prosecutor was floored. "The deputy used the truck for revenge. It was tit for tat!"

Johnson answered. "It was self-defense, in that there was never a dis-engagement of hostility!

Furthermore, Dell is being charged with the killing of a man she didn't even know was injured. When she was charged, it was a general charge of manslaughter, without specification of who might have been killed. She could not have attempted to kill a specific individual who she did not even know was present. To make that charge, the District Attorney will have to refile a specific charge on a particular individual. Furthermore, we submit that whoever is named, Dell had no knowledge of who she was defending against. The plea remains self-defense in this egregious and prejudicial charge."

The judge looked at the ADA. "Mister Prosecutor?"

"The attackers had already disengaged and had sought shelter and succor when they were ambushed. We contend that Dell stalked the victim and deliberately killed him, Your Honor."

The judge looked at Dell. "Is it true, young lady, that you rode on the truck that rammed you, to where they were staying?"

Johnson nodded to Dell, and she spoke. "That's right, Your Honor. It was pretty cold but I managed to hang on."

Jenkins banged his gavel. "Here's my ruling. The would-be killers were not seeking 'succor', they were celebrating their perceived outcome of the attack, and this 'celebration' was the final stage of that aggression. Therefore, they were still engaged when this young lady put an end to it." Judge Jenkins allowed himself a small smile. "I know you have been before this court before, young lady, and I told you at that time to stay out of trouble. But now, I am beginning to see how hard that might be for you. So, I will just caution you now to be careful in the future, please? And congratulations on your appointment as a deputy in our neighbor to the south. Case dismissed!" He banged the gavel again, and rose to leave the room.

When Dell stepped outside, she faced a crowd of reporters, many holding microphones in her face, asking questions about killers, and terrorists, and human trafficking. Not to mention due process, bombs, the homeless, what kind of boots she wore. The questions were endless, and it was up to Hughes County Sheriff Deputy Frank Chong to fend them off and give her a ride to wherever she needed to go at the moment.

"How about a Starbucks, Frankie?"

He was happy to oblige.

Chapter 47

"Why were they out there, Sheriff? I thought they were in jail for good."

Sheriff Warner examined the photos of sunsets on the walls of his office. Then his eyes drifted back to Dell. "I'm sorry, Dell. We had that guy on multiple charges, but he was on bail, pending his trial. Apparently, him and his associates have close to unlimited resources, and a high bail is not a deterrent, was not a deterrent in this case."

"I thought I nailed him, Vern. I didn't even see this other guy. I'm not sorry the bastard is dead though. It's just..."

"What, Dell."

"Well, this Savior guy is like an evil cat with nine lives. He always lands on his feet, and it is getting really frustrating having him after me all the time."

"I understand. And here's what we're going to do. We are going to dangle you out there. And when he comes after you, we'll nail him! Are you willing to act as bait?"

Dell was not entirely certain that this ploy had not been tried before. "How do you mean, Vern? Do you mean I should try and drive home again in a marked car? Should I wander around the Pierre Mall at night, after closing? How about, I stand naked outside the Capitol building after midnight and whistle?"

"Okay, Dell. You're right. It doesn't matter what you are doing at the time, you seem to draw his fire. So, here's what we're going to do."

Warner outlined his plan. Not an unusual plan, nor one that guaranteed a successful outcome. But it was a plan, and Dell was willing to risk a chance that while it might not be one hundred per-cent successful, Savior might stumble into its matrix and be unaware he had been caught.

Hours later, Dell lingered with Frankie Chong at his apartment for the second time this week. They had just finished another movie, complete with cokes and pop-corn. It was one of Chong's favorites, 'The Searchers', with John Wayne, Jeffery Hunter and of course, Natalie Wood.

"I can't believe it! He wanted to kill her, just because she fucked an Indian. He thought she was better off dead."

Chong displayed an enigmatic smile. "Yeah, go figure. But, to his credit, he decided to become human in the end, and figured that she had survived her ordeal, and that was good enough. Right?"

"I would hate to think what he would do with me."

Chong winked at her. "I'm sure he would give you the benefit of the doubt. We know who you are, Dell. You're a survivor, right?"

"You're cute, Frankie."

"You gonna let me kiss you, this time?"

"Only if you keep your hands where I can see them."

The next morning, Dell rode across the long bridge with Chong to the Fort Pierre Sheriff's Department, where he dropped her off. They put noses together, and shared a long kiss, before exiting the vehicle.

Dell's insides tingled and jumped about, as the contemplated the possibility of an actual relationship with a real person. That anticipation and the memory of the night spent with Frankie, put a smile on her face as she entered the Fortress.

Warner walked out to the reception area to greet her. "You're looking a lot better this morning, Dell." He held up a gold badge, pinned to a leather fold. "This is yours. I told you it would be no big deal. And I think you're going to need this." He offered a holstered HK semi-automatic. "I believe you are already familiar with its operation?"

"Is that my gun?"

"No, dear, this is County issue. That weapon I took off you last week, well, it had some problems, and you weren't the registered owner. So it was simpler to issue a service piece, with your name on it, and avoid any...complications."

Dell raised an eyebrow. "I thought I had to qualify first, before I was issued a weapon, Vern."

The sheriff scratched the back of his head. "Oh, you'll have to qualify, regularly, just like everyone else. But for now, you're not going to be let out there without protection. You might need the firepower, especially in the next couple of weeks, once we get this plan of ours underway."

Dell accepted the badge, and hefted the weighty pistol. "Thanks, Vern. I'm guessing you may be right."

Warner continued. "And as for qualifying, I'm pretty sure you'll have that weapons proficiency thing down in record time. Now let's get you situated into another vehicle."

Dell hit the highway alert for trouble, but encountered no incidents. Swerving north, she pointed the vehicle toward the Parker Ranch. Two days had passed since she had lain in her own bed at the ranch and she missed the comfort and security. No phantom truck would stop her this time.

When Francine arrived at the house after fetching Jimmy and Donnie from the bus, she was pleased to see Dell had made it home. The girl was sitting on the front porch with a book, and the boys clambered noisily up the stairs to greet her with shouts and hugs. "Hi, guys. How is school going?"

Donnie answered. "It's great!"

Jimmy added, "Donnie's got a girlfriend!"

"Do not!"

"Whatcha reading, Dell?"

"So, what's her name, Donnie?"

"She's not really my girlfriend! Her name is Rachael, and she's just a friend. We both like weird animals."

"Well that's good, Donnie—soulmates."

She looked at Jimmy. "Willa Cather, 'My Antonia'. It's the story of an immigrant girl who grows up in Nebraska, and her friend for life, named Jimmy, who leaves, but comes back years later."

"Sounds sad."

"It is sad, Jimmy. Happy and sad."

Francine intervened. "I gather you had an interesting week, Dell. Everything work out okay?"

"Yes, thanks Francie." She held up her badge in its leather fold. "Got my badge back. Met a lot of people, too—mostly suits, in court. A lot of them supportive, some not so much. But, it was good—we kept the bas..." Dell glanced at the boys, who were now rummaging in the kitchen, "the bad guys from drawing blood."

"Well, come on inside. We'll get started on dinner while you tell me about it."

"So, is Martin coming to dinner?"

Francie lowered her chin, giving her a measured look. "He'll be here in a couple of days, Dell. What are you asking?"

"Oh, I just thought maybe he was going to be around here a bit more often, now that you guys are in love." Dell ducked through the door.

Francine quickly followed the girl. "Now, how could you possibly know that?"

Dell cartwheeled onto the couch.

Francie abruptly stopped. "Dell, you'll break something!"

The girl leaned on her elbow and looked up at her benefactor. "Sorry. Just feeling good to be back. So, what about you and The Teach?"

"Well, if it means anything, l think this may be the beginning of a special relationship. And, yes, we are making plans together."

Dell became serious. "That's wonderful, Francie! I'm so thrilled you've allowed yourself space for your own happiness." She jumped up from her seat and threw her arms around the startled woman.

"You seem to be somewhat ebullient yourself, child. Is there something you'd be telling me?"

"Oh, Francie, it's just that things seem to be finally going my way. I met this guy, and I think there's a chance for a real relationship—somebody I can share myself with, who thinks of me as a real person! That's something I've never really experienced before."

Donnie had been listening. "Dell's got a sweetheart too!"

Jimmy corrected him. "Soulmate, Donnie. She's found a soulmate." He looked at Dell, and smiled wistfully.

Chapter 48

The next afternoon was spent working with the horses. They started with fly spray, then picked hooves and moved to grooming coats, manes and tails. Donnie and Jimmy did the grunt work, and Dell assigned herself the chore of brushing Jonny. Afterwards everyone saddled up and headed out for a short ride.

Donnie sat atop Lady, Jimmy rode Gretchen, while Dell had chosen Jonny. Dell had a sudden urge to head out over the prairie and ride into forever, but she knew that was not going to happen, so she settled for the river instead.

The boys followed, and soon they slowed their mounts at the river's edge. The water glinted in the late afternoon sunlight, like Damascus steel. They dismounted and stood together, listening to the whispering of the wavelets that lapped the shore. The horses grazed in the pussy toes and wild strawberry, as the company looked out over the water.

Jimmy broke the silence. "So, Dell. You going to tell us about your new boyfriend?"

Dell shifted her gazed to Jimmy, carefully considering her response, then tossed a stone along the water's surface. "You know, I love you guys like nobody else, but it's different with Frank. We just connect on a different level. It's physical and spiritual all at the same time. You know what I mean? It's really hard to explain, but it doesn't mean I love you guys any less. Okay?"

Donnie threw his stone, and answered. "I get you, Dell."

Jimmy shrugged his shoulders. "Yeah, I guess I see what you're saying."

They looked out over the blue-grey water for a moment, then Jimmy observed, "Next time we come down here, we should bring fishing poles!"

Donnie was pointing into the air. "Hey, what's that?

Dell and Jimmy looked where Donnie was pointing. They saw nothing there, but a slight whine crawled into their ears. Then Jimmy pointed. "It's some kind of aircraft. Over there!"

They examined the sky, here and there, zeroing in, eyes darting like dragon flies. Donnie affirmed. "Yeah, that's it!"

Dell looked where they were pointing, then glanced at the two boys. "I guess somebody must be playing with their model plane nearby."

"That's not a model plane. There's no one around here to fly a plane." Donnie was not convinced.

"Then what else could it be?"

Jimmy put his fingers to his chin. "There's only one thing it could be."

Donnie looked expectantly to his brother. "Well, what then?"

Jimmy smiled at Dell. "They've got us under surveillance, isn't that right, Dell?"

Dell peered at the speck in the sky, with the whine drifting in and out of hearing. "You got me, Jimmy." All the while she was thinking, if these two novices could spot a surveillance drone after about a minute, then what good was it going to be? Maybe in town it wouldn't be so noticeable. She would have to spend more time in the city and away from the ranch. Probably would be safer in the long run, anyway.

"Well, we don't have fishing poles this time, but Jimmy's right. We should bring them next time we're here. I have never caught a fish, but I hear it's a lot of fun...what kind of fish are out there?" Her questioning gaze darted between the two faces.

The brothers traded looks. "Lots of Catfish." Donnie stated. His brother thought a moment. "Probably, Stripped Bass is what you're most likely to catch." Donnie added, "Depending on your bait and tackle, of course."

Peter Savior was in pain. He tried to concentrate on the quiz show playing on the television, but his mind kept drifting back to the bruises on his ribs and legs, and the witch who was the cause of it all. He needed to put an end to that misery so he could get back to what he was good at—running the business and living the good life.

His gaze moved around the dingy motel room. He wasn't accustomed to living this way, definitely didn't enjoy being here, and now began to doubt the reasons used to justify going after the bitch. That impulse had brought him nothing but hassle and pain.

The phone buzzed and Savior answered immediately. "Talk to me."

Tulley's voice. "Hey, Savior, you still in Hicksville? I thought you were getting out of that place way before now."

"Yeah, don't rub it in, Fred. I know what I told you, but things haven't quite worked out as planned, yet. It's the local help—they ain't worth shit!" He related the story of the tow-truck, and how a sure thing turned into a disaster. "I'm still recovering from that fuckup! This bitch is the luckiest whore alive, and she is really getting under my skin."

"Well, it's probably just as well—things ain't going so hot here. The Feds are really stomping all over the operation. A lot of the girls are gone, and half our guys have been arrested. I'm telling you, Savior, it might be better if we all just lay low for a while."

"Are you fucking kidding me? This is all her fault, and I can't 'lay low'. That would mean she's won, which is not going to happen. I'm not really sure how we got to this point, but I'm definitely not going down because of a fucking teenage ninja whore! One way or another, this ends here."

A web of gossamer threads enveloped Dell while she slept. The dreams flashed in and out of her head like Burma Shave billboards strobing from a train racing through the night. Each one made little sense but, taken together, they formed a cohesive whole that one would joyfully put together with a sense of triumph. This is what we are seeking—the answers putting to rest all the unknowable pieces that have blown by. 'The-man-you-pursue-is-still-in-pursuit-of-you—Burma Shave!'

She awoke abruptly in a sweat. The prairie was warming up. The bedroom windows stood open, but no breeze stirred this night. *What the hell is Burma Shave*, she wondered?

She moved to the window and for a long time just sat listening to the night. The Cicadas whistled their desire, a nearby Mockingbird experimented with yet another melody, and the Crickets tuned their instruments incessantly. She found it difficult to believe evil might be lurking. Or was that just another expression of the endless chaotic porridge of life?

Dell decided this kind of thinking would lead nowhere. She could use some inspiration now, a new way to look at her problem. A way to track her tormentor and put him down forever! Dell never imagined how closely her thoughts paralleled those of Savior that night.

She was up early and almost beat Francie down to the kitchen. But the coffee already had wafted its distinctive wake-up aroma when she reached the bottom step.

"How'd you sleep, Dell?"

Dell peered at the woman with heavy eyelids. "Mornin', Francie."

Francine assessed the girl, noting that she hadn't bothered to put on shoes or pants, and her mop of red hair jutted out in oblique fashion. "Looks like you could use some java this morning, girl."

"Smells divine!"

"So, not a great night, then?"

"It was such a beautiful night—I just didn't sleep through it."

"Want to talk about it?"

Dell grasped the proffered cup and sipped experimentally. "Oh Francie, you've heard it all before. I don't want to have to deal with this gangster ever again, and I can't figure out how to make that happen..." Dell flopped into a kitchen chair, just managing to keep the cup from spilling. "It's so frustrating!"

Francine pursed her lips in thought. "I thought you and Vern had that all worked out."

Dell agreed, reluctantly. "Yeah, we did, but that doesn't keep me from being frustrated."

"So, what's the plan?"

The girl smiled a little. "Well, it involves drones and a tracking device, which I have upstairs."

Francine joined Dell at the table. "That sounds intriguing. Cloak and dagger stuff!"

"Yeah, something like that. I don't think it will work out here, though, so it means I will have to stay in town for a few days—hopefully only a few days, until this is resolved...one way or another."

Francine grabbed the girl's hand. "Dell, don't say it that way! You'll come through this. You always do. You've got good people backing you up—I wish there was something that I could do to help..."

Dell looked away, toward the kitchen window, to hide her misting eyes. "Francie, you've already done so much that I can never repay, and I'll try to take your positive vibes with me."

Chapter 49

Sheriff Wallace Jenkins tried to eat his breakfast and read the morning report at the same time. He kept missing his mouth, and milk drops clung to his chin. He cursed softly to himself. The usual calls had come in overnight, domestic violence, drug overdoses, runaways—involving mostly reservation girls, DUIs, and gang activity.

A homicide occurred earlier this week, perpetrated by that wild-girl deputy from the Fort, but that had been thrown out, thanks to his bleeding-heart brother who should have retired from the bench long ago. *There go two people who should never have been given positions of authority,* Wallace steamed. That pushy girl had been nothing but trouble ever since he first caught sight of her with that incompetent Sheriff Warner. They both need to stay off the bridge, and back in Stanley County where they belong.

First they expose our county to an influx of big city crime, then there's all the hoopla over a supposed terrorist bomb. The fake drama was unprecedented. He decided he would do something about it. The next time that girl showed her face around here, he would be on her like ticks on a sow. She was not welcome in his county, what with her quasi-legal bravura, and he would come down on her so hard that she would bleed from her eyeballs.

Martin headed up Highway 83 towards Pierre, at a good clip. He told himself he would have to make just one more stop at the roadside rest, there in the middle of the Fort Pierre National Grasslands.

At this time in the evening, his was the only passenger vehicle in the lot. Several big rigs could be seen parked across the way, but he saw nobody else wandering around.

He came out of the restroom and moved toward the vending

machines when he spotted her.

She sat under a 'no pets' sign, her legs pulled up and her head thrown back. She wore ragged blue jeans and a faded red sweatshirt and appeared to be exhausted. As Martin approached, her head suddenly straightened and swiveled as she drilled him with alert eyes.

Martin stopped and raised his hands, palms out. "It's okay, miss—I'm just passing by."

"Wait," she pleaded!

Martin stopped, hands still aloft.

"Are you going to the city? Can you take me?"

Martin lowered his hands and looked her over. She appeared to be a teenager, and her dark skin and black hair pegged her as Native American, probably Lakota. His first response was a question. "What's your name?"

The girl struggled to her feet and surveyed Planck, before she answered. "Irene. My name is Irene."

She was plump, with wide hips and thighs, stretching her tight, threadbare jeans to the limit. Her breasts were smaller, however, and her face had shed the baby fat. It was strikingly beautiful, with high, angular cheekbones, a small straight nose, and delicately sculpted lips. Martin was immediately drawn into her large dark eyes. Conflicting thoughts jumbled his head. "I'm not sure, Irene. Why do you need a ride?"

She glanced over to his vehicle. "I really have to see my Aunt in Pierre, and it's getting late."

"Don't you normally have family to take you places?"

She frowned, and looked out over the prairie. "I'm from the Rez, over near West Bend, an' I'm lucky to have made it this far. Look, you gonna take me, or not?"

Martin hesitated. There were a lot of danger signs here, saying—'keep your distance, Marty, do not get involved'. *But, what the hell,* he thought. He just couldn't leave this girl here to suffer an unknown and possibly dangerous fate. He shrugged and nodded. "Sure, I can take you. You ready to go? My name's Marty, by the way."

She rolled her eyes, and walked swiftly to his Ford.

Fewer than twenty miles separated them from Pierre, and the first ten passed in silence, with Martin occasionally glancing at the girl and wondering what kind of trouble she might be in to put herself out like this.

"Where's your phone?"

Startled, she turned away from the window. "Huh?"

Martin gave her a smile. "Normally, girls your age have a phone glued to their ear, or have the wires dangling from them." He checked the road, then continued trying to engage her in conversation. "You know, earbuds?"

"I don't have a phone. I had to leave in a hurry. Are you a pervert?" Her hand moved toward the door latch.

Martin tried to reassure the girl. "Relax, I'm a teacher. You appear to be someone who might be in trouble—am I right?"

"I'm fine! I just need to get to my Aunt's house, okay?"

"Don't worry. That's where we're going, and I'm happy to get you there. But, you know, if you are in trouble of any kind, we can help there, too."

"Nobody can help. I just need to get to my Aunt's place."

"I know, and that's just where we're going." Martin was silent for awhile, then glanced at the girl again, who had turned back to the window. "So, is it your boyfriend?"

The girl looked at Martin, then down at her hands. "It's my uncle. He thinks he can make me do whatever he wants, and I hate him!"

Uh oh, thought Martin. *Now, look what you've stepped into. Tread lightly.* "Is your mother around? At home, I mean?"

Her lips tightened with anger. "She's around, but she doesn't care about me. All she cares about is getting belted."

Martin assumed that to mean the mother was involved with drugs. "Have you spoken to anyone about this? Other family members?"

"It's just me and my brothers—they're never home. What's it to you, anyway? I really don't wanna talk about this."

Martin was quiet again, but for some reason he didn't want the girl to shut down on him. "Okay, instead, let me tell you my problems. I have this woman friend, see. She lives up where we're going, by the big river, and we've grown very fond of each other over the past few weeks, and she's asked me to come live with her..."

The girl was listening. "So you're in love, then?"

"That's right. Although we really haven't known each other that long, I think it may be what we're experiencing."

"You'd know if it was love."

He was starting to engage her. "Oh, you've been in love, then?"

She sat back, and began to relax. "Yah, a couple times, at least. You get all tingly and excited every time you see him. Then, when he's not around, it drives you crazy, 'cause you can't stop thinking about him."

"Yes, I guess you've been there. Well, you can see then when I'm away from this woman it's hard to get my work done since I'm thinking about her all the time. So I'm thinking of taking her up on the offer to move in. But, here's the deal—I live all the way across the state in Sioux Falls, and if I went to live with her at this time I would be forced to drive three hundred or so miles to work and back, at least three times a week! Then again, if I didn't make the move I would be driving myself crazy thinking about her all the time. You know the feeling."

"Wow," she said. "Well, if you're really in love, it's just a matter of which is worse, isn't it?"

"Well, you're a real problem solver, aren't you? So, you think that I should move in and damn the consequences, is that right?"

"I think you already know what you are going to do, so why ask me?"

Marty smiled, more to himself than anything. "Well, you know, it always helps when you talk to somebody about what's on your mind. Sort of helps you look at it from another side, don't you think?"

"I know what you're trying to do. I'm not stupid!"

"I can see that. Tell me, Irene, you're in school, in the tenth grade?" Martin was guessing high to increase her confidence.

She bit on a fingernail. "Ninth."

"Ninth. So, this uncle of yours, he bother you when you get home from school?"

Irene just watched the roadside, as it blurred by.

"You know, to make things better, you should talk about it, otherwise it just stays bad or gets even worse."

"I told you, I'm not talking about it! I just need to get to my aunt's house."

"Okay." Martin let it go, but continued trying to draw the girl out. "You told your aunt you're coming, right?"

"Well, she said she'd be there for me if I ever needed her."

Martin pulled out his phone, and offered it to the girl. "Do you know her number?

She looked at it like he'd pulled a toad out of his pocket. "Of course I know the number."

An hour later, Martin stopped the car in front of a white, manufactured home on Venus Street, in a subdivision where all the streets were named for nearby planetary bodies. Numerous potted plants had been placed on either side of the front porch, but any trace of a lawn had long since disappeared and the house itself looked to be badly in need of a coat of paint.

Irene made to open the door. "Thanks for the lift. I really appreciate it." She smiled her sincerity.

Martin stepped out the other side. "I'll walk you to the door. No trouble."

After a long stare, the girl proceeded up the walkway. Martin knocked, after ringing an unresponsive bell.

The door opened a crack, and Irene blurted, "Aunt Helen! I'm here!"

A small woman with gray hair and large breasts stepped onto the porch and embraced her niece. "Rena, I'm so glad to see you!" Then she took in Martin, looming a foot away. "Who's this?"

Irene indicated Martin with her little finger. "This is my teacher, Mister Martin. He gave me a ride out here." She turned to Martin. "Thank you so much, Mister Martin. I'm safe now, thanks to you."

Aunt Helen moved to take Martin's hand in thanks, but was pushed aside by a hard looking overweight man with long, greasy hair. The man took in Martin's form with an up and down sweep of his eyes. Then shut the door in his face.

Chapter 50

Martin stood stunned. He tried to process what just happened. As near as he could figure, this ogre who slammed the door on him was Irene's Uncle. That didn't bode well for the girl. Martin considered his options. He could probably get someone here from the Stanley County Sheriff's office in a half hour. Hughes County was out of the question, since he had only vague suspicions and that Sheriff Jenkins was such a hard-ass. But, wait. Didn't Dell know someone in Hughes County? Maybe he could get her to light a fire in that direction. He pulled out the phone and made a call.

"Hi, Dell? This is Martin. I was wondering if you could help me with something that may be an emergency, so we need to act quickly."

Fifteen minutes later, Martin observed a Hughes County Sheriff's patrol car pull up to the curb behind him, red and blue lights flashing. He jumped out of the Ford and went to meet the deputy. "Hi. My name is Martin Planck. I'm the one who summoned you out here."

"Martin. I'm Deputy Chong." He offered his hand. "Dell's talked about you. What's going on, here?"

Martin explained his fears, and he followed Chong to the door of the residence. The Deputy rang the bell, then knocked loudly. The knock was answered by the gray-haired woman, who opened the door a crack, and expressed great surprise when Chong flashed his badge. "Oh! The Sheriff's Department," she exclaimed loudly. "Is there some problem?"

"Ma'am; we have reason to believe a young girl is being held here, against her will." Chong pushed the door open, and Martin followed him inside.

"Please! There is no problem here!" She retreated behind a worn brown couch that faced the room's only window. "You have to leave!"

Chong observed candles covering the tops of several shelves along the wall. A dark hallway behind the kitchen led to the back part of the dwelling. A single glass fixture planted in the center of the ceiling illuminated the front room. "Ma'am, why don't you have the girl come out and tell us that everything is alright? Then we can talk about leaving."

Martin stepped toward the hallway and the woman moved to stop him. "You can't go back there. Leave now!"

Martin shouted down the hall. "Irene...can we talk to you?"

He thought he heard a muffled sob, and shifted his eyes back to the deputy. "Did you hear that?"

Chong nodded his assent, and reached for his holstered pistol. A door burst open in the hallway and a large man swiveled out, holding a shotgun. Martin ducked behind the kitchen counter and Chong dived over the brown couch, in a backwards twist, just as the man chambered a round and blew out the front window in an explosion of fire and glass!

The gray-haired aunt screamed, and Irene jammed into the shooter from behind, but was knocked to the ground with a swift backhand. He cocked the weapon again, looking for a target. Chong was on his knees in the small living room, trying to locate his pistol.

The man jerked his torso around toward Martin, who grabbed hold of a frying pan and hurtled it like a Frisbee toward the attacker. The man deflected it with the butt of his rifle and pointed the gun at Martin. "Tell the deputy to come out where I can see him, or I'll blow your fuckin' head off!" His words were somewhat slurred.

Chong raised his hands from behind the couch and peeked over a divot of flocking and threads in its back, the size of a turkey platter. "Okay, man. Let's be reasonable. We're only here to check on the girl. Why don't you put the weapon down?"

Aunt Helen had rushed to Irene's aid on the hall floor, where they sat embracing each other and crying softly.

The man holding the shotgun hesitated, and looked confused. "You have a warrant? Lemme see your warrant and you can see the girl."

"Well, we..."

"I didn't think so. You're trespassing, and I have every right to shoot you. What's your name?"

"I'm Deputy Frank Chong, of the Hughes County Sheriff's Department, here on official business. Put the weapon down, or you will be in serious jeopardy."

"What, you going to throw an ashtray at me? You," he gestured at Martin, "get over there with the cop!"

Chong had been considering throwing something, as the man was obviously out of control. Instead he tried to reason with him. "If you don't put that gun down now, you will be charged with several felony offenses, and you are certain to spend the next few years in prison."

"Oh, prison. Not again. I'm so frightened" The burly man shifted his weight from one foot to the other. "Chong. Why does that name...Deputy Chong! Hero of the Heartland. I remember now. You're the guy who found that big bomb some days ago and saved us all. Yeah, you're with that skinny red-head. Laid waste to all our plans. We would have really shown the whitey establishment that the time had come for payback. The beginning of the end for the years of slavery and genocide. But, no! You and that girl had to ruin everything."

Martin spoke up. "Listen, whoever you are, we are simply here to see no harm comes to Irene. We don't know anything about a bomb, or slavery." He pointed to the women in the hallway. "These folks have not harmed you, and it's time you let them go."

The big man glanced at the cowering females. "You can call me Uncle Henry. And these girls here, well, they're just tired. And nobody's going anywhere. We're going to have us a party. It's not the kind of party you're going to like, though. Where's that gun of yours, Deputy Chong. I'm going to need it." He gestured with the long gun. "Don't go making any sudden moves, 'cause I don't want to end this too quickly. That would spoil the fun."

Martin responded. "I'm not sure what your problem is. Just give us the girl and we'll be on our way."

Chong was moving his eyes only, searching for his missing pistol. "You are making this situation worse. What you need to do is..."

"I don't need to do nothing, mother-fucker! You must think I'm stupid or something."

The man pulled a phone from his coat and punched in some numbers. "Hey Gee, I fell into something here that might interest you." He paused to listen. "No, it's not that, you idiot! It's better."

Martin eyed Chong, still on his knees. He could see the butt of the gun just behind the deputy and tried signaling him with his chin.

Uncle Henry chuckled, and there came a static-like response from his phone. "Okay, make it quick!" He dropped the device back into a pocket and turned to the business at hand. "Now, Deputy, I'm going to need you to back all the way next to that wall there. He waved the shotgun at the far wall. His gaze flicked to Martin. "You too, white boy!"

Martin just stood and stared blankly.

"Did you hear me, cracker? Get against the wall!"

Martin cocked his head a little, like a cockatoo trying to figure out the ways of humans. "Henry. You are obviously suicidal. For some reason you want to die and take me with you...maybe all of us. It would be really stupid of me to do what you want, if that's the inevitable outcome."

Henry growled, and lunged at the defiant journalist.

Martin rolled over the counter, just out of the madman's grasp, landing in front of the couch. At the same time, Chong stood with his semi-automatic pointed at Henry's chest. He screamed at the big man. "Drop the weapon, fat boy!"

Henry stumbled and glanced down at the shotgun. He

smiled and brought it up level with Chong's chest. As the shotgun made its arc, a bullet blasted from Chong's pistol, knocking Uncle Henry into the kitchen sink.

Martin leapt over to the man and grabbed his weapon. Then he turned his attention to the women in the hallway.

Irene and her aunt were huddled on the floor, grasping each other tightly. Martin kneeled and addressed them. "I think we're okay, ladies."

Chong checked on Uncle Henry and found him still alive but losing large amounts of blood. He ripped part of Henry's shirt and tried to plug the hole, all the while talking into his radio.

Both men were surprised when the front door suddenly opened. A large black man, holding a military style rifle, stood in the opening, and surveyed the interior.

Martin stood, and Chong swung around reaching again for his holstered pistol.

The newcomer raised the rifle, and shook his head. "Uh, uh!"

A blast from the shotgun in Martin's hands sent the man careening back through the door

Chong and Martin traded glances, as the smoke cleared. "Who was that?" "What the..."

Chong stepped toward the door as Planck stood looking at the twelve gauge in his frozen grip. He let his gaze drift to where the women had risen from their huddle, then over to where Henry sat against the sink counter, clutching at his belly, his eyes staring blankly in shock.

Martin joined Chong outside. The deputy checked for a pulse on the downed black man. He looked up at Martin. "You put this one down for good, Martin."

A siren in the distance signaled the approach of an ambulance. Both men turned to the interior as Irene emitted a long moan. "You've killed him! You've killed Uncle Henry!"

Eventually two EMT units crowded into the short driveway, and a flurry of other vehicles, including six police cruisers from the City of Pierre and Hughes County sat in front of the manufactured home.

They transported a still alive Uncle Henry to the local medical center. The other man, still unidentified, was taken to the Hughes County Morgue.

Chong and Deputy Chavez remained outside the dwelling, where they attempted to question the distraught women. Martin sat on the curb in a kind of stupor, going over in his mind the significance of what he had done. He counted this the second incident recently where he had acted instinctively when a weapon had been thrust into his hands. He pulled his phone out to call Francine.

Francie urged him to 'please' get to the ranch as soon as he was able.

Deputy Chong finally sat down next to Martin. "So, Martin, hell of a thing, huh? I'm glad we made it through this okay." He looked directly at Planck. "Tell me again how you know the girl, Irene."

Chapter 51

Hours later, Planck sat at the Parker Ranch kitchen table with Francie and Dell. It was late, and the boys had retired to their rooms.

Martin stressed over recent events. "If I could live the rest of my life without ever touching a gun again, I would be a happy man."

Francine tried to be supportive, and placed her hands over his. "I know you're suffering, Marty, but it'll get better."

"I know I'm being unrealistic. If I'm to be out here with you on the ranch, then I may have to shoot a rattlesnake or coyote sometimes, but shooting a man, no matter how despicable he is, is something I hope to never do again."

He looked at Dell, and lowered his head.

Francie caught the glance, and voiced Martin's unasked question. "How have you been able to cope, sweetie, after you've confronted the monsters and the bad guys?"

Dell attempted to explain her momentary loss of what she could only describe as her sociability, when pressed to defend her life or others. "It's the rage. The rage takes over, and all my feelings and thinking goes away. Then, when it's finished, the rage takes any leftover doubts, and tucks them away in a little box, where I don't ever have to deal with them."

She locked eyes with Martin, who sat erect at her explanation. "Marty, I'm sorry if this is in any way my fault. I wouldn't want you saddled with my affliction."

As the tears trickled down Dell's cheeks, Martin answered. "This is none of your doing, Dell. Believe me."

Francine looked from one to the other. "It's okay, Dell. You don't have an affliction, and if you did, it's not catching."

"There is one thing though, Dell," Marty answered, "This guy out there knows about you. He seems to be connected in some way with that bomb of yours, and blames you and Deputy

Chong for making it go away."

Dell used both hands to wipe the tears away. "If that's the case, then I guess we have to pay him a visit tomorrow. Where is he being treated?"

Dell had contacted FBI Agent Maddis, who had agreed to meet her the next morning at St. Mary's. Dell paced across the travertine-tiled floor until she glimpsed Agent Maddis approach through the automatic sliding doors. She rushed over to embrace her.

"How you been keeping, Dell?"

"If you're asking whether I'm staying out of trouble, then the answer is 'not really', but I'm sure trying hard."

They continued to converse as they strode toward the elevator. The man they wanted to talk to was on the third floor, and reportedly able to speak.

Maddis asked about the suspect. "How did you happen onto this guy, Dell?"

"It wasn't me this time—it was Martin! The teach was trying to help a girl get to her aunt's, and away from the abusive uncle. He didn't know this guy, the uncle, would be there waiting." Her eyes got bigger in the telling. "And this Uncle Henry started blabbing about Chong and me and the bomb. It was just crazy luck!"

They left the elevator and headed toward the nurses' station. Someone was working behind the counter, and Maddis took the lead. "Excuse me!" She flashed her badge. "FBI. Could you direct us to the room where a Henry Grey-Wolf is staying?"

The male nurse peered at the Agent's badge, then pointed. "Room 318, down the hall."

They found Henry asleep, propped in a raised bed, one wrist handcuffed to the railing. He had monitor leads running out from under his gown in several places, and liquid of some sort was dripping into his body through a needle taped onto the crook of his arm. A continuous soft beeping sounded as they stood looking down at him. Somehow sensing their presence, the man's eyes opened and darted toward them, his head slowly following through.

"Hello, Mister Grey-Wolf. I'm Agent Maddis with the FBI. We're here to ask a few questions about your involvement in local efforts to disrupt power and civil structure in this area." Maddis nodded to Dell. "This is my associate, Deputy Dell, with the local Sheriff's Department. According to a Deputy Chong, you claimed that he disrupted your plans to set off a bomb that we had found. That indicates to us that you can be tied to this bomb and prosecuted for its placement. What could keep you from taking all the heat for this action is to tell us who else might be involved. We may be able to get you a lesser penalty for your cooperation in this..."

"Fuck you, bitch!"

Dell made a move towards the patient, but Maddis put out a restraining arm. "We are hoping you will reconsider, Mister Grey-Wolf. It would be to your advantage to do so. Otherwise, this whole thing will fall entirely on your head, which means you will likely never walk free again."

Uncle Henry did not respond. He just lay there, staring at the ceiling, the sound of soft beeping marking the time passing.

Dell and Agent Maddis spent the remainder of the morning in the hospital cafeteria, with salads and iced tea. Maddis's routine vicariously augmented with Dell's tale of her past week dodging tow trucks, and certain jail time for her efforts. A lesson lurked in that story somewhere, which the girl interpreted as 'finish the job you started, and don't leave loose ends'.

Maddis had a much more pragmatic message—when faced with a choice, choose the alternative that promised the most favorable outcome. "Next time, Dell, don't go crashing into trouble—get yourself out of the situation, then come back with reinforcements."

"That's extremely good advice, Rene, and I'll try and act on it if I ever get caught up like that again—but you know, whenever

I'm in the moment any planning seems to go out the door." She cut the air with her hand.

Chapter 52

Peter Savior listened impatiently while the man he had following Dell reported in minute detail what he had found when she had visited someone at the hospital. "The girl was with some kind of female cop. They rode the elevator up to the third floor, then they said something to a nurse. They talked with this guy awhile, then they left."

"Do you know why he was there, or who he might be?"

"All I know is that he was an Indian, name of Grey-Wolf. They had a meeting. I assumed they were concerned about the guy, but I really don't know why they were there."

Savior rubbed his chin. "Okay, I guess we need to find out if he is important to the girl and maybe we can get some leverage."

Grey-Wolf had another visitor. "Mister Grey-Wolf, how are you feeling?"

Uncle Henry slowly turned to look at this new annoyance. He saw a pale man with a dark goatee and a friendly smile. Henry grunted.

"Not so hot being here, all trussed up like that, is it?"

"Who the fuck are you?"

Savior sat in an armless chair next to the bed. The left side of his face was partially covered with a large white bandage. "I'm a good friend of Dell's, just checking in on you. You know Dell, right?"

Henry turned back and continued staring at the ceiling. "Don't know what you're saying, boy. Talk sense, or get out!"

It was then that Savior noticed the man was shackled to the bed. He quickly realized this man was not Dell's friend, but more likely one of her victims. It was almost embarrassing, but he deftly recovered. "I'm sorry. I'm talking about Dell, the tall girl with the wild red hair—she's responsible for you being in this situation, so she's definitely not anybody's friend, is she?"

Henry remained taciturn.

Savior persisted. "You know this tall redhead bitch, right? She the one that upset all your plans? We can put a stop to the bitch, you know. You have some friends we can count on?"

Henry turned his head back to look at Savior. "This the bitch who took away our device?"

"Yeah, that's her. She's always getting in someone's way, and we are going to make sure she won't ever interfere with anyone's plans again. But we're going to need some help, 'cause this bitch is lucky and seems to always be where we don't need her most."

Henry was beginning to comprehend. "So, you have a gripe with this woman?"

"Of course! This girl will do all she can to destroy my business. So, damn right I'm pissed!" Savior made a point of examining Henry's handcuff. "She's responsible for the mess you're in right now, and you should be pissed too."

Henry yanked loudly on his shackle. "Naw, she couldn't have anything to do with this. It was a couple of guys—one of them a cop."

"Yeah, well—she was in here trying to shake you down with a cop. They're all together in this. Believe me, if it weren't for her, you wouldn't be here." He pointed to his face. "Just look what she did to me!"

Henry mulled this over.

Dell met Chong at the Starbucks by the Mall. "I haven't had a chance to find out how you are doing after that whatever it was...shootout...you were involved in with Marty. What was going on?"

Dell took a sip of her grande double chocolate mocha-latte with whipped cream, while Frank sipped his regular black coffee. "You know Dell, I'm still trying to figure that out. Your buddy, Martin, got tied up with this rez girl somehow, and you got me involved. Next thing, I'm dodging shotgun blasts from this drunken 'uncle on the warpath', and next thing is your Marty blasts this new guy who showed up. He didn't feel too good about that."

Dell was sympathetic. She laid her hand on the deputy's arm. "I know. He told us about that. He had given a lift to the girl who was trying to get away from her uncle, but he took her right to him instead. And I'm sorry you had to be there, but Martin needed to get someone out there fast so the girl wouldn't be hurt."

"I know, Dell. You did the right thing. But now we are stuck with babysitting Uncle Henry who, so far as we know, may or may not be a terrorist."

Dell took another sip of her latte. "You have him shackled to his bed. With no other guard. How is that a good idea?"

"Not my call, Dell. Sheriff Perkins considers this guy low risk, and we have someone who comes around every couple hours to check on him. They have him on a catheter, so no need for getting him up, and the bedpan does the rest."

"Let's hope he stays there until we can get him talking about the bomb thing. You know, Rene and I were out there today, but he wouldn't say a word to us about anything."

That night, while Dell lay next to Chong's sleeping form, she thought about the surveillance. Was it fair to her boyfriend that the whole of Stanley County—well, the whole sheriff's department anyway, kept watch on Chong's sleeping arrangements? Whenever he slept with her, at any rate?

She tried to anticipate how he would feel about that, and vowed to tell him the next day. Life was sure getting complicated, now that she had a real relationship. And how about Frankie? Was his life becoming more complicated? She wondered about his real feelings for her. Were they complicated, or was it simple lust and convenience? Did he love and value her, like she loved and valued him as a person? Or didn't he know?

The more she thought on it, the less certain she became about her own motives. What the hell was she doing, thinking she could ever engage with a man on a spiritual level? The fact she was having sex with him somehow detoured the whole relationship to the most common and most familiar motive she was aware of—the pursuit of orgasm. For most people, that was the reward of a loving relationship. For people like her, it just may be the goal.

Was she being too hard on herself? She didn't really know. She needed to talk to someone. Frankie was asleep, but he was here, and if she couldn't talk to him about these things, then she may as well pack it in and head for the coast, as someone once said. Dell lifted herself on one elbow and gently shook the shoulder of her companion. "Frankie, we have to talk."

Chong groaned, and started to roll over. "Um...what time is it?"

"Frankie, what are we doing? I mean, are we going anywhere in this thing that we have going?"

Chong sat up, rubbed his right eye, and studied his bed partner. "I'm sorry. Are you upset about something?"

Dell chewed on her lower lip. "I'm not upset—I'm just wondering. Wondering what we're getting from each other, and whether we, you know, are headed for a life together, or whether I'm just taking advantage of your good looks and going for the easy score?" Dell cracked a smile as she asked and Chong studied her without expression, then swung at her with his pillow.

The ensuing pillow fight soon degraded into physical clinches with heavy breathing and some gasps and moans. Both lay exhausted for awhile, but as Chong was escaping back into slumber, Dell accosted him again. "No, really, Frankie! I'm worried. Could we have a good loving relationship if we weren't dependent on the good sex?" She modified her question. "If I weren't so willing to let you have your way with me?"

Chong considered. "I seem to recall some time back when you were more than willing to leave me terribly frustrated. Can't tell you how relieved I am, that we've moved on from that."

"It's just...well it's hard to say, but I'm not sure where, or how, or what, even..."

"Sounds like you have questions, Dell."

She pushed on his shoulder. "Don't interrupt—I'm trying to figure out the right words for what's bothering me. I'm just not sure what feelings I have when I'm with you." Chong opened his mouth for comment, but Dell waved him silent. "It's just that I want sex with you to mean more than it used to mean to me. You know my history with men. I want to know how to make sure that I'm with you, all the way, and not just in it for the sex—you get what I mean?"

Chong yawned. "I'm beginning to. Here's a question for you. Do you have a yen to jump in the sack with every handsome man you encounter?"

"Of course not, you dope! Actually, I never had a real boyfriend before, except I was attracted to that bastard, Savior, before he started working me...and I never really had a choice when it came to a sex partner. But I'm out of that life."

"Yet, here you are with me. So, what's different?"

"What do you mean? It's totally different!"

"Exactly! Now, let's catch a few more winks, okay?" Chong then plumped the pillow under his ear and closed his eyes. "Good night, my beautiful Amazon."

Dell was struck by the simplicity of Chong's argument, and she examined it from every angle until she drifted off, questions still banging around in her mind until they all blended into a warm pudding, thick and sweet, like blueberry compote.

The next day was routine. As were the following days, and a week slipped by. Dell hung around in Fort Pierre, working paper, then cruised the roadways, making a few traffic stops. She purposely stayed clear of the ranch, bunking with Chong, and mostly waited for the inevitable to happen.

The inevitable occurred at a little after five o'clock on Sunday, as she waited to meet with Frankie at the Perkins coffee shop, near the bridge.

The radio squawked and she heard Deputy Daniels voice. "Dell, I need you to assist with a situation out here on Verendrye, off Fourteen."

Dell answered immediately. "Whatcha got, Greg?"

"Hard to describe. Just get out here, ASAP! Okay?"

"Roger that, Greg. On my way." Dell wondered about the cryptic subtext of the call and why Daniels didn't just send a general request instead of her specifically but she figured that detail would make itself clear when she arrived on scene. She quickly dialed Chong on the cell and left a message that she would be late.

The intersection was several miles out of town. The late spring air felt brisk and the cloudless sky above seemed an infinite hemisphere of slate blue. Eventually, an off ramp took her to Verendrye Road where she slowed when spotting a clump of vehicles off to the side.

The cruiser's tires crunched slowly through the gravel until she glimpsed Daniel's SUV parked in between several other cars in the row. She pulled alongside and killed the engine.

He did not appear to be in the vehicle. Dell hopped from the cruiser, placing her palm on the HK at her belt, and surveyed the surroundings. She moved to the other side of the SUV, keeping close to its bulk, until she halted when the sound of locusts crackled in her ears.

She froze, puzzled by the noise, realizing almost too late that it had been generated by dozens of assault weapons being cocked, nearly simultaneously. The sound echoed in her ears and down her spine, creating a momentarily paralysis.

The only thing saving her from immediate death at that moment was the inexplicable hesitation of the assailants surrounding her. Then it became apparent to her and even the dumbest of the goons on all sides that had they opened fire, there was a good chance they would kill or maim their comrades.

Dell hit the dirt and rolled under Daniel's SUV—temporary shelter at best. Now they could shoot, aiming down instead of at their comrades opposite!

A barrage of bullets thumped and pinged into the vehicle above and the ground around her. She returned fire, swinging her HK across her chest, aiming at ankles on both sides of the vehicle. Then the shooting abruptly stopped.

The roar of other large vehicles, including the distinctive pounding of chopper blades, assaulted her senses, drowning out the ringing in her ears.

The dust roiled around her position, and the sound of renewed gunfire sounded in the distance.

The noise finally stopped. Dell lay still and took silent inventory, feeling herself where she could reach for any tell-tale stickiness. Finally mounting the courage, she scooted out from under the SUV, rolled over, coughed, and looked around.

Several men could be seen struggling with bodies and pieces of equipment. Some she recognized.

Sheriff Vern Warner of Stanley County had his hands full with something nearby. He looked up when he saw her, and gave her a 'thumbs up'. The sheriff was extracting a bundled figure from one of the parked autos. It was Daniels, and he appeared to be in one piece.

Dell watched the activity, as if it were taking place in an extraterrestrial diorama, until she was suddenly enfolded from behind in a familiar pair of arms. She started, then turned to peer into Frank Chong's deep brown eyes.

Chapter 53

"Frankie! You almost lost a kidney, you dope!" She wrapped her arms around him in a fierce clutch.

Sheriff Warner made sure someone took care of Daniels before turning his attention to his newest Deputy. Dell greeted him as he approached. "I'm sorry, Vern, I really blundered into it that time. How did you get everyone out here so fast?"

"Just glad you made it okay, Dell."

FBI agents Joiner, and Maddis joined the gathering. Joiner looked her up and down "I can't figure out why you are worth so much time and effort, girl, but I'm happy we're not dragging you out of here in a bag."

Maddis rolled her eyes at her colleague. "He's sweet, isn't he? How you doing Dell? Any worse for wear?"

Before she could reply, Warner interrupted with an answer to her previous question. "We had a task force ready to go for a while, now. One chopper we own and the Feds lent one of theirs. When Greg sent you that strange message, we heard it and put things into high gear. The drone and your device pinpointed your location. We came down on them hard, Dell."

Dell's eyes betrayed her only question. "Did we get him?"

Maddis answered. "It'll take some time to ID all these guys, Dell. More than a dozen of them here, and we killed half the bastards. We don't even know where they're all from. But if your guy is there, you'll be the first to know."

Dell nodded. "Thanks so much for your support Rene, Vern. How's Greg doing, Vern?"

"Oh, he got banged on the head pretty good, but he'll be okay in a few days. He's like you, Dell. Takes a lot of punishment."

Dell looked to where some ambulances were already rolling from the scene. "If you don't need me here, I'd like to take a couple days at the ranch—feed the horses, see Francie and the boys."

"Take whatever time you need, Dell." Warner looked up at the darkening sky. "And I'll see you on Tuesday!"

Dell smiled, and turned to Chong, who had been quietly standing by. "Hey, Frankie. We still on for dinner?"

The lights glowed a welcome warmth as Dell approached the ranch house. Her boots banged up the stairs. The door flew open in an instant, and two noisy boys, led by Panda, flurried out to greet her with hugs and tugs. Francie smiled at her from the open doorway.

They ushered her into the house, hurling questions like ping pong balls, some eliciting a response, others bouncing away, to be gathered up later. "Have you eaten?" "Did you get the bad guys?" "Did you get hurt?" "How's your boyfriend?" "How long can you stay?" "Want to go riding?" "Is that a new bruise?" "Did you miss us?"

Dell turned to Donnie and placed her hands on his shoulders. "Of course I missed you. I missed all of you, that's why I'm back. I want to spend as much time here with you guys as I possibly can. But, I think what I need most right now is a hot shower." Panda sat and wagged his tail.

After her shower, Dell promised Jimmy and Donnie that tomorrow after school would be devoted to what they wanted to do, and they trundled off to bed with clear ideas of what was to come.

Francie and Dell sat in the living area where they had sat together so many times before, discussing what was important for a good life. Dell talked of her relationship with Chong and how he had assuaged her fears about commitment, her relationship with Vern and how he had assured her that she had value, and most importantly, "My friendship with you, Francie, and how you have given me a home and a reason to believe in myself as a person. You are the mother I never had, and you've given me everything, without asking for anything in return. What can I possibly give back to you?"

"Oh, Dell! It's part of your charm, that you are unaware. That just by being you, that is enough. You are such a delight."

Francine grasped Dell's arms, and pulled her head into an embrace. They basked in the succor of each other's arms until Francine pulled erect. "Okay, enough. You will always have a home here, Dell. Never forget."

"I promise, Francie."

Francine stood. "Okay, if I'm ever going to get going tomorrow, I'd better get to bed. Sorry you missed Marty...he headed out shortly before you arrived. Another week of keeping busy, trying not to miss him too much."

"Oh, I'm sorry, Francie. I didn't even think to ask how he's holding up, now."

"He seems to be coping well enough—we can talk more tomorrow." She turned, with her foot on the stair. "Your room is as you left it. Good night, sweetie."

When Dell returned to the sheriff's office late Tuesday morning, she was not happy with the news. The man known as Peter Savior had not been among those identified or killed in the weekend confrontation. Savior was in the wind.

Dell decided to drive around and sort her thoughts. Fortunately, she was paid to do that, so it didn't seem unusual at the time. She told the dispatcher she was on patrol, if anyone should look for her. She felt she needed the time to herself without the distraction of schoolwork.

She drove aimlessly for an hour or so then decided to head across the bridge. The mist over the river absorbed every sound except the hypnotic whine of the tires. Aiming away from the river, she found herself close to the mall.

After parking the cruiser around the back under the branches of a sycamore, she eased out of the car. The damp air cooled her skin, but not uncomfortably so as it would in the fall.

She scrambled down the embankment in a cloud of dust, and sensed familiar ground. Juniper and mesquite bushes at first obscured her view. Then, a familiar blotch of orange betrayed the encampment of her particular sage.

After poking around a few minutes, Dell found who she sought. Pan. He stood near a wild lilac, quite obscured by the morning mist, which still clung to the bottom land. He appeared to be gazing out toward an invisible horizon.

"Pan! It's Dell. Can we talk?"

Pan slowly turned, and nodded an acknowledgment. "We can always talk to the goddess. We are well?" The tall black man stepped from under the tree and slipped into his camp chair, which was accessorized with cup holders on either arm.

"Pan, it's me, Dell. Since when am I a goddess?"

"A goddess appears from the mist—the red mist. You are the goddess."

Dell raised an eyebrow. "There are those who would laugh at that, and there are some who consider me more of an insect they are trying to squash."

Pan bowed his head. "An insect goddess, then, who has avoided being squashed."

Dell laughed. It was hard to control a conversation with Pan, whose mind worked like no one else's she'd ever known. "Well, Pan, I see you are still here, and in good health?"

"The aches and pains come, then go. It's good. You are not with your cop anymore? And you are unhappy—that's why you're here?"

Dell looked around, then chose an overturned bucket to perch on. "My cop friend is not with me today, but we're still friends. That's not why I'm unhappy. It's just that this man, the one who is trying to squash me--well, I just can't seem to shake him off."

Dell gazed at the ground, and Pan's eyes wandered from the cap she wore, to her boots, then off to the distance, as she continued. "They ambushed me over the weekend, and it was only luck that I escaped. Well, luck and a whole lot of help."

"Ah. Before, there was only me to help. Now there is lots of help. Hard to find good help, heh, heh. They all escape, then?"

Dell rested her chin in her hands. "Mostly not. But this devil of mine somehow did, and I don't know how many got away with him. So he's still out there, and still dangerous."

Pan moved his gaze to her face. "But not so much, I think. You have made messing with you expensive, and maybe unaffordable, even. Of course, watch your path. And we'll watch your back."

Dell smiled at this. "How are you going to watch my back? I'm hardly ever out here."

Pan stood, and stretched. "I have my spies. See all those people wandering around here and there, who don't look like they do anything? Most work for me!"

Chapter 54

Dell spent the hours before lunch in Lilly Park, reading her sociology, a text by C. Wright Mills. The park was only three blocks from the department, so she would be nearby if needed for something. Determined to work as hard as she could to mold herself into an individual who mattered, she had a lot of catching up to do. But it was hard to avoid daydreaming about the nebulous future.

Would she and Frankie continue to be together, and would children ever be part of the equation? Right now, she didn't feel the need ever to be more than maybe a loving aunt to a young child. Or a big sister.

Since the subject never came up, she didn't know what Deputy Chong might think on the subject, and didn't really need to know. Wasn't it just possible a woman could be 'creative', like a man, rather than in the traditional way of women, and still be as much of a person as anyone else?

It did surprise her to realize thoughts like this would never have flitted across her mind six weeks ago, noting also she had undergone more than just the one subtle transformation on this adventure.

An adventure for sure, and she was enjoying it, despite having bad people to deal with on occasion. Looking at the problem realistically, she concluded that tough assignments were part of the territory, and could handle whatever obstacle she stumbled upon, now more than ever.

As Pan had pointed out, she had quite a bit more help. She smiled as she thought about Pan, and vowed to pay him several more visits before he headed off to Arizona, or wherever, for the winter, like the rest of the snow-birds. Heck, by then she might even want to join him.

By mutual agreement Dell and Frankie would not spend all

their nights together now, since they both had other obligations. Hers was to spend as much time as she could with her studies and to help Francie and the boys around the ranch where the workload could be overwhelming at times.

The boys anticipated the last day of school tomorrow, and Jimmy would be doing his graduation ceremony, so that was a big deal. Everything would be more hectic than usual in the coming days leading up to the Planck Family reunion, set for next weekend.

They sat around the dinner table devouring a pot roast with potatoes and carrots from the garden, except for Francie who barely touched her plate. Preoccupied with her son's graduation and preparations for the gathering of the Planck clan in Sioux Falls on Saturday, she had little appetite.

They had all been invited, including Dell, who would be helping out where she could, since Francie had been charged with the bulk of the preparation for the big event. Martin's sisters would be of some help, but since they all were traveling, the logistics would not allow any significant efforts.

They would send mementos and stories to share, while Martin would choose beverages, have them ready at the hall he had rented, and play host at the event. Francine would plan the meal and hors d'oeuvres, select the caterer, and make sure everything happened on schedule.

Before finishing the meal, Jimmy had to ask the question rumbling around all their heads in one form or another. "Is all this work a test, Mom?"

"More salad, sweetie? A test for what?"

"You know, whether you'll make a good wife or not?"

Francie was speechless for a second, blinking her confusion. "A good wife test? For Martin? I don't think the subject of marriage has come up, sweetie. I mean, we probably love each other and would like to be together, but marriage? Well, that involves complications and implications that neither one of us has had a chance to think about, much less make a decision on." She hoped that would cover the subject.

"But Mom!" Francie and Dell's heads swiveled to Donnie. "We're all going out there to be checked out by Martin's family, aren't we? Even Dell. I mean..."

"That is far from the truth, Donnie. We are going to meet them because they are important people in Marty's life, and so are we. And we are going to meet them, and engage with them, and form lasting friendships, because of a common interest, which is Martin! And we're helping to plan this event, because Martin and his family are people we care about."

"Yeah," said Jimmy, "and because Martin would be totally lost without your help."

Dell tried to suppress a giggle, and Francie looked at her. "Help me out here, Dell."

"Sure. I'll take a little more of that salad, please, Francie."

Dell thought over the next few days about what Francie had said on marriage. If there were so many complications and implications for Francie to worry about, how could Dell be so presumptuous as to broach the subject in her own mind, let alone bring it up with Chong? She decided that subject was going to be off limits for a long while. Hopefully, she would be able to keep that vow the next time she saw him.

Wednesday was Jimmy's graduation ceremony. He brought tears to his mother's eyes when he appeared on the stage with the thirty-two other graduates at Stanley County High, and they announced he was graduating with honors. Francie reveled in the knowledge they had all come this far, and that most of the changes in their lives would be good ones from now on.

After the ceremony, when the caps went flying into the air, Dell thought she would be the first to reach him, but a female graduate, unknown to her, was already there, embracing Jimmy with gusto. When the girl finally let go, Dell moved in to hug him tightly and whispered, "Maybe you'll get a chance to introduce us someday." Then Francie and Donnie were there, to join with the celebration.

They decided to take the train on Saturday, since the old truck might not have what it would take to carry them to Sioux Falls comfortably and reliably. One of Jimmy's schoolmates had been given the task of looking after Panda and the other animals for the two days they would be gone.

Martin met them at ten in the morning at the station. He and Francie clutched at each other like they had been separated by endless war. They tossed the luggage into the trunk, and found their way to the hotel. There they were able to relax for an hour or so, and tidy up before meeting the family at the venue. Theoretically all the loose ends had been taken care of by the hired help, but Francie knew there were always last minute snags with things of this nature.

They made their grand entrance at noon. Six adult family members, with seven children of varying ages were on hand to greet them. Others were expected to arrive later, with a total of thirty-seven planned for. Introductions were made all around, with Marty proudly displaying the fact he was now a grown-up, and could join the ranks of his married siblings on an 'almost' equal footing.

"Sara, Sally, Sandy. This is Francine, a wonderful person, who I am devoted to. Francine, these are my sisters, and their husbands, Jack, Rory, and Edward. Sara and Jack are here from California, and Sally, Rory, Sandy and Eddie all live in the Carolinas."

How do's and glad hands all around, then everyone introduce their young ones. Jimmy and Donnie were taciturn and polite.

Lastly, Marty introduced Dell. "This is Francine's adopted girl, Dell. She hasn't been with us very long, but we've grown very attached, and don't know how we'd get on without her at this point."

Sally, Martin's oldest sister, took Dell's hand. "So happy to meet you, Dell. You don't look any older than these boys here.

May I ask, what it is you do that makes you such a treasure?"

"No treasure, ma'am. I'm just a force of nature."

Acknowledgements

Many thanks are due to my editor, Carol Beckham, who took on this project with enthusiasm and out of the goodness of her heart. Without her steadfast work from start to finish, the creation of this novel would have become too frustrating to bear.

My heartfelt thanks also to my partner in life, Peggy Biddison, who read through the first few drafts, red pencil always in hand, offering encouragement and support whenever required.

I also wish to thank Katherine Grave for a final reading of the book with her professionally trained eye on watch for all those typos and goofs that were missed in the first half dozen run-throughs.

And my thanks to all of those pre-publication readers who lauded the work and commented on the various characters as if they were real, which of course, they are—to me and hopefully to everyone who has enjoyed getting to know them for a while.

Readers new to this book are encouraged to review or comment on the story and send anything you care to share to the author at: **redmistgirl.com** or **mlbiddison@yahoo.com**. I thank you for your support, and encourage you to look for the next novel in the Red Mist Girl series, **DELL'S LUCK** in the fall of 2018. Leave an email address and I will let you know exactly when it becomes available.

Made in the USA
Monee, IL
02 July 2021